A Boy Off The Bank

Titles from Geoffrey Lewis:

Flashback
ISBN 978-0-9545624-0-3

Strangers
ISBN 978-0-9545624-1-0

Winter's Tale
ISBN 978-0-9545624-2-7

Cycle
ISBN 978-0-9545624-3-4

Starlight
ISBN 978-0-9545624-5-8

A Boy Off The Bank
ISBN 978-0-9545624-6-5

A Girl At The Tiller
ISBN 978-0-9545624-7-2

A Boy Off The Bank

Geoffrey Lewis

SGM
Publishing

ISBN 978-0-9545624-6-5

Reprinted 2008

Printed and bound in Great Britain by
Creative Print and Design (Wales)

First published in Great Britain in 2006 by

SGM Publishing
35 Stacey Avenue, Wolverton, Milton Keynes, Bucks MK12 5DN
info@sgmpublishing.co.uk
www.sgmpublishing.co.uk

This story is dedicated to the two men whose foresight, enthusiasm, and inspiration led to the founding of the Inland Waterways Association:

In memory of Robert Aickman and Tom Rolt

Acknowledgements

A few words of thanks are due to those without whom this tale would be but a shadow of its actual self. I am fortunate to have been around England's canals for many years, and am able to draw on my own knowledge of the ways and manners of the old-time boaters for much of the story, but it is always important that a writer like myself tries his best to make sure that the background and detail of his work is accurate: To this end, I have made use of such published works as William L. Shirer's *Rise and Fall of the Third Reich,* for a factual history of the second world war (how's that for dedication?). The account in David Bolton's *Race Against Time* of the meeting between Rolt and Aickman at Tardebigge in August 1945 was the basis of my chapter 38. Further thanks must go to Brian and Janet Collings, for confirming the overall 'feel' of the story in its canal context, and to Suzanne Maskell for memories of Wolverton as it used to be!

My trusty band of proof-readers merit a mention, of course – Pam, Mac, Sue, Bill, Janet, and Alison; not to mention Liz Payne of the I.W.A. who also read an early draft and made useful observations. And my thanks as ever go to Roger Wickham of Amherst Publishing, for doing the 'donkey-work' of getting my books into print!

Last but far from least, I have to thank young Joe Wallington, who so readily posed as 'Michael' for the cover picture; and his mum, of course, for letting him!

Geoffrey Lewis
May 2006

Introduction

The Inland Waterways Association was inaugurated in February, 1946, at a meeting in Gower Street, in London. It was the inspiration of two like-minded men, Robert Aickman and Tom Rolt, canal enthusiasts who were distressed at the state our waterways were being allowed to fall into after six years of war; two men who first met on a narrowboat at the top of Tardebigge Locks in August 1945, while the war in the Pacific was still raging.

Over the sixty years since then, it has grown to become not only a huge, democratically-run organisation of people who love Britain's waterways, but an influential force in their preservation and restoration – many of the canals we can enjoy today, whether it is as boaters, anglers, walkers, naturalists, cyclists, or just casual visitors, are there to be enjoyed because of the efforts of the Inland Waterways Association.

The spark of an idea, which was to become this story, had been with me for some years before it began to germinate, and it was during that process that it occurred to me that 2006, the year when I planned to have it ready for publication, would be the I.W.A.'s diamond jubilee. So it seems only fitting that a book which tells of the canals in the years immediately before the founding of the Association should commemorate that significant anniversary.

Geoffrey Lewis
May 2006

Chapter One

Hello Dad,

How are you? Are you managing okay? Try not to let things get you down – I know that's easier said than done, but Mum wouldn't want you to be sad, she'd want you to try and get on with life. I'm sorry I had to go so soon after her funeral, but like I told you, there's a bit of a flap on, they're saying we might have to sail any time – I couldn't tell you where, even if I knew myself, the censors would haul me over the coals if I did! But I'll get back to see you very soon, the Captain's promised me shore leave next time we dock in England so that I can make sure you're okay.

We didn't have time to talk about the future really, did we? I mean, you can't manage the boats now, can you – it must have been a struggle, even with Mum, and now... Will Mr Vickers find you a job on the dock, or would you rather get away from the cut altogether, go and work in a factory or something? That might be better, mightn't it, leave the old life once and for all, start again? I can't advise you, Dad – it was always you telling me what I should do, wasn't it? But whatever you do, you know I'll be there for you, as much as I can be with this damned war going on – and once it's over, I'll be home with you. Iris has said she'll wait for me – if we get married then, maybe we could get a pair, and you could come back with us, make up a crew of three? Yes, let's do that, Dad – you do whatever you think best for now, and when the war's over, we'll all go back on the cut! Perhaps we could buy our own boats, rather than run them for Fellers's – I'll try and put some money away from my Navy pay, save up – that'll give us all something to look forward to, won't it?

For now, Dad, take care of yourself, and try not to get too upset. I'll see you soon – give my love to Iris and her folks when you see them.

Your loving son,
Alex

Ben Vickers lowered the sheet of notepaper slowly to the table in front of him, slipped off his reading glasses as he looked up at the man sat opposite him. Sad grey eyes lifted to meet his, set in a lined, weather-beaten face that suddenly looked ten years older than he remembered, than he knew its owner to be:

'Thank yeh, Mr Vickers, Oi'm sorry ter trouble yer loike this' Albert Baker's voice was soft, choked with emotion.

'It's no trouble, Albert, you know that – I'm only too happy to help, especially at a time like this. Do you want to write back to Alex? I'll take it down for you now, if you like.'

'No – No, Oi'll send somethin' to 'im later, when Oi've 'ad toime ter think about it a bit. Toimes loike this, Oi wish Oi'd 'ad the chance o' some scholarin' – Oi wouldn't 'ave ter bother yeh then.' Vickers nodded sympathetically:

'I know, Albert. But as I said, it's no trouble. We all thought the world of your Rita, and we'll stand by you any way we can. That goes for the company, as well, you can take my word for it.'

'Oi know; n' Oi'm grateful fer it, Mr Vickers.' Baker leant back resignedly in his chair, fished a battered old pipe from his jacket pocket, began absently to fill it from the pouch he extracted from the other. Vickers watched him in silence for a moment, then he asked, gently:

'What *do* you want to do, Albert? Would you like me to give you a job on the dock here at Braunston? God knows, I've enough work keeping the fleet going at the moment! Or would you rather go to City Road, or Nottingham? That way, you'd be away from the memories, perhaps. Or do you think you'll do as Alex suggested, get away from the cut altogether, at least for now? Don't get me wrong, I don't want to lose you, but if that's what you'd prefer…?'

Baker didn't answer for a while, but concentrated on getting his pipe lit, puffing slowly until a cloud of aromatic smoke began to drift around the small office. Then, his eyes met those of the traffic manager once again:

'Oi'm not sure Oi know, roight now, Ben. Oi need ter think, get me 'ead around things – can Oi 'ave a day or two 'fore Oi decoide? Oi'd be most 'appy ter stay on the boats, a' course, boot even Oi can see as 'ow's that'd be difficult. Mebbe Oi could 'andle a single motor, on me own, boot… with this bloody war on, folks'll be wantin' things delivered quick, n' Oi'd be too slow, 'old oother pairs oop, ter boot. Wouldn't be fair, would it? Now – if yew could foind me a crew, a spare man or two…?' He raised enquiring eyebrows at his companion; Vickers chuckled:

"Don't get your hopes up, Alby! I've more boats than crews, at the moment, you know that. I'll give it some thought, for all that – meantime, you stay on the *Antrim,* where she is, until you're ready. I'll have your motor docked, perhaps next week, so that it's fit and ready to go, and then – well, we'll see, won't we? But – I'd like you to think seriously about staying here, helping me on the dock. You're good with the old Bolinders, I could use your expertise to keep them running now we aren't getting the money to replace them. All right?'

'All roight, Ben. Loike yer say, Oi knows me way 'round them old injins, mebbe Oi could be useful 'ere… Oi'll think about it, h'okay?'

'Okay, Alby! You tell me when you've decided. Now – another cuppa?' Without waiting for a reply, he rose and asked the girl in the outer office for two cups of tea. Albert Baker was as much a friend as an employee – the two had known each other most of their lives. Both born on narrowboats, Albert had stayed with the travelling life of the working boatman, while Vickers had taken the chance, once offered, to go 'on the bank' at the company's Braunston dock, and had since risen to be the local manager. Baker was one of the few boatmen who could, in private at least, get away with using his Christian name – in public, he would carefully maintain his friend's dignity by calling him 'Mr Vickers'.

Now, the two shared a friendly silence along with their mugs of hot, sweet tea, Albert reflecting on his luck in having friends like Ben Vickers, and all the other boaters who had taken the time to come to his wife's funeral, and express their sorrow and support, while Ben wondered how best to serve his old friend's needs at this sad time, as well as doing the best he could for the company out of the situation. He needed crews; if he could somehow keep Alby Baker on the boats... But he could see no way of doing that. The man in question interrupted his reverie:

'Oi couldn't *leave* the cut, Ben' his voice was low, contemplative: 'It's alwes bin moi loife, yew know that, Oi don't know nothin' else, n' Oi'm too old ter learn noo tricks at moy age, whatever Alex moight think. Oi'll be stickin' around, some'ow, proba'ly 'ere with you, on the dock – boot, gimme a day or two ter get use'ter the oidea, h'okay?' Vickers nodded, smiling gently at his old friend.

Later, Albert Baker made his way from the Dock Manager's office around the dry dock and along to where his butty was moored, near the iron bridge over the entrance to the old arm which now served as Fellows, Morton & Clayton Ltd's dock and basin, trudging through the fresh-fallen snow which was taking on a sparkle as the sun began to emerge. He was greeted by everyone he saw, with expressions of encouragement or condolence, making him reflect again on how lucky he was to be a part of the boating community, a resident in that nomadic village which was the world of the working boatman and his family. He acknowledged each of them with a word or a wave, at last climbing down through the cabin doors into the tiny home he had shared with Rita for twenty-five years. Usually, he would stand in the hatches in idle moments like this, puffing at his pipe, elbows on the open slide in front of him, the doors pulled to behind, and watch the world go by – but, despite the sunshine beginning to break through the cloud, the January day was bitterly cold, a chill breeze cutting through the heaviest of coats. And anyway, he didn't feel like being sociable, preferring to grab a little time to himself while he had the opportunity. Now, he slid the slide-hatch closed over his head, riddled the fire in the range to stir it back into life, and sat on the side-bed, resting the back of his head on the cabinside behind him.

Chapter Two

Reg Thompson was angry. Not that there was anything unusual in that – Reg seemed to live his life at varying levels of rage, nowadays: Rage at his job, which he had come to hate, where he felt trapped; rage at the home where he felt just as trapped; rage at the wife he had once loved, certainly, but incontrovertibly did no longer; rage at the children who only served to entrap him more effectively each and every day. And, most of all, rage at himself, for allowing himself to become so inextricably trapped in a life he hated.

There were times, still, rare moments of sobriety and reflection, when he regretted his own anger, wanted, tried, to dispel it. But it always got the better of him. There had been times, hadn't there, when life had been *good?* He'd been pleased, delighted, to be promoted to chargehand in the blacksmith's shop of the railway works – he enjoyed working with his hands, and the money, for the time, was very good. And Nettie – they'd been so much in love when they married, moved into the house in Windsor Street which the company had found for them. And he could still, if he really tried, remember the pride which had swelled with the birth of his first son. Michael had been, *was,* a fine kid – so why did he find it so difficult to to praise and encourage him occasionally instead of always shouting him down, *putting* him down?

Because it had all gone wrong. Gone wrong, from the day his second son had been born. Even Reg couldn't actually *blame*

Andrew – the kid couldn't help what he was, the doctors said it was just one of those things, something which went wrong sometimes, in the genes. Whatever they were. But, come what may, Andy was a Mongol – and that meant his brain didn't work properly, he'd never be really able to look after himself. Now, Nettie had to spend most of her time and attention looking after him; and that meant she had little time for Michael, for little Ginny – or for her husband. And so had begun the resentment which had, in turn, sparked the anger in Reg – anger which, because its root cause lay in an innocent, loving, disabled seven-year-old, had to find its outlet in other directions. Nettie, inevitably, took the brunt of it. Ginny, at five-and-a-half, had developed the knack of keeping her head down at the right moments. But Michael…

Michael Thompson was a typical, bright, lively, energetic ten-year-old, the kind who, even in a normal household, would have a tendency to get himself into scrapes, to get under your feet without meaning to. The boy tried, he tried very hard, to help his mother, he tried even harder *not* to upset his father – but he still got it wrong all too often. And then Reg's anger would take over, making him lash out at the boy, physically as well as verbally. Yes, there were times when Reg found himself filled with remorse at the way he treated his son, the way he treated all of his family; but those times were getting rarer and rarer as the years went by, the anger, fed by a liberal intake of mild and bitter in the *North Western,* becoming his habitual state of mind, all day, every day…

It was a bitter day, the North-East wind cutting you to the bone if you ventured outside. Snow had fallen intermittently, driving against the North-light windows of the workshops, piling up in the gulleys and making it darker than ever inside. Reg stumbled along Windsor Street, in Wolverton's terraced estate of railway housing, huddled in his heaviest duffle-coat, hands thrust deep in his pockets; his unsteadiness only in part the result of the wind. Four pints, downed in quick succession in the public bar, to help him forget the hard, mind-numbing labour of the day, to help him cope with the evening – the barely-adequate food Nettie would have prepared for him, the demanding, uncritical affection that Andrew would want to show him, the wary welcome he might, or might not, get from his daughter, and his oldest son's careful avoidance of his presence.

He walked in through the front door, slung off his coat and hung it on one of the hooks on the wall, where it began to drip disconsolately onto the floor. In the front room, Michael was sitting on the carpet in front of the fire, playing with the cheap (and second-hand) toy car which was all they had been able to afford as a Christmas present for him; Andrew sat watching, his habitual smile on his podgy face. As their father entered, both looked up; Michael greeted him with a quick 'Hello, Dad' and a flash of a smile which as soon vanished, but Andrew jumped up and rushed over, throwing his arms around Reg's legs and almost toppling him. Reg ruffled his hair, but disentangled himself:

'Come on, Andy, let me by, I need my dinner.'

'Through here, Reg, I'll dish up for you' Nettie called from the kitchen. Andrew went back to watching Michael playing on the floor as he pushed through into the other room; Nettie gave him a smile as she placed a plate at each side of the table. He sat down, picked up his knife and fork; and then realised what was before him:

'What's *this?*'

'Bubble and Squeak…'

'And *one* sausage?'

'I'm sorry, Reg love – it's all we've got.'

'How'm I supposed to put in a day's bloody 'ard work on food like *this?*'

'I know, love – I had a pork chop for you, but…'

'But *what?*'

'Well – Buster pinched it when I wasn't looking. I'd only turned my back for a second, really…' she was going on hurriedly as he interrupted:

'That *bloody* dog! Why we keep that mangy, flea-ridden bloody pest I'll never know! All it's good for is making a bloody mess and pinching our food whenever it gets the chance!'

'Reg! Buster's *Michael's* dog – you said he could have one!'

'Didn't know we were lumbering ourselves with a bloody thief, did I? No more – it's bloody going, soon's I've 'ad me dinner!'

'Dad! You *can't!*' Michael had heard the angry exchange; now he stood in the open kitchen door.

'Who the hell do you think you are to tell me I *can't?* That bloody dog's been nothing but trouble all it's life, n' I'm not putting up with it any more – it's going, I tell you!'

'But Dad – I'll make him stop taking things, I promise! I'll be responsible for him, I will – I'll keep him in the garden, so's he *can't* pinch things!' Michael went over to stand by his father's chair, put a hand on his arm entreatingly; Reg turned to him, took him roughly by his upper arms:

'No! He's going, and that's that. Where is he now?'

'In the garden' his wife replied, as her son gazed with horrified eyes at his father.

'He can bloody stay there for now, then. And I'll take him away later.'

'No, Dad, please!'

'I told you, don't argue with me, boy!' Reg shook his son roughly, then pushed him away and turned to his dismal plateful: 'Is there any tea?' he asked Nettie.

'Kettle's on, Reg.'

She didn't dare to mention, any more than Reg would have ever acknowledged, that the main reason that their larder was so poorly provisioned was because a large part of his weekly wage went over the public bar of the *North Western* or the *Craufurd Arms.* She sat, looking at her husband as he began to wolf down the meal which she, too, would have described as inadequate, wondering if her memory was playing tricks with her, if her life with him could ever have been as wonderfully harmonious as she thought she remembered from all those years ago. Now, they just seemed to struggle from one crisis to the next, whether it was a crisis of personalities, or money, or... Michael had dashed from the room after his father's last words – she wanted to go to him, comfort him, if she could, but she knew that to do so would raise Reg's anger to another, more catastrophic, notch. At least he hadn't hit the boy, this time, although she sensed it had been a close run thing.

She bent to her own dinner, ate without enjoyment, and then cleared the plates away, returning with a fresh pot of tea. Glancing into the front room, she saw that Andy had taken over Michael's toy, and was playing happily on the rug; muffled sounds of crying came from upstairs – and where was Ginny? She poured the tea for Reg, and then slipped quietly up to look into the children's bedroom, to see Michael laying on his bed, his face hidden in his arms, and his little sister sitting beside him, one arm curled around his neck in comfort. *She's doing better than I could!* Nettie reflected, and stole downstairs again, to try, at some risk of further riling her husband, to persuade him to relent on his sentence on Buster.

Chapter Three

'Gooin' ter be a cold 'un tonoight, Gracie!' Bill Hanney called across to his oldest daughter as she raised the paddles on the far side of Fenny Lock.

'Yes, Pop – be loocky if we're not boostin' ioce tomorrer!'

'Ar – could be n' all! Yer Ma getting the dinner?'

'Yeah. 'Ow far we gooin'?'

'Oi thought mebbe Cosgrove – or the Navvie, if we can do the extra 'alf-hour 'fore we all get too cold or too 'ungry!'

''kay, Pop. Oi'm glad that snow's stopped, though!'

'Me too, Gal!'

They pushed open the gates of the empty lock, and Bill waved to Little Bill to run the boats out. The motor slid slowly past; he stepped onto the counter deck as his son paid out the towline which he'd picked up from the foredeck of the butty. The teenager snagged it around one of the stern dollies, tied it off when they were about eighty feet in front; the stern dipped, as the motor took up the tow, started the loaded butty moving out of the lock in its wake. Gracie was already on board, taking up the heavy wooden tiller and slotting it back into place in the top of the rudder – the 'ellum, as she would have called it – and settling down to steer her silent, captive charge through the frosty darkness of the winter night.

'Yew goo down, get warm, boy' Bill told his son, taking the tiller from him.

'Roight y'are, Dad. Oi'll spell yer in a whoile, h'okay?'

'Foine, Billy.' The boy ducked out of sight, pulled the cabin doors to behind himself. Bill leant in the open slide hatch, the lower half of his body inside the cabin where he stood on the step inside the doors; warmth from within spilled up around his body, into the folds of his heavy jacket. Elbows on the hatch, he rolled himself a cigarette, cupped his hands around it to light it.

Three hours, to Cosgrove Lock. They had to get there, at least – the long pound from Fenny Stratford was pretty well all in open country, just the occasional remote village along the way. Not a place to get trapped if the ice took a real hold overnight. No, if they could make Cosgrove, they'd be okay whatever happened. Tomorrow, they should get to Braunston all right – normally, they'd be well past, Birdingbury Wharf maybe, but he and Vi wanted to stop in, see how Alby Baker was doing. They'd missed Rita's funeral, being all the way to Limehouse dock to load, but they both wanted to pay their respects to an old friend.

Thinking of Alby made Bill reflect on how lucky he was. Four good kids, and Vi as fit and well as ever… Alby and Rita'd only had the one boy: Alex was a fine lad, no mistake, but he'd decided to join up when the war started; his Dad had carried on, but now without Rita to help, he'd have to give up the boats, surely? Fellers's, Mr Vickers, would find him something, a job on the dock probably – but it wouldn't be the same, would it? Not to Alby, anyway.

Yes, Bill felt himself so lucky by comparison. Vi was the best missus he could have wished for; Gracie was a fine girl, coming up sixteen soon – she'd be finding herself a feller before long! Little Bill wasn't so little now, either, nearly fourteen; Stevie, capable, reliable, quick-witted, at nine years old; and Jack, bright and unstoppable, and pushing eight. No, he couldn't have a better family!

The boats cruised steadily on their way, making a good four miles an hour, the old Bolinder engine going as strong as ever, its exhaust echoing a constant tonk-tonk-tonk-tonk-tonk from the banks, reverberating hollowly under every bridge. The towpath, the surrounding fields, all glowed eerily white under the moonlight now that the cloud had broken, making it seem almost as bright as day – a help, to their night-time journey, but one which held its own menace. Clear skies meant an inevitable frost; a hard enough frost, a layer of ice on the water, and their way would be drastically slowed the next day. Only an exceptional frost would stop them going altogether, but even a light skim would have an effect on their progress...

Past the village of Simpson, past the Plough... On through Tinker's Bridge... Skirting away from the village of Woolstone... By Great Linford Wharf, Little Bill came up from below to join his father:

'All roight, Dad? Cuppa tea fer yeh.' Bill gratefully took the steaming mug:

'Thanks, Billy.' The youngster, muffled in a heavy donkey-jacket, a thick scarf around his neck, squeezed under the tiller to stand on the gunwale to one side of the cabin:

'Gonna freeze, tonoight?'

'Reckon so.'

'Yew pressin' on ter Cosgrove?'

'Yeah. We could'a stopped 'ere, I s'pose, walked oover ter the Nag's 'Ead, or toied boy the Black 'Orse. Boot oi want ter be as far ahead as Oi can be, tonight. We should be oop Cosgrove Lock, in the village, 'fore it gets too late.'

'Roight. Oi'll tek 'er now, Dad, yew goo 'n warm oop.'

'H'okay, lad.'

Bill glanced back as he clambered down into the cabin, saw that his wife had relieved Gracie from the 'ellum of the butty; his daughter would be down in the warm, doing her best to keep the two youngest boys amused. Earlier in the day, they'd had a fine time, running and playing on the snow-covered towpath, keeping pace with the moving boats, rushing to help at every lock. But now, in the dark, their mother wouldn't allow them to stay out; no more would Bill himself! There was too much danger of an unexpected slip, a sudden fall into the bitter cold water – and a couple of minutes in water this cold could kill a child, even before he had time to drown.

Down in the confines of the cabin, Bill sat on the sidebed, reached forward to riddle the fire, threw on a couple more lumps of coal. The little range was almost glowing, the kettle singing merrily on its top-plate; golden light from the oil-lamps gleamed on the brass of the fiddle-rails, the polished knobs and handles of the drawers and the table-cupboard, made the gold edging of the hanging-up plates sparkle. A feeling of deep contentment filled the boater: Folks on the bank could keep their fancy houses, their upstairs and downstairs rooms, their electric light; all he and his kind needed was a good boat, a cosy cabin, and a steady flow of orders to keep them loaded and travelling, to keep the money coming in.

In the hatches, Little Bill leant on the slide with one arm, the tiller tucked under the other, peering forward into the bright gloom of the winter night. They hadn't lit the headlamp – with so much light coming from the fields under the moon, there was no need for it – and he steered to follow the gleam of water, under Black Horse Bridge and out around the hill at Stantonbury, round Target Turn, by the old army firing range, and on, under the turnpike road again to pass the old derelict windmill on its hilltop at Bradwell. A brief stretch of open countryside, and then they were skirting behind the railway works of Wolverton, the glow and clamour of the night shift shattering the peace of the canal, all but drowning out the Bolinder's steady beat: *Air-raid men'll 'ave their goots fer garters if they see that loight!* the teenager grinned to himself.

Less than an hour, now; Billy, like his father, loved their way of life, couldn't imagine giving it up to work in a dirty, noisy factory like the one he was passing. But that night, he wouldn't be sorry to tie up, sit in the warm of the cabin and get on the outside of a big plate of his mother's stew, and then go across to the 'Mow for a pint of ale with his Dad. They began to leave the noise and bustle of the works behind them; he shifted his feet, settled into a more comfortable stance, leaning on the tiller as the sides of the cutting began to rise around him.

Chapter Four

Nettie Thompson eased the door of the children's bedroom open. Ginny had taken herself off to her own bed, in the far corner, and was now snuggled down, only a tangle of golden hair visible on her pillow; Michael lay curled up on his side, face to the wall. His breathing was slow and even – asleep? Or was he pretending, not wanting her attention – she knew full well that he had taken to doing that, lately, when he was hurt or upset by his father's anger. Only a year or two ago, he would have turned to her, reached out to her for comfort, held her close to ease his suffering…

Now, it seemed as if little Ginny was the only one who could get close to him. Nettie knew, understood, why he would feel that way, and blamed herself – but Andy was the root of the problem. The Mongol boy was so sweet-natured, so affectionate – but he wanted *her* affection, her attention, all the time. Even he was wary of approaching his father. And – the doctors had told them, Mongolism affected different children in different ways. Some were only lightly disabled, almost capable of living a normal life; but Andy was more severely handicapped. She needed to be with him, watching him, protecting him from himself – he didn't understand things, would quite likely try to lift a boiling pot from the stove, or play with the flames in the grate…

And poor Michael was the only pair of reliable extra hands she had around – he would run errands for her, wash up, sweep the floors, tidy the children's room, as soon as he was asked. But she had begun to sense a growing reluctance, a resentment at being called upon like that, all the time – what could she *do?* She needed all the help he could give her, just to stay ahead of life; if she didn't, if things got out of hand, the house untidy, food not ready on time, Reg's mood would descend from anger into a real fury, vented, more often than not, in violence – violence against herself she could handle, but so often, too often, he would lash out at Michael…

But not tonight. She rubbed the fresh bruises on her arms, stroked the tender side of her jaw, as she gazed down at the son she loved, but so frequently used, ignored, when all she wanted to do was hold him, hug him: *Oh, Michael…*

Michael heard the quiet click as the door closed behind his mother. He had known she was there, but, as she had guessed, hadn't wanted her fussing over him. He rolled onto his back, lay staring at the ceiling of the darkened room, hearing his sister's quiet breathing in the opposite corner. Andy would be curled up asleep next to their mother, on the settee in the front room – that was how it always happened. She would carry him up to bed, soon, tuck him in… *She used to do that for me!*

There came a muffled clattering from downstairs, a stifled whimper: *Buster!* He heard his father's voice, his words inaudible but his tone angry; then the bang of the front door, and he knew that his faithful puppy, his companion of the last months with whom he'd played and romped around the fields up by Manor Farm, and along the old canal towpath, was gone. Gone for ever: *I hate him!* Unlike his father, Michael knew where to focus his anger. He lay there, thinking about his life, his family – if his hatred was directed solely at the father who seemed only able to curse him or hit him, anywhere else he looked he found only emptiness. His mother only spoke to him to give him another job, the love he vaguely remembered vanished from her tone; Andy's love was open and carefree, true, but then Andy loved *everyone* the same way, so that his affection counted for little. Only Ginny really seemed to care about him – but then, since she'd started school, she had found new friends of her own, and had less and less time for her big brother.

I'm just in the way, all the time... If he wasn't there, Mum could give all her attention to Andrew; Dad wouldn't get so angry, shout at her, or knock her about: He'd heard the row, the scuffling, from downstairs. Again. And Ginny? She'd be better off, too, probably, if he wasn't around – Mum could give more time to her as well, maybe; and she wouldn't get so frightened, if Dad wasn't so angry all the time...

I wish I was *dead – heaven can't be as miserable as this!* The thought, nebulous at first, brought a shiver to his spine – but the shiver wasn't only of horror, there was an element of hope, of inspiration, about it. He lay still, his mind in a whirl, his thoughts unformed, not daring to follow his ideas to their conclusion – but slowly, a decision, a resolve, took hold of him...

Michael swung his legs from the bed, got silently to his feet. He groped around under it for his shoes, sat on its edge to put them on, lace them tightly. Moving as quietly as he could so as not to wake his sister, he found, pulled on, a thick jersey, then let himself out of the room. He stole down the stairs, took his coat from the hook in the narrow hallway, and slipped out of the front door, his heart in his mouth in case his mother heard him. Closing it behind him, he struggled into the coat, and began walking.

The snow on the ground muffled his footfalls; out into the street, left towards the works he trudged, his head bent, chin sunk into the collar of his coat, his thick golden hair moving gently with the breeze. He shivered, and not only with the now-intense cold of the night. Left again, into Stratford Road; across to the far pavement and along the unending wall of the railway buildings; then past the expanse of the printing works. Few people passed him on such a bleak evening, and none ventured to speak. At the far end of the works, a path led away from the road towards the canal.

He reached the black, silent waterway, in its low cutting, paused to peer down over the parapet of the high bridge. *Suicide Bridge...* That was what they called it – from the time, many years before, when a lady had thrown herself from it, to her death. He could follow her example... But somehow the idea of plunging from its height into the freezing water gave him pause – he walked on, turned around the end of the abutment wall and scrambled down to the towpath below. There was another bridge, a little way along here, wasn't there?

Barely a hundred yards on, that other bridge loomed out of the darkness. Beyond it, he could hear the sounds of revelry echoing from The Galleon, the pub next to the old coal wharf; at its side, he turned and tried to climb the bank towards the road level. He couldn't get up – it was too steep, and everything was under inches of snow! *Damn!* He let the naughty word he'd heard his father use so often echo round deliciously in his mind while he wondered what to do next: *Now or never, Michael!*

He began to climb again. He got as far up the steep bank as he could, hauling himself up with the bushes which grew there, pushing himself up against the rough stonework of the bridge itself; he turned and looked down at the black, inviting water...

Goodbye, Ginny! He ran, not caring any more if he fell, launched himself across the towpath...

Chapter Five

'Dad! Coom oop, quick!' Billy Hanney set about bringing the boat to a stop, whipping out the oil rod, winding back the speed wheel as his father squeezed up the steps past him:

'What is it, Billy?'

'Soomeoone's joost joomped in the cut, up a'ead boy the bridge!'

'Yew sure, boy?'

'Sure Oi'm sure! Yew think Oi'm bloind or stoopid? 'Ere, bring 'er in ter the soide, Oi'll goo see what's afoot!'

Ignoring the boy's unaccustomed rudeness, Bill took the controls, threw out the clutch lever, pulled the reversing rod, and listened to the big single-cylinder diesel slow, miss a beat, and then pick up once more its steady tonk... tonk... tonk. Now running backwards, as he threw the clutch back in, the propeller began to turn in the opposite direction, slowing the heavy boat to a halt as he steered for the bank, let the fore-end run against the edge of the towpath. As he let the stern swing in, Little Bill jumped for the side, ran forward to the bridge-hole; glancing back, Bill saw that Vi had already steered the butty into the bank, using its friction to slow the boat, preventing the towrope from going slack, getting caught in the propeller.

'Dad! There's soomeoone 'ere all roight – bring the cabinshaft!' Bill grabbed the eight-foot-long shaft, with its hooked end, and leapt onto the bank, throwing the clutch out again as he did so. He ran, following his son's voice, to the bridge; Billy snatched the shaft from him, reached out and snagged a dark bundle with the hook, dragged it as quickly as he could to the side. It took both of them to lift the limp body out of the icy water:

'Booger! It's joost a kid!'

'Yeah…' Little Bill's voice was hushed.

'Coom on, yew two, out o' the way. 'Elp me get 'im inter the motor cabin, 'fore 'e freezes to death!' Vi had come up behind them, having leapt off the butty; now, she supervised her two men as they carried the child back, lifted him onto the boat and took him carefully down into the warmth of the cabin. They sat the boy on the sidebed, opposite the heat of the range; Bill began to massage the limp, cold hands in his own. Vi took one look at the closed eyes, the slackness of his neck; she set about undoing his coat, pulling it off, then stripped the woollen jersey over his head, instructing her son over her shoulder:

'Goo 'n get some o' Stevie's things from the butty, they should fit 'im. Warm trousers, a shirt, 'n one of 'is thick pullovers. 'N a pair o' thick socks!' She called after him as he hurried to do her bidding. Fumbling with freezing fingers, Bill tried to find a pulse in the thin, cold wrist:

'Yew think 'e's still aloive, Vi?'

'It woon't be fer want of oos troyin' if 'e ain't, Bill.' She stripped off the boy's shirt, whipped his vest over his head: 'Lay 'im down, troy 'n get some o' the water out of 'im, will yer?' Bill turned the boy, lay him on his back on the sidebed, turned his head to one side; but, before he could start squeezing the child's chest to expel the water from his lungs, he gave a sharp cough, then another, and spat a mouthful of the canal onto their clean floor. The boy's eyelids fluttered, but stayed firmly shut; Bill looked up at his wife, a delighted grin on his face:

'E's still with us, Ma!' She smiled back:

'So Oi 'ear! Now, get me the spare blanket out o' the bed cupboard, Bill.'

He stepped past her into the bed-hole, reached up to open the big top cupboard and pulled out their one and only spare blanket. With the half-drowned boy laid on the sidebed, Vi had taken off his shoes and socks, and was sliding his trousers down, pulling them over his bare feet. She paused; he was stripped to his underpants, now – but even they were soaked through, freezing cold. She shrugged, and pulled them off him, throwing them to join the heap of his clothing on the floor of the bed-hole:

'Ere, Bill, 'elp me get 'im sat oop again!' Between them, they eased the lad back into a sitting position; Vi gently drew the blanket around his shoulders, tucked it in around him, and sat beside him. She looked up at her husband with a mother's smile on her face as she drew the unknown child into her arms and held him close:

'If that kettle's 'ot, Bill, mek oos soome tea, will yer? Let's get soomat 'ot down 'im.' He nodded, and turned in the tight confines of the cabin to reach for the teapot.

Silence, disturbed only by the thud of the engine, reigned for a minute or two as he spooned tea into the pot, poured on the water, sought out three mugs from the table-cupboard. Little Bill returned, a bundle of dry clothing under his arm; then the boy in his mother's arms gave another snort, began to cough long and hard, as the remaining water came up from his lungs. He slumped against her; but now his breath was coming fast and deep as his body threw off the effects of the cold and his near-drowning. Vi lifted the mug of tea to his lips, coaxed him to take a sip; and then, at last, his eyes gradually opened, a look of disbelief in them – big, grey-green eyes with curling golden lashes which matched his thick, wavy hair. *'E's a handsome little lad,* Vi thought to herself as he gazed around the cabin:

'Is… Is this *Heaven?'* His voice, thin and shaky, held a tone of utter disbelief. Vi laughed:

'Noo, bless yew, boy! Is that where yew expected ter be?'

'Er – well, yes – only…' She chuckled again:

'Yeh're in the back cabin o' the *Acorn,* young feller. Moy man, 'n moy son 'ere, they fished yew out o' the cut.' The boy just gazed up at her, disbelief still written in his expression. He shook his head slowly, let it fall forward until his face rested in his hands. Bill squatted under the arch of curtain which served to screen off the bed-hole, spoke softly to the boy:

'What's yer name, lad? Where're yeh from?' The big bright eyes lifted to meet his:

'Michael…' the boy's voice cut off abruptly; he sat with his mouth hanging open, thoughts racing through his head: *I'm* not *going back there!*

'Moichael what? 'N where do yeh live, lad?' The boy just shook his head. Vi looked at her husband over the bedraggled golden locks:

'Leave it fer now, Bill, 'e's all shook oop. We'll bed 'im down 'ere fer tonoight, Billy can manage in the butty wi' the oothers.' Bill frowned:

'Oi wanted ter get on a bit more, tonoight, Ma. Boot if we do, we'll only 'ave ter bring 'im back when 'e tells oos where 'e's coome from!' To his surprise, it was the boy who intervened, his voice suddenly strong and forceful:

'I'm not going back there! Take me with you? Please?' Bill and Vi exchanged startled looks; Vi shrugged her shoulders:

'Pull 'em through the bridge-'ole, Dad, we'll toy there. You 'n Billy can get a beer in the Galleon, later – 'n we'll only be an hour be'ind in the mornin'. Then, if Moichael 'ere changes 'is moind, we can still get 'im 'ome 'fore we goo on.'

'Yes – roight yew are, Ma. Coom on, Billy, let's do as yer Ma says – Oi'm ready fer a plate o' that stew, anyway, aren't yew?' Little Bill gave a heartfelt sigh:

'Aye, not 'alf, Dad!'

The two rose and climbed out of the cabin. Michael felt himself drawn back into the soft, cosy embrace of the buxom boatwoman, let himself relax; his eyes closed as he rested his head in the hollow of her shoulder: *Mum used to hold me like this!* But that had been a long time ago; no-one had shown him such physical affection in months, years... *If I tell them who I am, they'll send me back...* He felt weariness creeping over him, sleep overtaking his brain – his eyelids drooped, closed.

Vi held the boy, sensing his slow descent into sleep. Even the bumping of the boat, as Bill ran the pair through the bridge and tied them on the towpath opposite the pub, didn't cause him to stir; no more did the sudden silence when he stopped the engine. When her husband looked down from the hatches, she smiled up at him:

''E's asleep, Bill! Oi'll leave 'im 'ere, took 'im in fer the noight – we can eat in the butty cabin.'

'H'okay, Ma.'

Chapter Six

'Wha's gooin' on, Ma?' Stevie's voice was eager, excited; his little brother gawped over his shoulder, eyes wide. All six Hanneys were crammed into the cabin of the butty boat; Vi, descending the step as the last one in, exchanged glances with Gracie, who'd missed it all, keeping her younger brothers out of the way while her parents and Little Bill had dealt with the emergency – her brown eyes too held questions:

'Yer Pa and Little Bill 'ave pulled a kiddie out o' the cut – 'e's warmin' oop in front o' the range in the motor.'

'E's still aloive, then, Ma?' The girl asked; Vi nodded, over the clamour of her two youngest asking;

'Oo is 'e?' 'Where's 'e from?' ''Ow old is 'e?' 'Is 'e a boatee?' She raised her hands in protest, shook her head:

'Tek it easy, the two o' yer! We don't know 'oo 'e is, or where 'e's from – 'e's pretty shook oop, 'e can't tell us.' Bill's eyebrows went up at this, but he said nothing; his wife went on: 'E's about your age, Stevie, Oi reckon – 'n no, 'e's no boatee! When 'e coom to, 'e didn't know where 'e was – 'e thought 'e'd doied 'n gone to 'Eaven!'

'Cor! Oi wouldn't call a boat cabin 'Eaven would you, Jack?' Vi's youngest shook his head vehemently. They started to ask more questions, but she waved them to silence before they could get a couple of words out:

'We'll foind out all about 'im in the mornin', Oi 'spect. Now, toime fer dinner, h'okay?'

'Yeah!' five voices chorused. Vi smiled around her family:

'Well, if yeh'll all get out o' me way, Oi'll dish oop dinner then, shall Oi?'

There was a hurried scramble to open a space for her to get to the range, in the corner of the cabin. Gracie opened the table-cupboard and got out six plates; Vi took them from her, placed them down on its open flap and began to ladle stew out into the top one. Filling it well, she handed it to Little Bill:

''Ere, Billy, yew go sit in the bed-'ole out o' the way.' He ducked under the lace curtain, sat on the locker at the side as he was told. The next plate went to Gracie; she sat in the far corner of the sidebed, pulling her two little brothers down beside her – the next two plates, a little less heavily loaded, went to the two boys. A well-filled one again, to her husband:

'Oi'll eat in the 'atches, Ma.' He stood on the step, put his plate on the slide outside the cabin, and began to shovel the stew down with his fork. Vi tapped him on the leg, the signal that she wanted to get past him; he stood aside as she climbed out, her own plate in her hand:

'Where're yew off to, Vi?'

'Oi thought Oi'd go sit with our guest, in case 'e weks oop 'n don't know where 'e is. Oi don't want 'im throwin' 'imself in the cut again, not with moy only spare blanket wrapped 'round im!' Bill gave a snort of laughter:

'H'okay, Ma! Oi'll coom see 'ow yeh're doin' in a minute.'

Twenty minutes later, feeling more human again with a full stomach, Bill and his oldest son stepped across from the butty onto the motor-boat's counter – they'd tied them up side-by-side, as was normal practice with a pair of narrowboats. Bill climbed down into the cabin, echoed his wife's smile as she looked up at him from inside the bed-hole. Michael was curled up on the sidebed, well wrapped up in the blanket, and sound asleep, a tangle of golden hair all that was visible of him. Vi handed her empty plate to her husband; he passed it out to his son:

'Tek this oover ter Gracie, will yer, Billy?' The boy nodded, stepped back onto the butty where his sister was filling the hand-bowl with warm water from the kettle for the washing-up. Bill squatted on the step, pulling the cabin doors closed behind him:

'What're we gooin' ter do with 'im, Ma?'

'Oi doon't know, Bill.' She looked down at the sleeping child with the puzzled, loving expression that only a mother can put on when faced with the vagaries of youth:

'If 'e was troyin' ter drown 'imself...'

'Is that what yeh think 'e was doin?' Bill interrupted. Vi gave him a withering look:

'What else was he doin', all alone, boy the cut, on a noight loike this? 'N Billy said as 'e thought 'e'd *joomped* in, didn't 'e?'

'Yeah – Oi suppose...'

'And think about what 'e *said,* Bill! *Oi'm not gooin' back there!* 'E was runnin' away from soomat, fer sure.'

'Yeah... Oi s'pose yeh're roight, Ma. But what about 'is folks? What'll they be thinkin'? What'll they be *doin?'* Vi shook her head:

'Oo knows, Bill. Mebbe 'e ain't *got* any folks, mebbe 'e's from an orphanage, or soomat. One thing's fer sure – if 'e doon't tell oos, we ain't gooin' ter know!'

'Unless they coom lookin' fer 'im, foind oos 'ere!' She shrugged her not-insignificant shoulders:

'If they do, they do.'

'Boot – they moight accuse oos o' tekin' 'im!'

'Don't talk soft, Bill! We *saved* 'im – there's 'is clothes, all soakin' wet, 'n 'im wrapped in me best blanket! If they do coom, we'll 'ave to give 'im back to 'em, whatever 'e thinks about it.' Bill gave her a knowing look:

'Boot not if yew can 'elp it, eh, Ma?' Vi laughed out loud:

'Yew know me too well, Bill Hanney! Oi can't leave any o' God's creatures in distress, leave alone a little kiddie loike 'im. Oi don't know what on Earth we're goin' ter do with 'im – boot if 'e was that desperate to get away from soomat, Oi'll not be the one ter send 'im back, not if Oi can 'elp it!' He shook his head, smiling helplessly:

'H'okay! We'll leave 'im be, fer now, see what termorrer brings.' He stood up on the step, poking his head out into the bitter night, ducked down again:

'It's freezin', now. We'll be brekin' oice in the mornin''

'Will yer goo on any'ow, Bill?'

'Shouldn't be too bad – oone noight o' frost'll only leave a skim on the top, 'alf an inch mebbe, 'n we can boost that h'okay. Slow oos oop, though, 'specially oop the locks – we moight be loocky ter mek Stoke Bruin.'

Vi grunted: 'Hnh. 'N if it freezes agen, termorrer noight, we could be stook there a whoile.'

'At least we'll be with oother folks, there. Not loike 'ere. Any'ow – Billy 'n me are gooin' over the Galleon fer a beer – yew coomin'?'

'Not tonoight, Pa. Oi'll stay 'ere, keep an eye on this young 'un – yeh could bring me a bottle o' stout back wi' yeh?'

'Roight-Oh Ma. We'll not be long.'

Bill stepped back over to the butty, collected his eldest son; the two set off over the hump-backed bridge to the old pub on the other side. Vi settled back to her vigil, watching over the sleeping child, wondering about him: Who was this small stranger who had so spectacularly landed himself on their hospitality? And what could it have been in his life, that was so terrible as to make a kid his age try to kill himself? *Mebbe 'e'll tell oos – anoother day, if not now!*

Once or twice, the boy stirred, shifted his position without waking; each time, Vi gently, lovingly, tucked the blanket back around him. It was warm in the cabin, with the range still burning, but he'd taken quite a chilling in the few minutes he'd been in the icy water: *Doon't want yer catchin' the newmony, on top of everythin'!*

When her husband came back, let himself softly into the cabin, she smiled her thanks for the bottle in his hand. He flipped off the cap, poured the contents into a glass from the table-cupboard; Vi drank it gratefully. Gracie and the two little ones were already bedded down in the butty's cabin; Billy had gone to join them for the night, sleeping on the floor in front of the range – usually, he occupied the sidebed in the motor's cabin. Vi finished her stout; Bill had a last cup of tea, and then lowered the cross-bed into place. Husband and wife retired behind their curtain for the night, snuffing out the oil-lamps, leaving the boy to sleep out his shock and distress – Vi knew, as any mother does, that her instinct would warn her if he woke and needed her attention.

Chapter Seven

Blackness. Warm, cosy, comforting blackness. Michael's awareness rose, oh, so slowly from the depths of sleep. Half dreaming, half waking, his body stirred, stretched; his feet hit an obstruction: *I've wriggled right down in the bed!* He languidly pushed the bedclothes away from his face, but lay still, his eyes closed, not wanting to wake up, wishing he could sink back into the warm cosiness of sleep and not have to face the reality of his waking life.

He was so warm! *It's still winter, isn't it?* Their unheated bedroom was always freezing cold in the mornings – he and Andrew would often amuse themselves scraping the frost from the inside of the windows. *Why am I so warm?* Wondering at his unexplained comfort, he let his eyes drift open; and saw nothing! Pitch blackness, not even the usual faint glow of the night sky from the window. More awake now, he reached out, and realised with a shock that he seemed to be sleeping on a shelf! Barely wider than the width of his shoulders, a wall to his left, empty space to his right, and only a thin cushion beneath him to serve as a mattress…!

Where am I? His mind was gradually coming into focus, memory returning… The pain of yet another tirade from his father, the threat that Buster would be taken away – *I walked out! And jumped in the canal…* Was he dead – was this warm, comfortable blackness all that the afterlife held, was Heaven just a silly myth put about by priests and grown-ups? But no – more memories were coming back as he returned to full wakefulness: *They pulled me out…*

Now, it all came back to him. The short, stocky man in the old clothes, a thick scarf wrapped around his throat, tucked into his heavy coat, a battered old hat on his head; the boy, a few years older than himself, dressed the same but without the hat; and the woman, short and round, that funny bonnet on her head, the wide, full dress and frilly pinafore… They'd saved him, dried him down, kept him warm… where? What was it she'd said: *…in the back cabin of the* Acorn… He was on a boat! One of the cargo boats which he would often see travelling the canal when he and some of his school-friends went to play on the towpath…!

With that revelation, he reached out again, tentatively, exploring his surroundings by touch, pushing himself up on one elbow. He felt the gentle coarseness of the blanket against his skin, realised that he was naked under its covering; then laughed silently at his momentary sense of shock: *You didn't bring your pyjamas, Michael!* He felt the wall, rising above him on one side, leaning in slightly as it rose; reached down over the other side of his strange bed, to touch a floor maybe eighteen inches below – bare wood, with a rug laid over it. Behind his head, a partition of some kind, its edge cut away in a curving shape, and below his feet another wall – if he stretched out, he would be wedged between the two. *What a funny, tiny bed to sleep on!*

There was a feeling of warmth, radiating from somewhere to his right, and down near his feet. His memory of being in the cabin, before he had fallen asleep, was hazy, confused, he found he could not picture its interior in any detail – but there had been a stove there, hadn't there? He could remember its warmth then, sitting there wrapped in this same blanket, the woman next to him, holding him, *cuddling* him…

Tears suddenly rose to his eyes, the thought of such affection from a stranger, the memory of the lack of it from his own mother, too much for him. He swung his feet to the floor, holding the blanket around his body, rested his elbows on his knees and sank his face into his hands, crying quietly. Crying for the pain and sorrow of his own life, crying for his past, and his future: *What future? What will I do now?*

Take me with you! He'd asked it, hadn't he, last night? But how could he expect these people to do that, to take a kid they didn't know, make him a part of *their* family? Why would they want him, anyway? They obviously had a son of their own; and hadn't they said something about other children? No, they wouldn't want another mouth to feed! They'd send him home... He'd stopped short of telling them who he was, where he lived – but could he keep that up? If he didn't tell them, they'd *have* to take him along, wouldn't they? But they only had to go into the town, ask a few people – someone would soon tell them who he was...

His heart sank; his tears kept coming, despite his best efforts: *Cry-baby! Act your age, Michael!*

The curtain dividing the cabin was pulled open beside him, and the comforting bulk of Vi Hanney eased herself around to sit on the edge of the cross-bed. Michael felt her stand up, reach over him; a match flared, and an oil-lamp came to life as she replaced the glass chimney over the wick. The lamp, attached to the cabin wall near the range, spread its light around the confined space; Michael raised his eyes, curious, despite his empty heart, to take another look at his strange surroundings. The wooden walls reflected a golden glow; brightly-coloured decoration in the form of painted flowers and a picture of a castle by a river enlivened their plainness; and the soft light sparkled from polished brassware, from decorated plates hung on the walls around and above the stove.

Vi sat down again, looked at the boy whose awakening she had sensed, whose sadness she had heard; the look of fascination in his eyes which now masked the tears made her smile:

'Good mornin', Moichael.' He turned to her:

'Good morning…?'

'Oi'm Vi'let Hanney. We didn't get interduced, last noight, did we?' He smiled at her, shook his head, as she asked: ''Ow are yeh feelin' this mornin'?'

'Better, thank you, Mrs Hanney.'

'Mm. Glad ter 'ear it, Moichael.' She fixed him with a steady gaze: 'Now – 'ave yeh had toime ter think things oover, choild? Are we gooin' ter tek yeh home 'fore we go on our way? Or what?'

The boy hung his head, unsure what to say. Vi held her silence for a moment, gave him time to think; at last, when he still said nothing, she went on, gently:

'Things are pretty bad, are they? They moost be, fer a nice kid loike you ter troy 'n do away with 'imself. Boot – do yer *really* want ter leave 'ome? What about yer folks – aren't yeh goin' ter miss 'em, after a day or two?' He hesitated, but then shook his head:

'No – I'm only in the way, they don't want me, they don't…' Sadness swallowed his words, and the tears spilled from his eyes again. Vi's heart went out to him; she completed his sentence:

'They don't *love* yeh?' Michael's head sank forward onto his chest as he shook it again:

'No – there's only Ginny… She's my little sister…' Vi gazed at the forlorn child:

'Oh, *Moichael…*' She reached out, drew him into her arms and held him, stroked his hair as he sank his face into her shoulder, smiled as she felt his arms worm their way tentatively around her, as if still fearful of rejection.

After a few minutes, she gently pushed him away, held him at arms length:

'Moichael? Look at me, choild.' He raised tear-stained eyes

to hers, the look in them half-afraid, as if he expected to be told that he had to go home. Her smile began to reassure him; her words made his heart sing:

'Moichael – we'll tek yew along with oos, fer a day or two, any'ow. If yeh change yer moind, we'll see about getting' yeh back 'ome, roight? If not… well, Oi've got the beginnin's of an oidea…'

'You mean it? Really?'

'Not a word ter moy man, though, boy! Let me 'andle 'im, oonderstand?' Michael nodded, eagerly; then he stretched up to plant an impulsive kiss on Vi's plump cheek. She laughed him off:

'Git away, boy! Yew don't knoo what yeh're lettin' yerself in for, yet!' Michael just smiled up at her, feeling as though the warmth to which he had wakened had spread to fill the whole of this strange, compact world that he'd found himself in – the warm glow of the oil-lamp on his surroundings, the cosy heat radiating from the little iron range by the cabin doors, but above all the warm comforting presence of the happy, buxom woman at his side.

'Moy man'll be about soon – yew feel oop ter getting' dressed, Moichael? Would yeh loike a coop o' tea?'

'Yes, please, Mrs Hanney. What time is it?'

'Oh, it'll be 'bout six, Oi'd guess. We'll be on the move pretty soon, once moy Bill's oop.' She stood up and lifted the kettle from the range, where it had been quietly murmuring to itself all night, and set about making a pot of fresh tea. Michael looked around:

'Mrs Hanney?'

'What is it, boy?'

'Where are my clothes?'

'Oh, they're 'anging oop in the injun-'ole, Oi put 'em in there las' noight, ter droy out round the motor. There's soom of ah Stevie's things there, boy yer feet, they should 'bout fit yeh.'

He looked down, groped about in the folds of the blanket and found a pair of heavy grey cloth trousers, a white shirt with no collar, a pair of rather threadbare underpants and some thick woollen socks, an obviously-handknitted red pullover. Vi poured the tea, added milk and sugar to one mug and placed it within his reach; she gave him a broad smile before reaching up to slide open the hatch above the cabin doors. Climbing up onto the step, she took her own tea with her and stood, elbows on the slide, sipping it, her head and shoulders in the frosty air, to give the boy a little privacy in which to slip out of the blanket and dress himself.

Michael stood up and dropped the blanket behind him on the bed. It felt so delicious to get up in such a cosy, warm place after his own cold room; he stretched luxuriously, ducked instinctively when his hands hit the low roof of the boat's cabin, smiled at his own reaction. He looked down at himself and smiled again, feeling rather embarrassed – he'd never slept without his pyjamas before! He picked up the pants, slipped them on, then sat down to pull on the socks. Everything fitted, more or less – a bit short in the legs and arms, maybe, but otherwise okay. He was just finished when sounds of movement from behind the curtain made him jump – he'd almost forgotten that the boatman was still asleep in there. Vi had heard the noises too, and ducked down into the cabin once more:

'Good boy, Moichael! Sit here in the corner whoile Oi pours a coopa fer moy man.'

Chapter Eight

Dawn rose to a day as beautiful as only a fine English winter day can be. The *Acorn* and the *Angelus* were making their way along the six-mile pound which separates the single Cosgrove Lock from the flight of seven at Stoke Bruerne as the sun edged above the horizon, its pale golden rays striking across the fields, bringing a sparkle like diamond to the frost on the grass and the hedgerows. The air was still, the sky brightening to a clear, pale ice-blue with just the faintest, scattered wisps of thin white cloud; all the world's colours were rendered in the finest pastel tones.

The first part of their journey had been slow, difficult: The overnight frost had been harder than Bill Hanney had anticipated, the water of the canal bearing a solid layer of ice from bank to bank. He and his son had had to walk around the gunwales of the boats, breaking the ice with their long shafts, to be able to move at all; and then, progress had been hampered by its thickness, the stem of the motor boat forcing its way through to a cacophony like the continuous shattering of glass. Close to the aqueduct which passes over the River Ouse, the canal is so exposed that the ice was even thicker, making Bill back up to take a run at it several times when the sheer weight of it brought the boat to a halt.

They had made it to the lock while darkness still reigned, worked through with the help of the keeper, who had had to rake the broken ice out from behind the gates before they could be opened.

* * *

Once Bill Hanney had risen, Vi had given a knock on the butty's cabinside to wake the rest of her brood. In fact, as she well knew, they were already on the move, Gracie up and about and brewing tea for her brothers as they dressed around her. Soon, all four piled out onto the snow-drifted towpath; Bill climbed around the outside of the motor boat's cabin and down into the engine-room, where he began the half-hour procedure which was needed to start the big single-cylinder diesel, while his daughter and eldest son began breaking the ice around them – Stevie and Jack enjoyed a raucous snowball fight alongside the boats, their voices shrill and happy in the bitter morning air, their breath blowing like steam around them as they ran and ducked through the pre-dawn darkness.

Before long, Bill heaved the flywheel over, and the engine started with a loud report and a cloud of black smoke, settling to its off-beat thudding as he emerged once more into the open. Vi had stepped over to take the tiller of the butty, beckoning Michael to follow; her two youngest sons had dropped their snowballs, remembering the presence of their strange, uninvited guest, and had quickly climbed onto the cabin-top, staring at him in frank and slightly awe-struck curiosity. But Vi had ushered him down inside:

'Yew stay down there in the warm, Moichael. Yeh had a real chillin' las' noight, n' yeh doon't need ter be catchin' yer death now. Coom oop later, when the soon's oop – yeh'll be able ter see what's what then!'

Michael had done as she suggested, grateful for the warmth as he sat on the side-bed: The cabin on this second boat appeared all but identical to the one on the motor, only a different array of plates hanging on the walls above the stove, a different rug on the bare floor, telling him that he had changed abode. He felt the movement from alongside as the motor boat pulled away, the broken ice scraping and jingling as it pushed its way through;

then the gentle tug as the towline drew taut, starting the butty on
it way. Feeling cosy and content, he leaned back, resting his head
against the wooden cabin wall behind him, hearing the distant
throb of the *Acorn's* engine, and the hushed voices of the two
boys sitting on the cabin-top, their words almost but not quite
audible. He smiled: *I bet I know what they're talking about –
or who, rather!*

He had passed the next hour relaxed, half-dozing, in the
cosiness of the warm cabin, listening contentedly to the sounds
of the canal in winter – the low murmur of water against the
boat's hull, the rustle and tinkle of the ice, the occasional stirring
of the stocky boatwoman at the tiller, whose lower body intruded
upon his world from the hatches, her heavy black boots firmly
planted upon the step next to the range. Every now and then, she
would bend to peer in at him, and smile proprietorially at the sight
of his closed eyes, the peaceful look on his face. Once, she caught
him looking up at her:

'Moichael? Be a good lad 'n put soom coal on the range, will
yeh?'

'Yes, Mrs Hanney – but…?' he looked around, puzzled.

'It's oonder me feet, choild, in the box! 'N use the iron, boy
the stove there, or yeh'll burn yer fingers, roight?' Michael nodded
up at her:

'Right!' He found the iron, spent a minute or so working out
how to use it to open the firedoor of the range, and then located
the supply of coal – big bricks of best house coal, stacked in the
wooden box which was designed to double as a lower step under
the cabin doors. There was no shovel, so he put a few lumps
carefully into the fire with his fingers, and sat back again,
disproportionately pleased with himself at having achieved even
so small a task for her.

At the lock, she had looked in on him again:

'Stay where yew are, Moichael – we're goin' through the

lock. 'N doon't mooind the bumpin' about.'

'Can I come up and see, Mrs Hanney?' She shook her head:

'Not now – when we get ter Stoke Bruin locks, later, all roight? It'll be dayloight then. It'd be too risky 'ere in the dark, til yeh know what yeh're doin'.'

'Oh – all right.' She smiled at the disappointment in his voice:

'Yeh'll 'ave 'ad enough o' locks boy the toime we get ter Braunston, boy, yew mark moy words!' He smiled back at her, settled into his corner of the bench again, listening to the sound of voices, the cracking of the ice, the creaking of the lock-gates, the rattling of the paddle gear – all so mysterious to a boy who had never seen a lock worked! Itching to see what was happening, he held his curiosity in check against Vi's promise to let him watch at the next flight they came to.

* * *

Now, in the fragile sunlight of the January day, their passage was a little easier. From Cosgrove village, above the lock, they had been following a broken track through the ice, left by a pair of boats which must have gone ahead of them after stopping at the Barley Mow overnight. Even the already-broken ice slowed them, its shifting floes pushing lazily aside as they passed through. Still, they had encountered no other boats travelling in the other direction – there was nowhere that the boaters would choose to stop for the night below the top of Stoke Bruerne locks, so any pairs moving South would probably still be working down the seven as dawn broke over them.

The going was still slower than Bill Hanney would have liked. He stood at the tiller of the motor, fretting quietly at their progress, considering his options – that night, it might be best to stay in Stoke. He hated the idea of losing time, delaying the end of the trip and his pay-day: They could make it through the tunnel to Blisworth – the sheltered water of the cuttings would be clear of ice in all probability – but if they did, and it froze hard again, they'd find themselves stuck until the thaw. They could probably make it to Whilton, at the bottom of Long Buckby locks, even if the sixteen-mile was slow, but, despite the presence of a pub there, it wasn't a good place to be frozen in for any length of time… He'd talk to Vi, when they got to Stoke, decide then whether or not to stop there until the weather bucked up; and they had to talk about Michael, too – she'd overruled his doubts, insisted on taking the boy along with them that morning, and he'd bowed to her judgement in his haste to get ahead, but he still puzzled over what they were to do with the boy.

For her part, Vi was thinking deeply about him, too. Once they'd left Cosgrove Lock, she'd relinquished the tiller of the butty to Gracie, and stepped down into the cabin to make breakfast. She'd managed to 'acquire' a few eggs and a handful of sausages – fried up on the range with some thick slabs of bread, they'd keep her brood going through the day! Michael was dozing in a corner of the cabin again, propped against the partition which separated off the bed-hole; Little Bill was with his father on the motor – *Oi moost stop callin' 'im that, 'e ain't so little any more!* – and the two youngest had resumed their perch on the cabin-top, watching the sun come up over the fields.

Moving as quietly as she could about her cooking, her thoughts turned again to their mysterious passenger. Who was he, what was his background, whatever could have got him so depressed as to try to end his own life? And what was she to do with him, now? She had begun to doubt the idea which had come to her earlier, wondering if it was sensible after all – she'd talk to Bill about it, perhaps when they got to Stoke Bruerne. In the end, she knew, it would be her decision – they were a team, and a damned good one at that, but while she would always defer to her husband when it came to the boats and the way they worked, the family was her responsibility, and now that she'd taken this errant kid under her wing, he fell into that category, too.

She glanced down, found him looking up at her:

''Ow are yeh feelin' Moichael?' He gave her a wan smile:

'Okay, thank you, Mrs Hanney.'

'Oi'm doin' Breakfus' – would yeh loike soome?' His smile widened noticeably:

'Yes, please – it smells great!' Vi chuckled, scooped a sausage and an egg on top of a slab of bread on one of the plates she had ready, handed it to the boy:

'There yew goo then! Tea ter foller in a minute, h'okay?'

'Okay! Thank you.'

She piled two more plates, stuck her head out of the hatches to quickly confirm their location, called to her second son:

'Stevie! Coom 'ere boy, tek these plates and joomp off in that bridge-'ole, run forward to yer Dad 'n Billy on the motor. 'And 'em oover, 'n coom back 'ere fer yer own, roight?'

'Roight y'are, Mum.'

He stood, balancing on the gunwale, as she swung the stern over until it was close enough for him to step down onto the bank. Running forward as best he could through the snow to the next bridge, he got there in time to hand the plates over to his father and brother – Bill had slowed the engine to allow him to overhaul them – and then wait until the butty caught him up again. Meanwhile, Vi had handed a plate out to Gracie, and one for little Jack – she had Stevie's ready for him when he tumbled eagerly back into the stern well, let him inside to sit at the table-cupboard to wolf it down.

Michael had finished his, handed the plate back to Vi to have it replaced with a mug of steaming tea. Stevie's brown eyes flicked up to him in frank curiosity as he munched on each mouthful of his breakfast; Michael looked back, trying not to feel uncomfortable under such scrutiny. Mopping a runnel of egg from his chin with the last mouthful of bread, Stevie asked:

'What's yer name, then?'

'Michael.'

'Moichael what?'

'Just Michael.'

'Ah. Oi'm Stevie – that's moy Ma.' He indicated Vi, sitting beside him as she ate her own sausage.

'Yes, I know. I'm pleased to meet you, Stevie.' The brown eyes widened at such formality:

'Er – yeah, Oi guess so…'

'If yew two've finished, whoy doon't yeh go 'n sit outsoide? Lend Miochael yer spare coat, Stevie.'

Chapter Nine

Ferreting in a drawer that he'd pulled out from below the sidebed, Stevie handed a heavy serge jacket to Michael. He picked up his own, and slipped it back on ready to brave the outdoor chill:

'Put that on, Moichael, it's cold enooff out ther' ter freeze the…'

'Stevie!' The boy grinned cheekly at his mother:

'It is though, Ma!'

'Oi'm sure it is, but that's noo excuse! Now git yerself out o' moy way whoile Oi start on yer dinner!'

Stevie led the way outside, tapping his sister on the leg to signal his wish to leave the cabin; he clambered nimbly up onto the cabintop and sat on the right hand side, his legs dangling over the edge. He reached back, offered a hand to Michael who was moving somewhat more cautiously, helped him as he scrambled rather inelegantly up to join him. Grace stepped back into the hatches, resumed her easy stance, one arm draped casually over the heavy wooden tiller; Jack had turned to stare over his shoulder from his own perch at the front of the short cabin roof.

'Jackie – this is Moichael.' The seven-year-old, big brown eyes under a thatch of dark hair a smaller echo of his brother, gazed in frank curiosity at the newcomer:

'Moichael what?'

'Joost Moichael.' Stevie forestalled the subject of their discussion from answering.

'Oo's boat yew off'n, then?'

'I'm not off a boat – I've never been on one before!' Michael got to answer for himself this time.

'Oh – wher' yeh from, then?' Michael hesitated, not wanting to give away more about himself that he had to – the fear that they might still insist on returning him to his parents was still in his mind, but after a moment he relaxed, realising that he wasn't telling the boys anything they couldn't have worked out for themselves:

'Wolverton.'

'Oh.' There was a pause, while the three boys regarded each other thoughtfully.

'Yew roon away from 'ome, then?' Jack asked. Hearing the words of that dramatic phrase spoken so bluntly set Michael back on his heels, its implications striking deep into his mind in a way that his words with Vi had failed to do; but he nodded:

'Yes – yes, I suppose I have!'

'Oh. Yew goona stay with oos now, then?'

'We'll 'ave teh see, Jackie' Grace joined the conversation for the first time: 'That'll be oop ter Ma 'n Dad.'

'Wher's 'e goona sleep?'

'We'll manage loike we did las' noight, fer a whoile, if that's all roight with yew, master Jack Hanney!' The boy shrugged his shoulders, giving his sister a mischievous grin:

'H'okay, Gracie!' He turned his gaze back on Michael: 'What d'yeh knoo about boatin', then?'

'Nothing, I'm afraid. Like I said, I've never even been on one before!'

'Oh!' This time, Jack's response held an ominous tone.

'We'll 'ave ter teach 'im, eh, Jack?' Stevie suggested; his younger brother's face lit into a broad smile;

'Roight! Tha'll be foon, eh?' Both brothers beamed at their new apprentice; Michael, both pleased and nervous at the prospect, smiled back:

'It'll make a nice change from school!' The Hanney brothers exchanged significant glances:

'Yew bin ter school, then?'

'Course 'e's bin ter school, stoopid! All kids 'oo live on the bank goo ter school, don't they, Moikey?'

'That's right, Stevie.' Michael was amused at the other's vigorous manner of correcting his younger sibling; and then the implications of their exchange, and of his new situation, hit him: 'You don't go to school?'

'No – leastways, not offen. We soometoimes git teh go fer a day or two, if the boats are 'eld oop at the stop soomewher'. Boot that don't 'appen mooch.'

'So – How do you learn things? Do your parents teach you?'

'What sort o' things d'yeh mean?' Michael could only shrug. Stevie looked at his brother for a moment, then went on: 'We learn about boatin', 'n the cut, 'cos we're 'ere, see? Oi can steer the pair, breasted or on cross-straps, 'n Oi can work a lock quicker'n moy Dad!'

'Soo can Oi!'

'Noo yeh can't, Jack! Yeh're too small ter steer yet!'

'Oi can steer the butty – can't Oi, Gracie?'

'Only if'n yeh're stood on a box – yeh can't see oover the cabin else!'

'Stop it, the two o' yeh, 'fore yeh git the back o' me 'and!' The grin on Grace's face as she silenced their bickering gave the lie to her words. She turned her smile on Michael:

'We don't get mooch chance fer any proper schoolin', livin' on the boats, Moikey. Loike Stevie says, we moight get a day or two, now 'n then, boot it don't amount to anythin'.' Michael took this in, a frown on his face as he absorbed the idea; he looked around at her:

'So-o…?' Her smile crinkled the corners of her eyes, as dark as were her brothers' – her voice was gentle as she explained:

'So, there's noone of oos can read 'n wroite, Moikey. Stevie's doon quoite well, when he's got ter goo ter the school at Bull's Bridge – 'e can make most of 'is letters, if'n 'e troys 'ard. 'N we can all do figurin' – we 'as teh, fer the toll tickets, see?'

'But – can't your Mum and Dad teach you?' She laughed:

'*They* can't read nor wroite, neither! They didn't get any scholarin' when they were kids, either!'

'Oh…' Michael's thought returned to his own situation: 'So – if I *can* stay with you…'

'Yew won't be getting' any more learnin', Moikey! 'Cept what *we* teach yeh – 'bout the boatin'!' Stevie sounded pleased at the prospect.

'Doos that woorry yeh, Moichael?' Grace asked, a concerned frown on her face.

'I don't know… My Mum's always said I should get a good education, then I'd do better for myself when I grow up – but… I don't know' he repeated; then the smile returned to his face: 'But I *do* want to learn all about your boats!'

'Good fer yew, Moikey! We'll show 'im, woon't we, Jackie? We'll be at Stoke Bruin 'fore long, 'n we can show yeh 'ow to work locks up'ill then – 'n 'ow ter toy the boats fer breastin'-oop, 'n things. Then there's the toonnel…'

'A *tunnel?*'

'Yeah – Blizzerth Toonnel! It's more'n a moile long, teks 'alf an hour teh goo through…'

'You have *tunnels* on the canal, like railways?'

'Yeah – 'course we do! En't yew seen oone b'fore?'

'Moikey 'asn't bin on a *boat* before, remember?' Grace reminded her brother.

'Oh – Oh, yeah, Oi'd forgot.' Stevie's face took on a mischievous smirk, as his voice dropped to a mysterious whisper: 'It's ever soo dark, 'n wet, 'n spooky, insoide! They says as there's the ghost of an ol' boatee, 'aunts it, 'n throws things at yeh…'

'Stop it, Stevie – yew knoo very well there's noo ghost in Blizzerth! Stop troyin' ter froighten Moikey loike that!' Stevie subsided as his sister admonished him, but he threw a cheeky grin at Michael:

'Not 'fraid o' the dark, are yeh?'

'No – of course not!'

'What else did they learn yeh at school, then?' Jackie asked.

'Oh – arithmetic, and history, and geography, and – all sorts of things!'

'O-oh!'

A brief silence fell, while the Hanney brothers regarded their new companion with a degree of awe. Michael took the opportunity to look around him, taking in some detail of the boats which he hadn't noticed before – the tall chimney at the other back corner of the cabin, above the place where the range stood, with its polished brass bands gleaming in the thin winter sunshine; the two big jugs, rather like enormous watering-cans to look at, which stood in front of it, brightly painted with flowers and a scene like those he'd noticed inside the cabins, the handle of a long mop poked through their own handles, its business end lying on the cabintop near the front. And the scenery through which they were passing – open fields on both sides of the canal, the low morning sun sparkling on the frosted hedges and occasional tree, the clear pale blue of the sky… A townie boy all his life, Michael experienced for the first time that lifting of the heart which the beauty of nature can bring, so much so that it made him shiver momentarily:

'Yew cold, Moikey? Go in the cabin 'n git warm if yeh loike.' He smiled at Gracie's concern, shook his head:

'No, thanks, I'm fine. It's – so pretty, isn't it?' He gestured at their surroundings. The girl laughed:

'Oi s'pose so! We see it all the toime, so we don' notice it any more.' She looked around herself, then smiled back at him: 'It is, in't it? Boot this is wher' we *live,* Moikey.' He looked at her for a moment, absorbing the meaning of her words:

'You're so lucky, all of you!' A thought struck him: 'These are *your* boats, are they?'

'They're our'n, teh live in, yes, as long as we're workin' 'em. Boot they *belong* ter the coomp'ny.'

'Oh…' Michael bent to look between his own legs at the cabinside: 'That's the name on the side, is it, the company?' She laughed:

'Oi s'pose so! It's Fellers's – Fellers, Morton 'n Clayton, we work for. Or Pa doos, 'e's the oone as gets paid. Coomp'ny tells 'im what ter load, 'n wher' teh tek it, 'n pays 'im when it's ther' 'n unloaded.'

'They have sort of managers, to tell you what to do, like my Dad does in the rail…'

'Oh-ho! Yer Dad's in the works, is 'e?' Stevie butted in, his voice gleeful at his discovery. Grace glared at him, seeing the horrified look on Michael's face, then said:

'Boot we en't goin' ter *tell* anyone that, are we? Not unless yeh want oos to.' Meaningful eyes still weighed on her younger brother, until he shook his head:

'No – 'course not!' Gracie's smile returned, directed upon Michael:

'Ter answer yer question, yes, Moikey. Ther's a man at each stop wher' we go, 'oo directs the loads, tells oos wher' to go, what we're carryin'. Loike Mister Vickers, at Braunston – yeh'll meet 'im in a day or two, when we gits ther'. If this oice'll let oos! Ma 'n Dad want ter stop ther' a whoile – an ol' friend o' theirs 'ad 'is woife doie a week or two back, 'n they want ter see 'im, cos we missed 'er buryin'. Oi 'spect we'll…' She broke off, a look of revelation on her face: 'Stevie – tek oover 'ere, will yer? Oi want ter talk ter Ma fer a minute!'

The boy jumped up on the cabintop, made his way past Michael and slipped down into the hatches, took over the tiller as she stepped down into the cabin, a proud grin on his round face.

Chapter Ten

It was Michael's turn to regard his new friend with awe, as Stevie settled comfortably over the tiller, gazing casually forward past him, to where the motor boat led the way through the broken, drifting ice. Jack was still twisted round, looking at his brother:

'Can Oi 'ave a go?'

'No! Gracie tol' *me* ter steer!'

'Oh – go on?'

'Mebbe later, then.' Jack turned away, shoulders slumped grumpily, to watch the scenery sliding by. Aware of Michael's continuing scrutiny, Stevie had a little smile on his face as he gazed into the distance, carefully avoiding eye contact so as not to seem too proud.

'How big *is* this boat, Stevie?' Michael's curiosity came to the fore; Stevie turned his smile on him:

'Seventy foot' he said, the pride resonating in his voice despite his attempt to sound casual: 'All narrerboats are the sem soize, give or tek a bit. Gran' Union's are a foot 'n a 'alf bigger'n ourn – they can carry a toon or so more'n oos. Boot moy Dad sez they're big oogly boogers.' The two boys shared a grin at his repeating of such colourful language.

'How much do you carry at once, then?'

'We got 'bout twenny-eight toon on this'n, 'n twenny-three or –four on the motor.'

'What is it?'

'What's what?'

'Your load?'

'Oh – Inkits. Alloo… Allyoomin…'

'Aluminium?'

'Ah – that's it. Allyoominum inkits.' Michael paused, trying to make sense of this – then the light dawned:

'Aluminium Ingots?'

'S'what Oi said!'

'Where're you taking them?'

'Birnigum'

'Birmingham?'

'Yeah - Birnigum! Yew deaf or soomat?' Afraid he'd angered his new friend, Michael hurried to smooth things over:

'No – sorry – it's just that your accent's a bit…' Stevie suddenly grinned at him:

'Yew can talk! Yew sound all la-di-da – moost coom from spendin' all yer toime in school, Oi s'pose.' And then they were laughing together, the townie boy and the boater's kid sharing the understanding that the joy of childhood is the same, whatever your circumstances. Stevie went back to his explanation of their trip:

'We 'ad ter go teh Loime'us ter load, 'cause there weren't no loighters ter bring the stoof ter Brentford for oos. That's all the way 'round the Paddin'ton cut, see? It's a bit scary there, 'cause they load oos straight out o' the ship, wi' big cranes – if'n they gits it wrong, they could sink oos, no trouble! Now, we're 'eadin' back oop the Joonction, 'n Oi 'spect it'll be middle road inter Birnigum 'n oop the Ol' Main Loine ter James's fact'ry on the So'o loop.'

Most of this 'explanation' meant nothing at all to Michael; Stevie grinned at the blank look on his face:

'Yew doon't know what Oi'm on about, do yeh?' Michael shook his head:

'I don't know the places you're talking about, I'm afraid!'

'Loime'us dock's on the London River, roight? Where the big ships coom in. They usually send the stoof oop ter Brentford – that's at the end o' the Gran' Joonction cut, where we meets 'em – on loighters, on the river. Only this toime, they 'adn't got noo spare loighters, roight?'

'So you had to go to the dock?'

'Yeah! Noow, we're goin' back ter Birnigum – this 'ere's the Gran' Joonction Canal, roight? Goes all the way from Brentford teh Braunston – then, we'll go on the Warwick cuts inter Birnigum, oop 'Atton locks – that's what they call the middle road, see? 'N Oi 'spect we're goin' ter James's wi' this lot – that's the usual place we tek Allyoo…'

'Aluminium.'

'Yeah. That's on what we call the So'o loop, off'n the Ol' Main Loine o' the BCN.'

'BCN?'

'Er – Birnigum Canal… Navigash'ns.'

'I see…' Michael was still not entirely clear about what Stevie had been saying, but he didn't want to appear too stupid. Hearing the doubt in his voice, the boy at the tiller gave him a big grin:

'Yeh'll see, when we gits ther'!'

A friendly silence fell between them as they passed an old derelict wharf at the canalside, only the big whitewashed house, with its sway-backed roof, showing signs of occupation. Michael found himself bursting with questions about life and work on the boats – the more he learnt, the more he realised there was that he *didn't* know, and the more he wanted to ask. But for now:

'How difficult is it to steer a boat?'

'S'easy! Yeh can see 'ow mooch Oi've bin doin' 'ere. 'Course, the butty 'as ter foller the motor, 'cause o' the tow – boot yer still 'as ter keep it roight. Let it git out o' the channel, 'n roon on the mud, 'n yer can snap the loine, so yew 'as ter stay in the middle o' the cut, see?'

He gave Michael a speculative look: 'Yew want ter 'ave a go?'

'I don't know…' Stevie caught the look of thunder on his little brother's face as Jack looked around at him:

'Oi'm *teachin'* Moichael, Jackie! Yeh can 'ave go in a bit, h'okay?' The youngster turned away again, not entirely mollified but knowing that it was no use arguing with his brother. Stevie turned back to Michael:

"Old on whoile Oi tek it 'round this turn – then yew troy, okay?'

'What do I have to do?' Michael was still unsure of himself.

'Yew joost move the tiller oone way or t'other, 'n the boat turns – loike this:' He pushed the tiller away, to the right: 'Put the 'ellum oover that way, 'n the boat cooms 'round this way, see?' He gestured ahead with his free hand, and Michael turned to watch the front of the boat swing gently to the left. Stevie pulled the tiller to the left, and the *Angelus* came back straight, and began to turn right instead; he brought the butty back into line and centred the tiller. The boats swept around the bend in the canal, passing under a blue-brick bridge at its apex; a long straight section now loomed before them as Stevie turned to his apprentice: 'See? S'easy, en't it? Coom on, yew stand 'ere, wher' Oi am, 'n tek 'old o' the 'ellum.' He stepped out into the well, making room for Michael to take his place; but the other boy hesitated, scared of the responsibility:

'I'm not sure…'

'Oh, Coom *on,* Moikey! Yeh'll 'ave teh 'ave a go soomtoime, if'n yer goin' ter stay on the boats!' Michael gave him a nervous smile, but did as he was bid, climbing down carefully from the cabintop to stand in the hatches. He took the end of the long wooden tiller, polished from years of use, in his right hand; Stevie stood behind him, his own hand still resting on the shaft, ready to guide his pupil.

Down in the butty cabin, Vi and her daughter had been holding a prolonged conversation over the dinner preparations, one peeling the potatoes while the other scraped and cut up the carrots. Their voices were hushed, so that the subject of their talk didn't overhear, although the sound of the children's chatter from outside suggested that they had their attention elsewhere. When the shuffling of feet on the step in the cabin doors interrupted them, Vi looked up with a grin:

'Seems loike ah Stevie's tekin' 'is new job serious-loike!' She gestured with the knife, and Grace turned to see Michael's feet, clad in Stevie's spare boots, step nervously into place. She smiled, her dark eyes alight:

'Yew think it'll work oot alroight, Ma? What we bin talkin' about?'

'We'll see, love. Oi'll talk teh yer Dad, later – Oi reckon 'e'll go along wi' it.' The girl turned back to her task, the smile still on her face.

Billy Hanney looked over his shoulder as his boater's sixth sense told him that the tow wasn't behaving the way it should, the butty's weight at the end of its line pulling the motor-boat's stern fractionally to one side, shifting the tiller in his hand:

'Eh, Dad!' He gestured back with a toss of his head. His father, stood on the gunwale to one side of the cabin, his knees leaning against it to keep him balanced, looked up from rolling his cigarette, and glanced in the direction indicated. Even at that distance, the trepidation on Michael's face was clear to see; he turned back to his son with a grin:

'Doon't look too 'appy, doos 'e?' Billy laughed:

'Stevie'll keep an oiye on 'im, 'e woon't let 'im cock it oop too bad!' They exchanged grins which had an element of the conspiratorial about them.

'No! Not so mooch!' Stevie's guiding hand fought Michael's over-enthusiastic push on the tiller: 'Gently doos it, Moikey. Yew only want ter move it a little way, see? Joost enooff ter keep it straight. Moy Dad sez the more yeh steer a boat, the more yeh *'as* ter steer it.'

'What?' Michael was trying to concentrate on the task at hand, and this obscure statement had him perplexed.

'If yeh steer it too mooch oone way, yeh 'as ter steer back the oother, 'n so on, roight? Yeh'll end oop goin' from soide ter soide 'til yeh 'it's the bank or soomat, see?'

'Oh – right!'

'So – joost move the 'ellum a bit at a toime, 'n watch the fore-end, wher' it's goin, keep it loined oop joost teh the roight o' the motor's starn-end. That way, yeh're out o' the blade-wash, roight?'

Michael focussed all is attention on doing as he'd been instructed. Moving the heavy tiller to keep the boat from wandering off-course, he could feel the pressure of Stevie's hand guiding what he did, and slowly found himself getting the feel of the boat as it responded to their joint control. And as he relaxed, he realised that he was beginning to enjoy himself, his fears subsiding behind the pride at having such a huge vessel under his inexperienced command. But there was a problem:

'Stevie?'

'Yeah?'

'There's a bridge coming up.'

'Yeah.' Michael risked a quick glance at his instructor, saw the devilish grin on his face:

'What do I do?'

'Best oidea is ter aim fer the 'ole in the middle.'

Vi and Gracie exchanged cheerful looks as the boys' laughter echoed down into the cabin, even if they could both hear the nervous edge to Michael's.

Chapter Eleven

A journey which they would usually have completed in the course of a morning had taken them most of the day. They'd reached the bottom of Stoke Bruerne locks about lunchtime – Despite his impatience, Bill had insisted on taking the six-mile quite slowly, aware that the butty's wooden hull could be damaged by the sharp-edged icefloes, even if the *Acorn,* a newer boat with an iron-sided hull, would be quite safe in such conditions.

Forewarned by the family on a southbound pair they'd passed near Bozenham Mill, all hands had turned to for the flight, fortified by mugs of steaming hot soup resurrected by Grace from the remnants of the previous night's stew and passed around as they rose in the bottom lock. With too much broken ice floating on the water, it was impossible to get the gates fully back into their recesses in the lock walls, preventing the boats from being breasted up as would have been the usual practice – instead, at each lock, Bill and Vi would run the motor and butty in separately, manoeuvring them alongside each other before Grace and the boys closed the gates and raised the paddles to fill the lock. And even that could only be done after some time spent using the long shafts to clear the ice from behind the gates. They crossed several more pairs headed in the opposite direction, and Vi got a report of Rita Baker's funeral from a southbound FMC family who had been there, their boat undergoing repairs to its engine in the Braunston yard.

Despite being a year the younger, Stevie had now taken Michael firmly under his wing; with Jack tagging along, the younger boys had worked one side of the cut as a team, Michael eager to learn all that Stevie and his brother could teach him. Vi watched them, her proprietorial pride in her own offspring matched by a growing admiration at the way in which her new charge was prepared to throw himself into whatever task he was given. It was mid-afternoon by the time they had cleared the flight, a job which would normally have taken little more than half an hour; Bill and his wife had conferred briefly beside top lock, and decided that it would be folly to go on further that day, preferring the civilisation of Stoke Bruerne to the desolation of the sixteen-mile pound if they were indeed going to be ice-bound for a while.

* * *

'Two points o' moild, 'n a stout fer me Mum, please, Zoe!' Joey Caplin stood at the diminutive bar of the *Boat Inn,* beside the canal by Stoke Bruerne top lock. Oldest of the Caplin children, Joe was just seventeen – too young, in the eyes of the law, to be drinking ale, let alone buying it. But that was a law which, on the waterways as in many rural communities, was more often ignored than observed. His parents sat side-by-side in the bay window, his father idly picking at his banjo, listening and finely tuning the strings. Zoe Woodward, the landlady, plonked the two pint glasses down, turned to reach for a bottle of stout from a shelf behind her, as Joe fumbled in his pocket for a handful of change.

'How old are you, young man?' Joe looked around at the question; his eyes lit on a man sat in the corner of the bar, whose attire placed him as a member of the farming community who regularly shared the *Boat* with the people of the waterway. The man rose to his feet – taller than Joe, and broadly-built, dark hair greying at the temples, he looked down at the teenager with an expression of some disdain as the boy, mindful of the law, replied:

'Eighteen!'

'Oh? Then what are you doing here?' The man's voice was educated, but still carried the local Northamptonshire accent. Unsure of his intentions Joe answered:

'What d'yeh mean? We're workin', on our way ter Brentf'd.'

'Why aren't you off fighting for your Country, like all the other young fellows?' The man's manner was becoming intimidating, and Joe took a step back, unsure how to reply. His father stood up, and answered the man's question:

'We're boaters, mate, doin' our job, h'okay?' The man turned to him, looked him up and down:

'Maybe – but this young fellow should be serving his Country, in the forces, at a time like this!'

'Oh no 'e shouldn'! Soom o' the boatee boys 'ave joined oop, boot that's their choice – we're what they call a deserved h'occipation, so 'e doon' 'ave ter go if 'e doon' want teh, roight?'

'It's not right! *My* son's had to go, risking his life in the army, while you get to stay here and take it easy – it's not right!' he repeated.

'We're doin' ar bit, mate! Roight now, we got a load o' shell cases, goin' ter be filled oop 'n sent off ter France fer your bloody army – if we didn' carry 'em, 'ow'd yon fellers be able to foight, eh?' The landlady chipped in, trying to calm things down:

'Leave the kid alone, Tony – like Henry says, they're doing their bit for the war! Let 'em have their drinks in peace, after a long hard day, all right?' the man glowered at her for a moment, drained his glass, slammed it down on the bar and stormed out. She turned to Joe:

'Don't take too much notice of Tony, lad, he's just upset 'cause his boy's been called up. Worried about 'im, you understand?' Joe gave her a smile:

'Yeah, I guess so.'

'Tell 'im we 'ope 'is kid's all right, when yeh see 'im again, eh, Zoe?' Henry added; the landlady nodded;

'I will, Henry. You 'ave those drinks on me, right, for the upset?'
Always glad of a free beer, father and son both grinned at her:
'Thanks, Zo! Yeh're a star!'

'Not now, Bill! We're not goin' noowher' fer a day or two, 'n
ther'll be toime enooff ter talk about 'im termorrer.'

For the umpteenth time that evening, Bill Hanney had tried to
raise the subject of their unexpected guest, only to have Vi shush
him. He was the boss, the captain of the boats, and would brook
no interference with his decisions on that front – but he gladly
allowed Vi to take charge when it came to the children. He sensed
that she had come to some decision regarding Michael, and knew
that she would discuss it with him when she was ready, even
take note of any objections he might have; but for now, all he
could do was shake his head and return to his pint of mild.

They too were now sat in the bar of the *Boat Inn.* It was later
in the evening, and the atmosphere had become thick and smoky
in its tight confines; a lull had fallen in the music, melodeons and
Henry Caplin's banjo laid aside for the moment. Gracie was sitting
in one corner in her best dress, her hands clasped primly in her
lap although she was deep in animated conversation with Joe;
Billy had volunteered to stay with the boats, keep an eye on the
young ones, while his elders had gone to the pub, understanding
his sister's eagerness to be in the company of her beau even if
both of them thought their parents were unaware of it. He'd
seen his two little brothers settled in the butty cabin, top 'n tail on
the sidebed as was their usual sleeping arrangement, and then
taken Michael over into the motor in accordance with his mother's
instructions – the boy was to sleep where she could keep an eye
on him, even if it meant Billy himself having to manage on the
butty's floor again. Not that he minded – it seemed like the kid
could do with a break, if what he'd gathered of his life was true
– but he quietly hoped it wouldn't be for too long!

He felt the boat move gently as someone stepped onto the butty – the pair was once more tied side-by-side in conventional fashion – then heard the scrape of boots on the counter. The cabin doors opened, the hatch slid back, and his mother stepped down inside, her eyebrows raised in question:

''E's foine, Ma. 'N the other two're asleep nex' door.' His voice was soft, not to wake the sleeping child.

'Roight – thank yer, Billy. Gracie's 'ome – give 'er a minute 'n yeh can git ter bed 'n all.' He nodded, and climbed out onto the counter; his father took his place in the cabin, passing Vi to sit on the edge of the cross-bed where she had already lowered it before brewing them a last cup of tea. She poured, and sat on the stool beside the open table-cupboard, leaning on her elbows to take a sip from her cup, her eyes raised to her husband. She smiled at the look on his face:

'Yew en't gonna sleep oonless we talk about 'im, are yeh?' She knew he was troubled by the boy's presence, concerned at what to do with him. She held his gaze for a minute; then: 'All roight, Bill. Oi'll tell yeh what Oi think – me 'n Gracie 'ad a long chat about it, coomin' oop the six-moile terday.'

'Go on, Ma?'

'Well – we can't keep 'im, can we? We don't need any 'elp, wi' four of our own, 'n we en't got the room fer 'im, really, 'ave we? 'N they say as 'ow food's gooin' ter git rationed any toime now, what with the war 'n all, so Oi don't need an extra mouth ter feed. We won't git rations fer 'im, 'cause 'e en't one of our'n.'

'So we should send 'im 'ome, is that what yeh're sayin'?' Vi glanced briefly at the shape huddled under the blanket on the sidebed:

'No, Bill. 'E woon't thank oos fer that, not if 'e troied teh drown 'imself teh git away from ther'.' She leant forward conspiratorially: 'Ow about we give 'im ter Alby?'

'Alby Baker?'

'Yeah! 'E's got no-one, wi' Rita gone, 'n Alex away in the Navy, 'as 'e?' Bill looked puzzled:

'What good's a kid off the bank goin' ter be ter Alby? 'E don't know anythin' about boatin', 'n Alby can't teach 'im if ther's joost the two o' them troyin' teh work the boats!'

'No – boot we could lend 'im our Gracie, as well. Wi' the three of 'em, they could manage the pair, 'n Moichael could learn as they go along, see?' Bill sat back, considering this idea. He had to concede that it did make a kind of sense – with two experienced boaters, the boy would have every chance to learn and become a valuable member of the crew; and it would get Alby Baker back into the work he loved, with some prospect of continuing as they both knew he would want to. But there was one thing he didn't like…

'Oi know what yeh're gonna say, Bill. Boot, she's goin ter go, one day, yeh know that. She's near growed oop – 'n she's got an oiye fer that Joey Caplin, too.'

'She 'as?'

''Course! Din't yer see 'em, tonoight? Thick as thieves, in that corner! She'll be weddin' that boy, one foine day, you see if Oi'm not roight!'

This news set Bill back on his heels. He'd known his only daughter was growing up, becoming a fine woman as she did so, but the idea of her married… Like any father, he found the thought of his precious girl being old enough to have children of her own both scary and rather painful. But Vi was right. He heaved a sigh:

'Yeah – mebbe yeh're roight, Vi. Boot what's Alby goin'ter think?'

'We'll 'ave ter ask 'im. Oi 'spect Bert'll 'ave a tellyphone in 'is cottage – if not, Oi'm sure Zoe's got oone in the poob. We'll get oone of 'em teh ring Mr Vickers, in the mornin', ask 'im ter talk ter Alby, see what 'e says.'

'Yeah…' He glanced down at the sleeping child: 'Can 'e 'andle the work, though, Vi? Yew saw 'im las' noight, when yeh'd got 'is clothes off of 'im – 'e's a skinny little thing!'

'Aye – boot 'e's woiry with it, Bill. Yew saw 'im, terday, with our two, gettin' stook in, pushin' the gates, 'n woindin' the paddles once Stevie'd showed 'im 'ow.'

'Mebbe… Boot what about 'im? Will 'e loike this idea o' your'n?' Vi chuckled:

'Whoy doon't yeh ask 'im?'

'What? Wek 'im oop, at this toime o' noight?' Now, she gave a full-throated laugh:

'E's bin listenin' to oos all the toime! Bin awake since we coom in – 'aven't yeh, boy?'

The mound on the sidebed rolled over; Michael pushed the blanket down from his face, gave her a rueful smile and nodded sleepily:

'I woke up when the boat moved – and then I heard you talking about me. I'm sorry…'

'Doon't yew be, choild! Yew've 'eard what we said, it'll save oos 'avin' ter explain it teh yeh tehmorrer.' The boy nodded again.

'So – what d'yeh think, Moichael?' Bill asked.

'I'm not sure…' Vi smiled gently at him:

'Oi know, Moikey – yeh wanted ter stay with oos, didn't yeh? Boot, yeh heard what Oi said ter moy man – it's joost not practical. Goin' with Mr Baker, yeh'll be able teh 'elp 'im no end, 'n ah Gracie'll be there teh keep an oiye on yeh, 'elp yeh along.'

Michael went to speak, but she shushed him: 'Yew get soome sleep now, choild, we'll talk about it in the mornin', h'okay?'

Quite why he wanted to cry, Michael couldn't understand, but the tears rose to his eyes nonetheless. Vi saw them, and hitched her stool closer, drew the boy into her arms as he reached for her, holding his slim bare shoulders as they began to shake:

'Yew poor kiddie! It'll all work out, yew'll see!'

Chapter Twelve

Eight o'clock in the morning. Janet Eastwood looked up from the sink as the news bulletin came on the wireless in the back room: *He'll be clockin' on now* – clocked *on if he doesn't want to lose a quarter of an hour's money!* She'd got Eric away in good time for work, as always – even if he'd been in half a mind to take the day off, help their neighbours look for the boy. She hadn't seen Reg go off – presumably, he was staying home...

They were calling it the Phoney War, even the newsreaders. Four months in, and not a lot seemed to be happening – not that that was necessarily a bad thing! Oh, there was news of the Expeditionary Force in France and Belgium, of course, and even the odd air-raid, back and forth across the North Sea. At home, things were going on much as usual, in many ways; petrol had been rationed, but that didn't matter too much to the Eastwoods – they couldn't afford a motor-car. There was talk now of food being put on ration any time – she heaved a sigh: That would make life more difficult; but they'd get by, they always did!

She'd persuaded Eric that it wasn't worth losing a day's pay – it seemed pretty certain, if what she'd heard was true, that little Michael had run off of his own accord. And who could blame the kiddie? All the neighbours knew what a rough time he had from his father – she had, herself, heard their rowing through the too-thin walls between the terraced houses, seen the occasional bruises on the lad's arms and face... No, who could blame him for wanting to get away from such abuse?

The only question was, where on earth had he gone? The authorities, police, ARP and all, had their minds collectively on other matters, even if it was still just a 'phoney war'; too preoccupied to take the disappearance of a schoolkid very seriously, especially as it seemed he'd taken himself off, would probably bring himself back home just as surreptitiously, in his own good time. Granny Thompson lived in the town, just a few streets away, but she'd seen neither hide nor hair of the boy, hadn't known of his disappearance until roused by her daughter-in-law's frantic knocking on her door the previous morning. The police had gone to see Nettie's parents, Granny and Grandpa Morris, over in Buckingham, but they'd not heard from Michael either.

Just as long as he was okay – that was all that mattered! Janet was not a religious woman, but lately she'd taken to offering a quiet prayer each night for the protection of her own two sons – Edward, learning to fly fighter aeroplanes with the RAF, and Martin, training as ground-crew because they wouldn't let him fly, not with his eyesight. Last night, she'd added little Michael's name as a third on her list: *Please, God, just let him be safe!* In the back of her mind, and, she was sure, in the back of Nettie's, if not Reg Thompson's, was the fear that he might have decided that life wasn't worth living... But they hadn't found his body, either, so that had to be hopeful, didn't it?

'I'm off to school, Mum!' Janet turned to wave goodbye to her daughter:

'Okay, Susan love. Don't work too hard!'

'Don't worry, I won't!' The girl chuckled as ever at their daily joke, swept out of the door in her uniform, the battered old satchel over her shoulder. Janet turned back to her washing-up, her mind still on her neighbours: *Poor Nettie – and poor little Ginny!* The little girl had come to her yesterday, while her parents were out looking for Michael, distraught at the absence of the big brother she loved more than anyone. Janet shook her head, told herself with feigned certainty *he'll turn up in a day or two!*

* * *

Ten miles away, the subject of her thoughts was enjoying a robust snow-ball fight with a bunch of boatee kids. Stevie and Jack had dragged him out, quite early – seven or eight pairs of boats had opted to stay in Stoke Bruerne the previous night, and now weren't going anywhere until the thaw came, at least enough for the ice-breaker to get through and free them all. Now, about a dozen youngsters, ranging from four to about twelve, were hurtling around, their eager voices shrill in the frosty air, on the old disused mill wharf, snow-balls flying indiscriminately in all directions.

A brief pause in the random, good-natured hostilities, as the snarl of aero-engines made itself heard. Heads turned, eyes raised to the ice-blue skies, as a vic of three fighters passed overhead:

'Spitfoires!' The cry from several small throats, but Michael shook his head:

'No – those are Hurricanes.'

''Ow d'yeh know?' Stevie was the inquisitor.

'Their wings are straight, with round ends, look! Spitfires have curved wings, and the ends are pointed.'

'Oh – yew sure?'

'Yeah!'

The planes flew on, and a snowball hit Stevie on the shoulder, bringing him back to the battle at hand.

Nothing more had been said about Michael's future, and he hadn't wanted to raise the subject, still unsure of just what he wanted. He'd understood Vi's explanations, and accepted, albeit with a feeling of sadness, that he couldn't stay with the Hanneys – the choice between going back home and going to work with this Mr Baker was a difficult one: He found himself now beginning to miss his mother, and little Ginny – even Andy – so to have to choose between seeing them again, and launching out into the unknown, even with Gracie's company, was a hard choice for a boy of ten. As the snow-ball fight went on, his mind kept returning to the subject despite his attempts to ignore it – one moment he'd decide to give up and go home; the next, to go on to Braunston and at least meet this Mr Baker, see what he was like...

* * *

Ben Vickers replaced the telephone's handset, a thoughtful look on his face. He got to his feet, left the office, and made his way around FMC's dock to where Alby Baker's pair were tied, near the iron bridge. He knocked on the butty's cabinside – the pair were breasted up, the motor as always on the outside, where the water could more easily accommodate its deeper draught. The hatch slid back, and Baker's head poked out into the bright morning air:

'Mornin, Ben! Coom on in the warm – yeh got toime fer a coopa?'

'You know better than to ask, Alby!' Vickers stepped down into the cabin as Albert pushed the doors open for him, pulled them closed again behind him. He seated himself where his old friend indicated on the sidebed, while his host reached into the top cupboard above the table and extracted a striking brown and white Measham teapot which had been Rita's pride and joy. Seeing this, Ben commented:

'I'm honoured, Alby!' The boatman shrugged his shoulders:

'She wouldn'a wanted it joost sittin' in the coopboard gatherin' doost.'

Ben sat silent while his friend spooned tea into the pot, added water from the kettle which had already been singing quietly to itself on the range. That was the inviolable convention which had to be observed – business could be raised only when the ceremony

73

of brewing and pouring the tea was concluded. Alby would give him the opening, when he was ready!

At last, each sat with a mug of good strong tea in front of him on the lowered table-cupboard:

'So, Ben – coom ter pester me about this job on the dock, then, 'ave yer?' Vickers laughed, shook his head:

'No, Alby! I think we might manage to keep you on the boats after all!'

'Oh? 'Ow's that, then?' The boater's voice was as noncommittal as his expression – but Ben had seen the light in his eyes:

'I've just had a call from Bert Jones, lock-keeper at Stoke Top…' he went on to tell Baker about the runaway that Vi and Bill Hanney had picked up, and of Vi's suggestion that he could go to work with him. The man's reaction was exactly what Bill Hanney had expected:

'Coom on, Ben! What bloody use is a little kid off the bank goin' ter be ter *me?* 'E'll know nothin' o' boatin', 'n Oi can't teach 'im on me own 'n work a pair at the same toime! 'N Oi 'spect 'e'll be 'ankerin' teh go 'ome to 'is folks 'fore we git anywher', any'ow!'

'Hold on, listen, Alby! Vi also says you can take their Grace along – she'll help you, and help to teach this kid at the same time. Between you, you could manage okay. Gracie herself is all for it – Vi reckons she's taken a fancy to young Joey Caplin, and won't mind her folks not being about when they meet up around the cut.' Alby laughed:

'Aye, Oi reckon! Remoinds me o' the way moy Rita alwes troid teh git away from the soight o' her Ma when we was courtin'! Old Ma Wain didn't think mooch ter me, at fust – boot she coom 'round in the end.'

'Grace is almost sixteen now – she's a good boater, and even if she goes her own way in a year or two, by then you can have the boy trained up. The two of you could run the pair, then – after all, you and Rita managed okay with just two, didn't you? And this lad's young and fit, from what Vi says, and only too keen to learn.'

''Ow old is 'e?'

'Ten, coming on eleven. His name's Michael – he's on the skinny side, but tall for his age, apparently.'

"Wher's 'e coom from?'

'They don't know, exactly. They found him by Galleon Bridge. And I don't think you need worry about him wanting to go home – Vi reckons he'd tried to drown himself by jumping in the cut. He won't talk about his home, but it must have been pretty awful for him to do that.'

'Hmm, yeah, mebbe so.' Alby sat back, sipping his tea thoughtfully for a minute or so; then he nodded: 'H'okay, Ben, Oi'll give 'im a go, if young Gracie's along ter 'elp. Loike yeh say, she's a good girl.' He drained his mug, set it down: 'What about me boats?'

'I was going to put the *Sycamore* on the dock later today. The *Antrim* is fine, we only docked her what, last year?'

'Yeah. Boot the motor needs doin', Ben – it needs a coat o' paint, and the bottoms are weepin' joost back o' the mast, need fixin' 'fore they git any worse. 'Ave yeh got a change boat Oi could 'ave?'

'I could get you one…' The conversation lapsed into a thoughtful silence, only to be broken by Alby, going off on another tack:

'When's 'Anneys loikely ter git 'ere? Oi tek it they're froze in at Stoke Bruin, roight now?'

'That's right, Alby. But the weather men say the thaw's on its way, tonight or tomorrow – if they get the Gayton ice-boat working and break them free, they could be here, probably the day after.'

'Hmm… Wher' are they 'eadin' for?'

'They've got Aluminium on, fifty-two ton, for James's foundry on the Soho.'

'Hmm. 'Ow about if this little lad stays wi' them fer a bit longer? If they tek 'im oop teh Birnigum, 'n drop 'im 'ere on their nex' trip, boy then yeh could 'ave moy motor about ready, couldn' yer? 'N 'e'll learn more, 'n quicker, wi' them – they got a good crew, with all them kiddies o' their own, 'aven't they?' Vickers just smiled at the boatman, who went on: ''N Oi'll mek meself useful round 'ere, in the meanwhoile – get soome of them old Bolinder's o' your'n roonnin' properly! 'Ow's that?'

'If you hadn't suggested it, I was going to! You can start by setting up your own engine – then the old *Envoy* is by the dock, she really needs a new motor but I haven't got one spare, with the war and everything. You could see what you can do with her, for me?'

'Roight – it's a deal then, Mr Vickers?' He put out his hand; Ben took it, shook it warmly:

'A deal, Mr Baker!'

Chapter Thirteen

'No stars tonoight, Mr 'Anney!'

Bill had been standing in the hatches of the *Acorn,* waiting and puffing on one of his notorious roll-ups while Vi got herself into her best skirt and blouse, ready for another foray over the road to the *Boat*, to sample whatever impromptu entertainment the evening might provide. Now, he looked around at the sound of a voice:

'Yer roight ther', lad!' Joe Caplin stood on the bank, by the butty's stern: 'Bert said ther'd be a thaw tonoight – 'e could even be roight, mebbe!'

'Wind's bin gone 'round since mornin', 'asn' it?'

'Ar – yeh roight, boy!'

'Shall yeh be away in the mornin', then?'

'Reckon so. 'E says Gayton Yard'll troy 'n 'ave the oice-boat out fust thing, s'long as its softened oop enough, brek it through ter Bugby; we'll get away, through the toonnel, see 'ow far we can git. Should make the New Inn, at Bugby top; mebbe even Braunston. Yew 'eaded off, too?'

'S'oop ter moy Dad, Mr 'Anney – boot Oi'd say so. We're goin' ter Brentford, wi' what they're callin' machine parts – bits fer tanks, Oi reckon they are, bound fer France or soomwher'.'

'Shan't be seein' yeh fer a whoile, then?'

'Reckon not, Mr 'Anney.' The youth hesitated: 'S'whoy Oi'm

'ere, really – is your Gracie coomin' oover the *Boat* wi' yeh tonoight?' Bill laughed:

'Moy Missus was roight, then, was she? You two're sweet on each oother?' Joe's blush was mercifully lost in the darkness:

'We loike each oother foine, fer sure, Mr 'Anney – But Gracie's not sixteen yet, it's too soon ter be thinkin' loike that!'

'Oi know, lad – Oi'm only teasin' yeh! Teh answer yer question – no, she's stayin' wi' the boats tonoight, ter keep an oiye on the young 'uns. Our Billy's coomin fer a beer with 'is old Dad, instead!' He stood aside, feeling Vi's tap on his leg, to let her emerge from the cabin beside him.

'Yeh could stay 'ere, talk to 'er, if yeh wanted, Joey?' Vi had clearly overheard the conversation. Bill gave her a doubtful look, but she just smiled serenely at him: 'Joey's a good boy, Bill, 'e'll not do anythin' 'e shouldn't.'

'Of Course Oi won't, Mrs 'Anney! We'll sit on the starn-end 'ere, wher' yeh can keep an oiye on oos!' Vi laughed:

'Yew do that, Joey, keep moy man 'appy! Coom on, Bill, that ale woon't keep all noight!' She knocked on the top of the butty cabin: 'Yew too, Billy, shift yerself! Gracie – soomeone ter see yer, girl!'

* * *

Bert Jones' message for the Hanneys, that afternoon, hadn't just concerned the weather:

'Mr Vickuss said te tell ye that Owbert Baker'll gi' yore noo boy a try, Bill – as long as 'e's got yore Gracie te 'elp 'im. 'E wants ye te stop and see 'im, when ye gets te Brarnston, okay?'

'Roight-oh, Bert. If what yeh say 'bout the weather's roight, we'll be away termorrer, with any loock.'

'Okay, mate! Cloud's buildin' up a'ready, ennit?'

So the next morning saw the family up and about as usual, making ready to get under way. By soon after seven, the big Bolinder was making its habitual off-beat throb echo off of the surrounding buildings; the ice, while still present, was visibly thinning, withdrawing from its margins, leaving a clear edge around the boats and along the bankside. During the night, Bill had wakened to the sound of a gentle rain on the cabintop, and smiled to himself before turning over and going back to sleep, secure in the knowledge that they would be able to move come morning.

Through the Blisworth tunnel, of course, the water was clear – in the cuttings at each end, they broke a thin skim of ice, but once into Blisworth village, past the old mill by the bridge, they found the surface already broken, either by other pairs moving in front of them, or by the ice-breaker from the canal company's maintenance yard by Gayton Junction. From then, their journey was much easier, despite still having to plough their way through the softening, broken ice; once past the junction, where the arm to Northampton and the River Nene turns off to the right, they began to meet other pairs travelling in the opposite direction. Each steerer would call across, confirming that the way ahead was passable; Bill would respond in kind, telling them that the road to Stoke was clear.

There was still enough broken ice to make the working of Buckby Locks slow and difficult, causing Bill to mutter under his breath at the delay; but the summit was clear, and once through Braunston Tunnel, the run down the six locks was made in quite good time.

The old Bolinder's beat echoed under the bridge below Braunston bottom lock as Bill wound it up to power the laden pair out into the length. Last to scramble back aboard, the three boys perched themselves around the gunwale of the butty's stern well, under Vi's watchful eye as she leant in the hatches. Dinner was simmering on the range, below – Billy and Grace stood one each side on the motor's gunwales as their father took the still-breasted pair past the old boat-building sheds, and under the towering gaze of the engine-house chimney.

'Tonk….Tonk Tonk….Tonk….Tonk….Tonk Tonk' The engine settled to its irregular tickover as Bill wound back the throttle, letting the boats travel slowly along, past the reedy, overgrown reservoir and under Butcher's Bridge. And so to the iron bridge over what had once been part of the Oxford Canal, now a truncated arm which was home to Fellows, Morton & Clayton's dock and offices. Along the length they passed tied-up boats – some obviously out of service, waiting to be docked, or just abandoned for want of crews; others occupied, perhaps awaiting a quick, minor repair, or perhaps stopped for family reasons – birth or sickness, marriage, even a funeral.

Michael gazed around, taking it all in even through the gathering gloom – the dank greyness of the day was beginning to descend into a deeper darkness which was slowly killing all the colour in the scene that met his eyes. Just past the iron bridge, Bill knocked out the clutch, turned the boats in toward a vacant space on the towpath:

'We'll toy ther', Ma!' he called across.

Two small figures climbed nimbly onto the butty's cabin roof, and ran forward along the top planks, jumped down onto the foredeck. As the fore-end came close to the bank, the skinny one with the mop of golden hair leapt off, taking the mooring line with him; his companion, shorter, stockier, and black haired, followed suit, showed him how to tie the line, through the ring and back onto the butty's fore-end stud. Bill smiled to himself: *Vi was roight, 'e'll mek a boater yet!*

All that day, he'd been watching young Michael, seeing how he threw himself into any task that was set him – winding paddles, pushing gates, even steering the butty on easier parts of the long pound from Blisworth to Long Buckby. *'E won't give oop, neither!* A number of times, the boy had rebuffed Stevie's attempts to help him, insisting on doing things for himself: On the heavy, cantankerous paddle-gear of Buckby Locks, he'd heaved and strained, refusing to give in, making Vi exchange amused smiles with her husband even if Bill's impatience to get ahead would have preferred him to let Stevie lend that helping hand:

'Ere, Oi'll give yer a 'and' Stevie's voice had carried down to them over the sound of the engine.

'No! I can *do* it!' And he had, even if he'd almost collapsed into the boat when they finally cleared the top lock of the seven. Working downhill, at Braunston, he'd found the going much easier, found himself enjoying the labour, beginning to find a satisfying rhythm in the swing of the gates, the pulling of the paddles, the movement of the boats. Now, as, under Stevie's expert direction, he tied the fore-end to the mooring ring outside the old Stop House, he was feeling deliciously tired, and happy with his lot in a way he hadn't known for so long...

Billy had secured the stern ends to the bank; now, his father stepped down into the engine-hole and stilled the Bolinder's off-beat idling. Emerging once more into the deepening night, he found his wife standing on the towpath:

'Yew gooin' teh see Alby?' He asked.

'Yes, Bill. 'Is butty's joost oonder the bridge, but Oi doon't see the *Sycamore* anywher'.

'H'okay, Ma. Oi'll goo foind Mr Vickuss, tell 'im we're 'ere, n' stoppin' til the mornin', Oi'll join yeh in a minute. Yew tekin' Moikey wi' yeh?'

'They ortta be interdooced, doon't yer think?'

'Sooner the better, Oi reckon.'

With that, Bill turned away, pulling his hat down more firmly over his ears as the drizzle which had plagued them on and off all day began once more to fall. He strode off towards Ben Vickers' office; Vi turned to the two boys, waiting beside the boats:

'Ow yeh feelin', Moikey?'

'Tired, Mrs Hanney!' But she received the brightest smile

she'd seen from the boy so far. Smiling back, she told him:

'Coom wi' me, lad! Oi want yer teh meet Mr Baker, the man 'oos boats yeh're goin' on.' Seeing the boy's smile take on a nervous look, she assured him: 'Yeh'll loike him, 'e's a really noice fella. 'E's got a boy of 'is own, Alex, boot 'e's older'n yew, joined the Navy, fer the war, see?' Michael just nodded, suddenly feeling as nervous as his expression had suggested; but he followed her as she set off along the towpath:

'Yew coomin' too, Gracie?'

'Yes, Ma!' She fell into step with Michael, giving him a reassuring smile. As they turned under the bridge, Vi glanced back:

'Stevie! 'Oo said yew could coom along?'

'Oh, Ma – can't Oi? Oi want teh see Ooncle Alby, too!'

'Oh – h'okay, then. Wher's Jack?'

''E went down in the cabin, wi' Billy.'

'Huh! Oi 'ope the two of 'em'll keep an oiye on the dinner, then!'

Chapter Fourteen

Albert Baker was enjoying a fresh cup of tea, when the knock came on his cabinside. That afternoon, they'd lifted his motor boat onto the dock; having watched that process with proprietorial anxiety, he'd gone to take a look at the *Envoy's* tired engine, but given up trying to start it with the onset of the early dusk. He thought he knew what was needed – but it would be more sensible to tackle the job with the aid of daylight.

He got to his feet, slid back the hatch and looked out:

'Vi! Good ter see yeh, 'ow are yeh?'

''Ello, Alby – 'ow's things?'

'Oh – h'okay, Oi reckon. Yew coomin' in fer a coopa?'

'If yeh've got the kettle on, Oi will!'

'Coom on, then!' She stepped over into the stern well, followed him down into the cabin as he beckoned Gracie to join them. Michael went to follow, but Stevie held him back:

'Not 'til yeh're arst, Moikey!' Seeing his companion's puzzled look, he explained: 'Yeh never step onta soomeoone else's boat 'til yeh're invoited – if yeh go callin', yeh knock on the cabin, then wait - 'n don't look *inter* the cabin, neither, that's very rude!'

'Oh – right!' *Careful, Mikey, don't get off on the wrong foot!* He reflected that there seemed to be rules of etiquette that went with the boater's life – and he'd need to know them, or risk upsetting people! Vi's head appeared out of the hatches:

83

'Yew two – step on, 'n sit yerselves on the gunwales, there, fer now. Tea?'

'Please, Ma!'

'Yes please, Mrs Hanney.'

They did as they were bid, sitting on the edges of the stern well – moments later, two steaming hot cups of tea came out, and they sipped them gratefully. Michael was back in his own clothes, now that they had dried out, and he felt vaguely out of place: His school trousers were too smart, too well-creased, for these surroundings – and too thin! He envied Stevie the heavier, warmer fabric of his, as the cold of the winter night began to penetrate. And his coat – too long! It had tended to get in his way, especially working the locks. But Vi had taken a look at it, while they were travelling the summit, said that she'd alter it for him to make it more suitable – and she'd promised to find him a few extra things, from Stevie's wardrobe, to keep him going for a while. Not, he suspected, that any of them had much clothing to spare.

The two boys sat in companionable silence for a few moments, sipping their tea, hands clasped around the cups for warmth. Then, their eyes met through the rising steam; a twinkle surfaced in Stevie's as he asked:

'Well? 'Ow're yeh loiking' the boatin' then?' Michael hesitated, trying to find words to express his feelings:

'It's – brilliant! Hard work – I don't think I've ever felt so tired – but it's still brilliant!' Stevie laughed:

'Better'n goin' ter school, then?'

'Heaps better!'

'Goin' ter be a boater, then, are yeh?'

'Yeah! If Mr Baker'll have me. But there's so much to learn!'

'Oh, yeh're getting' the 'ang o' things a'ready! Moy Dad says yeh never stops learnin', on the boats – when yeh think yeh know it all, soomat cooms along n' catches yeh out, shows yeh 'ow mooch yeh *doon't* know!'

'That's good advoice, Moikey, even if Oi didn' think moy son 'ad teken it in! Coom insoide, lad, n' meet Mr Baker.' Vi gave him an encouraging smile from the open hatch, beckoned him forward. Nerves fluttering in his tummy again, Michael rose and followed her down into the cabin's bright interior. Looking around inquisitively, he found himself in familiar surroundings – apart from slightly different decoration, a different set of hanging plates on the wall, different curtains over the bed-hole, he could have been on board the *Acorn* or the *Angelus*. His gaze went to the occupants – Vi and Gracie were squeezed in side by side on the sidebed, and a man who must be Mr Baker sat facing him, on a stool the far side of the table-cupboard.

The two studied each other for a moment – Michael saw a man, not unlike Bill Hanney in height and build, maybe a few years older, his hair greyer, his eyes also a dark grey in colour, with the creased, weatherbeaten, but somehow ageless complexion of someone who spends his working life out of doors. The man rose to his feet, held out a hand, as Vi spoke:

'Moichael – this is Mr Baker.'

'Pleased to meet you, sir.' Michael took the proffered hand and shook it; Albert Baker smiled at his new recruit:

'Mr Baker'll do! Moichael – is that what folks call yeh?'

'Yes, sir – Mr Baker – but… the others have been calling me Mikey…'

'Oothers?'

'Mr and Mrs Hanney – and Gracie and the others.'

'Oh. D'yeh prefer that, then?'

'I… I think so, yes, s… Mr Baker.' The smile widened:

'Moikey it is, then!' Albert returned to his seat; Michael stood there feeling slightly embarrassed under his continuing gaze. The boatman turned to Vi:

'Yew were roight, 'e's' a bit on the skinny soide – Yew sure 'e's oop to the work?'

'Oo-ar, Alby, 'e can do it! 'e meks oop in determination what 'e ent got in strength!'

'That's roight, Ooncle Alby! Yeh should'a seen 'im, today, coomin' oop Bugby – 'e wouldn' let me 'elp 'im wi' the paddles or nothin'!'

'Joost 'oo arst yew, Stevie 'Anney?' Albert grinned as the boy subsided in the open doors, having spoken over his new friend's shoulder. His smile shifted to Michael:

'Sit down, boy – on the step, be'ind yeh. 'N yew'd better coom 'n join oos, bein' as yeh've a'ready poked yer nose in, Stevie!' The younger boy did as he was told, sitting beside Michael with a cheeky grin:

''E's a scholard 'n all, Ooncle Alby!'

'That roight, Moikey?'

'I've been going to school since I was five, Mr Baker.'

'Ah! Yeh can read 'n wroite, then, can yeh?'

'Of c… I mean, yes, I can.' Michael stilled his initial, indignant reply as it occurred to him that the man facing him quite probably, himself, could not.

'Ah – Yew could wroite a letter fer me, ter moy son, if Oi told yeh what ter say then, could yeh?'

'I – yes, I could, Mr Baker.'

''E's away in the war, see, boy – in the Navy.'

'I know – Mrs Hanney told me.'

''Ow's 'e doin, Alby?' Vi asked

'Pretty good, Oi reckon! They won't let 'im tell me wher' 'e is, what 'e's doin', boot Oi know 'e's on oone o' them destroyers. 'E wroites ter me when 'e can – that's wher yew coom in, Moikey, yeh see?' Michael nodded:

'I'd be glad to help, Mr Baker.' The boatman turned to the girl sitting beside her mother:

''Ow about yew, Gracie – yeh're 'appy to coom wi' me, 'elp me teach this 'ere lad the ropes, are yeh?'

'Oi am, Ooncle Alby. Ma 'n Dad 'ave got enooff 'elp wi'

Billy 'n Stevie 'n Jack, they can manage foine without me.' His gaze went from the girl to her mother; Vi nodded her agreement.

'H'okay, as long as yeh're all sure. That's settled, then.' A knock sounded on the cabinside: 'That yew, Bill? Coom on, join the crowd!'

The butty rocked as Bill stepped into the well, leant in through the open hatch; looking at the crowded state of the cabin, Vi spoke up:

'Yew two, go on back ter the boats, wi' Billy 'n Jack. We'll sort out yer things in a whoile, Moikey, h'okay?'

'Yes, Mrs Hanney.'

'Oh, Ma!'

'Go on, Stevie. Yeh can coom 'n see Ooncle Alby later, when we've eaten.'

There was a resentful droop to the youngster's shoulders as he obeyed his mother, which lifted under the challenge as Michael said;

'Come on Stevie – I'll race you!' Vi chuckled at her husband's raised eyebrows as he stepped down into the space they had just vacated:

'Two minutes ago 'e was wore out! Ent it great ter be a kid?' The grown-ups and Gracie shared a good-natured laugh:

'Sit down, Bill. Tea?'

'Oi could use a coopa, thanks, Alby.' Moments later, the steaming cup in his hands, Bill asked:

'What d'yer think o' the boy, Alby?'

''E seems loike a good kid, Bill. A bit on the skinny soide, boot Vi says 'e's oop ter the job, got a bit o' grit to 'im. Wher's 'e from, though? What about 'is family?' Bill laughed:

''E woon't tell oos! We fished 'im out o' the cut, boy Galleon bridge...' he went on to tell Albert the story, from the moment Billy had spotted the boy diving into the canal: ''N now 'e still won't tell oos 'is surname, or anythin' about 'is folks. Boot as Vi says, if 'e was so keen ter git away from 'em as ter troy 'n drown 'isself....'

'Roight... it's a sad state ter be in, ent it? 'E's keen ter stay on the boats, is 'e?'

'Seems so, Alby. Yeh goona tek 'im?' Baker nodded:

'Reckon so. Wi' Gracie's 'elp, we'll mek a true boater out of 'im! Boot, what Oi suggest is...' he told them of the plan for the boy to stay with them for the trip to Birmingham and back: 'That way, 'e'll 'ave learned a bit more than 'e could standin' around 'ere, 'n moy motor'll be back in the water.' Bill and Vi exchanged glances:

'Yeah... Sounds loike sense, Alby. Mr Vickuss is 'appy wi' that, is 'e?'

''E is, Bill. If only 'cause 'e wants me ter look at the *Envoy,* troy 'n sort out 'er injun!' They laughed again; Gracie suggested:

'Dad – 'ow about if Oi stay 'ere wi' Ooncle Alby? Oi could 'elp out, do 'is cookin' 'n the loike – 'n yeh don't really need me, do yeh? Not wi' Moikey as well the oother boys?'

'What d'yer reckon, Ma?' Vi nodded:

'Meks sense, Dad. Give oos more space in the cabins, 'n all.' Bill hesitated, reluctant as any father to let go of his only daughter any sooner than he had to; but at last he gave in under the girl's imploring gaze:

'H'okay, all roight, if yeh want, girl!' Boot no 'obnobbin' wi' that Joey Caplin when they coom boy, oonderstand?'

'Yes, Dad!' A cheerful silence held sway, until Vi turned to Albert:

'Oi'm so sorry we missed Rita's buryin', Alby. 'Ow are yeh copin'?'

'Oh, not seh bad, thanks, Vi...'

Chapter Fifteen

The next morning saw the *Acorn* and the *Angelus* on their way North once more. Gracie had left the adults chatting, Vi and Bill enquiring sympathetically about Rita's funeral, and gone back to their boats where she'd fed the children. When her parents had come back for their meals, the two boys had returned to the *Antrim* to see their 'Ooncle Alby', taking a still rather nervous Michael with them.

Over the next hour, he'd found himself developing a deferential liking for the older boatman. Baker was clearly a man who expected children to be respectful of their elders, but he could still enjoy their company, laugh with them at their fooling, amuse them with his own japes and tales. Later, they had settled to their beds while the adults, with Billy in tow, had walked back to Butchers Bridge and up the hill into the village, to enjoy the hospitality of the Old Plough.

Michael had felt an odd emptiness at waving goodbye to Gracie, but consoled himself with the thought that he'd be seeing her again in a week or two; she had settled easily into her role as his big sister, taking him under her wing just as she did with her own brothers, and he had developed a deep affection for her. But the prospect of boating all the way to Birmingham and back with the Hanneys filled him with anticipation at the same time, as he and the two younger boys settled themselves on the gunwales around the butty's stern well. Vi leant on the massive wooden tiller; Bill and his elder son were, as usual, together on the motor boat.

The two heavy-laden boats swept around the turn, under one of the two elegant iron bridges which span the triangular junction between the Oxford and Grand Union Canals. Two hours would take them to Wigrams turn, and so onto the Northern part of the Grand Union, and the first locks of the day.

Over the days which followed, all the members of the Hanney family threw themselves into teaching Michael as much as they could about the art and technique of running a pair of narrowboats. He found himself involved in, expected to cope with, everything from working the locks to breasting the boats up, from steering the butty to mopping down the cabinsides:

'A *real* boater won't go nowher' wi moocky boats. Alwes keep 'em clean, 'n the brasses shoining, Moikey!'

Not all the locks were the same, either. He had to tackle the huge new locks of the Northern G.U., which Vi called the 'Candlesticks', including the impressive flight of 21 at Hatton; and then, at the other extreme, the narrow locks of the Birmingham canals, where they had to bow-haul the butty through separately. By the time they reached their destination, he was getting beyond the exhaustion he'd first experienced at such constant exercise, and was feeling fitter than he'd ever known; and then came the back-breaking work of unloading, lifting the ingots of aluminium onto the dockside, within the factory walls. It had come as a shock to him when Bill had swung the pair in through a narrow aperture under a towpath bridge and actually inside the building, where a private dock allowed materials to be discharged, and finished products loaded direct into waiting boats.

A message had been waiting for them at the factory, ordering them to load at the Coombeswood Works with steel tubes to go to Brentford; and so, once empty, they had set out to cross Birmingham, navigate the Netherton Tunnel and so onto the Dudley Canal. Loaded once more, they began the return trip – it was now that Michael was surprised, and Stevie seriously put out, when Bill told him to come onto the motor boat:

'Boot *Dad*, yeh've never let *me* steer the motor, 'cept in the locks!'

''E's older 'n yew, Stevie – 'n any'ow, 'e needs ter be able ter 'elp Alby Baker all 'e can, roight?'

'O-oh! Oi s'pose so – boot can Oi 'ave a go wi' the long loine, soon?'

It was mid-morning when the boats turned once more under the iron junction bridge and ran down to the Stop House in Braunston. They'd tied overnight at Birdingbury Wharf, just above Stockton Locks; Michael hadn't slept too well that night, knowing that the time was rapidly approaching when he would have to leave his enthusiastic tutors, say goodbye to his new friends. He was looking forward to seeing Gracie again, and only vaguely apprehensive at going boating with Mr Baker – his self-confidence had grown out of all proportion during the Birmingham trip, as had his skills, and his knowledge of the canals.

He had had little time to think about his life before that fateful night, about his own family; but now, as another upheaval grew closer with every mile, he found himself wondering how they were, what they were doing. His Mum – did she miss him, or was she relieved to have one less to worry about, to be able to focus her attention on Andy? Andy – happy, loving Andy – he'd be missing his brother, for sure, but he'd probably soon forget him. And Ginny: His heart gave a lurch as he thought of his sister, a feeling of guilt creeping over him at the thought that he'd run off and left her, the only one who'd really loved him. Was she all right? Was she managing to avoid her father's anger, now that he wasn't there to be the target?

Bill, standing on the gunwale at his side, reached over and grabbed the tiller, straightening his course as his attention wandered from the job in hand:

'Yew all roight, Moikey?'

'Yeah – it's just – I was thinking about my sister…'

'She'll be 'ome, with yer folks, will she?'

'Yeah – what day is it?'

'Toosdy, Oi reckon.'

'She'll be at school, then.'

''Ow old is she?'

'Five, nearly six. She only started school in September.'

'Yew got any more brothers 'n sisters, Moikey?'

'Only Andy – he's my younger brother. He's what they call a Mongol, he's… his brain doesn't work right, you know?'

'Yeah, Oi know. Oi'm sorry, Moikey.' Silence fell for a while; then Bill chanced the big question: 'What about yer parents, lad – they'll be missin' yeh, won't they?' Michael shook his head:

'I shouldn't think so. My Dad – all he ever did was get angry with me. And my Mum was too busy with Andy, and Ginny, to take much notice of *me*.'

Bill glanced across at the boy, whose eyes were looking straight ahead, apparently intent upon steering the boat, but somehow unfocussed, as if staring into the past. His heart went out to this quiet, capable kid, who had proved his quick brain and eager adaptability so often, so effectively, over the last days. Impulsively, he reached over and put a hand on his shoulder; the grey-green eyes turned on him, glittering with unshed tears. Michael smiled:

'Thank you, Mr Hanney.'

'Noothin' ter thank me fer, boy!' Bill heard the gruffness of emotion in his own voice.

'You saved my life, you and Billy. And you've given me a *new* life, all of you, one I want to live. Not like….' Bill cleared his throat, looked around:

''Ere, watch wher' yeh're gooin, boy!' Michael looked up, pulled the tiller over to straighten their course, a sudden grin splitting his face:

'Sorry, Mr Hanney!' And they were both laughing, the joy of life overcoming their embarrassment.

* * *

They found the *Sycamore* back in the water, tied up alongside the *Antrim.* Gracie had settled into the butty cabin:

'Yeh'll share the motor wi' me, Moikey – yew can 'ave the soidebed, h'okay?'

'That's fine, Mr Baker.' Michael had got used to the confines of a sidebed; he'd remained in the cabin of the *Acorn,* with Bill and Vi, while Billy and the two boys had used the butty cabin. He collected his few possessions from the boat, and carried them along the towpath to his new home; stepping down into the cabin, he found a pile of clothing already heaped on his bed. He looked up, puzzled, to see Albert smiling down from the hatches:

'Folks 'oo've coom boy these last few days 'ave left 'em fer yeh. They've all 'eard about 'ow 'Anneys found yer, 'ow yeh 'aven't got no kit 'o yer own.' Michael could only stare, open-mouthed – he'd seen how little most boating families had, and for them to give of their limited resources to an unknown kid like him...

'Boaters stick tergither, Moikey. We look after our own – 'n yeh're a boater, now.'

'I am? I mean...' Baker laughed:

'Look at yerself, boy! Yeh're browner, 'n broader – 'n Oi swear yeh've grown two inches in a week!'

''E 'as that, Alby!' He heard Vi confirm from the towpath outside.

The moment had come: They all stood by the side of Hanneys' pair, looking at each other, until Vi gathered the boy into her voluminous arms:

'Tek care o' yerself, Moikey – we'll be seein' yer oop 'n down the cut.'

Chapter Sixteen

The July sunshine blazed down as a pair of boats swung around the series of long turns to the North of Cosgrove village, on the Grand Union Canal. The long cold of the winter was gone and forgotten – the 'phoney war' had become a real war at last, with the Nazi onslaught on the Low Countries, followed by the invasion of France. A triumph of propaganda had changed the ignominious retreat from Dunkirk into at least a qualified victory, the almost miraculous survival of more than three hundred thousand apparently-doomed soldiers justifiably trumpeted to the heavens.

Now, many miles from the peaceful vista of the canal, warplanes snarled and jockeyed for position over the coasts of Kent and Sussex, the sleek shapes of Hurricane and Spitfire pitted against the black-crossed hordes of Heinkels and Dorniers, and their Messerschmitt protectors. At sea, the U-boats were threatening to decimate allied shipping – and the abortive raids on German-occupied Norway had proved a disaster despite early successes.

It was late in the day – an emergency stoppage to replace a split paddle-board at Stoke Bruerne locks had held them up for several hours. The boats swept under Solomon's Bridge, and into the village; many years before, Cosgrove had been sliced in two by the building of the Grand Junction Canal, and now the passing boats still travelled under the watchful gaze of the church and the Barley Mow, looked down on the old stone cottages of Main Street.

At the tiller of the motor boat, its paintwork bright and clean, its brasses gleaming in the evening sunshine, stood a tall, slim boy of eleven, clad in a grey check shirt a good few sizes too big for him, a flat cap crammed low over his soft grey-green eyes. Passing under the bridge, he lifted it and wiped his brow with the back of his hand, revealing a thatch of unruly straw-coloured hair. He bent to call down into the cabin:

'Solomon's, Mr Baker. Lock's coomin' up.' He stood aside to allow the older man out onto the counter; Albert Baker dropped a battered old trilby hat onto his head, tucked a windlass into his belt:

'H'okay, Moikey. Yeh'll tek 'em through?'

''Kay, Mr Baker.' He eased in the oil-rod, slowing the Bolinder from its rapid, steady beat to a slower rhythm, allowing the speed to come off the boat slowly, so that the butty didn't over-run them but kept the towline tight. At the narrows of a long-dismantled swing-bridge, Albert stepped off the boat and hurried to the lock, which stood open for them – a pair, crossing them a mile or so North of the village had told them of its readiness – as Michael let the motor run in on one side, skilfully reversing the single-cylinder engine to bring it to a halt neatly within its confines. He turned to reel in the tow as the butty floated up, guided into the narrow space beside him by Gracie's hand on the tiller. She brought it to a halt by strapping a rope over one of the motor's stern dollies as he stepped off to push the gate closed behind the motor; Albert was already heaving on the butty's gate. The two of them walked to the tail of the lock, simultaneously pulled both bottom paddles; in barely a minute, the lock was emptied to its lower level, and they pushed the gates open. Hurrying back to his tiller, Michael started the motor out of the lock; Albert stepped onto the counter beside him, paid out the towline again. As it drew taut, Michael eased down the throttle, allowing the rope to take the strain gently, then wound it on again, the butty now following them, a silent, captive shadow.

Over six months, the three of them had become a skilled, efficient crew. Each task which was a part of commercial boating would be tackled almost without conscious effort, without thought; Albert Baker may have been the nominal captain of the pair, but he would rarely if ever need to utter a word of command. They would, with an easy rhythm, whistle the boats up a flight of locks, spin them into inch-perfect place on a wharf to load or unload, without the need to talk, each knowing what the other would do, working in concert like the various parts of a well-oiled machine. Michael's respect for the old boatman had become a part of his way of life, and, while he didn't perhaps recognise it, the man's confidence in him was reflected in that lack of command. For his part, Albert saw and appreciated the boy's abilities, his ever-growing self-confidence in the new life he had so eagerly adopted. Careful never to over-praise his young apprentice, he would nevertheless allow himself a quiet, proud smile as Michael casually slipped the motor past an oncoming pair in the confines of the tunnel, or passing over an aqueduct, with barely an inch of clear water between them.

''Ow far we goin', Mr Baker?'

'It's getting' late, boy – we'll toy at the Galleon fer tonoight. Oi'd 'oped ter be ter Talbot's, mebbe 'Ammond Three, boy now, boot...' He shrugged: 'Galleon'll do.'

The boy regarded him silently, sudden memories possessing his thoughts; Baker saw the look in his eyes:

'That's wher' 'Anneys found yeh, wasn' it?' Michael just nodded.

'Yeh'll be close ter 'ome, then?'

'My home's here, on the boat, with you!' It was Albert's turn to look at his young companion in silence for a moment, before he said gently:

'Yes, boy, but yer *old* 'ome's 'ere, isn' it? Yer *family?*' The boy nodded again; now, the look in his eyes was one of sorrow. Albert went to speak again, but thought better of it; he leant on the cabintop, watching the evening scenery pass by as Michael took the boats out onto the long embankment and over the old 'iron trunk' aqueduct above the River Ouse. Some ten minutes later, they were tying the boats on the towpath opposite the disused Wolverton Wharf, by the bridge carrying the Old Wolverton Road from where Michael had launched his abortive suicide attempt six months before. The boy was unusually silent, and Albert left him to his thoughts, his memories, as they tucked into the evening meal which Gracie had prepared as they ran around the pound. Gracie herself, even more aware of the significance of the spot, kept an eye on Michael, trying to judge his mood and react sympathetically.

The meal done, all three of them trekked over the hump-back bridge to the pub for a last refresher before bed. Over his pint of bitter, Albert said casually that he thought they might make a later start the next morning:

'But we're all be'ind already, after that stoppage!'

'Exac'ly, Moikey! Anoother hour or two woon't 'urt, then, will it?' Grey-green eyes regarded the boatman, knowing full well what he was offering, uncertain whether to take advantage of the unspoken suggestion. Gracie broke the silence, at last:

'A loy-in moight be noice, fer a change, at that!' Desperate to change the subject, not wanting to discuss the possibilities, Michael wondered what they'd be likely to load for the return North from Brentford, this trip, and the conversation, by mutual, unspoken agreement, stayed with other matters until they returned to the boats, and their beds.

Albert Baker rose the next morning at his habitual six-thirty a.m. He smiled at the already-vacant sidebed – he'd heard Michael rise a while before – but his smile held an overtone of concern, as well.

Climbing out onto the counter, he tapped on the side of the butty cabin; the hatch slid open, and Gracie's head popped out:

'Tea, Ooncle Alby?' She passed him a steaming cup without waiting for his reply.

'Thank yeh, Gracie.'

''E's gone, then?'

'Ah. 'Eard him git oop a whoile back.' They both sipped tea in silence, until Gracie expressed both their thoughts:

'Will 'e be back, d'yeh think?' Albert hesitated:

'Oi 'ope so, Gracie. We need a third 'and wi' the pair.' She stared at him, angered by his apparently mercenary attitude to the boy:

'So do Oi, Albert Baker – boot only 'cause Oi'll miss 'im if 'e don't!' He glanced over, then avoided her gaze:

''E's a good little boater, near as good as Alex was at 'is age.' He looked up again: 'All roight! Yes, Oi'm fond of 'im, too. Oi'd miss 'im – boot Oi'm already missin' Alex, 'n Rita, 'n…' The girl reached out and took his hand:

'Oi know, Ooncle Alby. When the war's over, Alex'll be 'ome – 'e'll marry 'is Iris, 'n then yeh'll have four o' yeh, wi' Moikey. That'll be a good crew, oone o' the best on Fellers's!' Baker smiled at her, grateful for her words, but still reluctant to admit his feelings:

'Wher's that boy got teh? We should be gittin' ahead!'

'We'll wait 'til 'e gets back, Albert! 'E'll not be any longer'n 'e can 'elp.'

'What if 'e's 'ad enooff, decoides teh stay wi' 'is folks?'

'We'll give 'im toime teh git back!' But her heart told her that the boatman might be right, that the child, for child he still was, might so easily sink back into the bosom of his family, now that the opportunity was there.

Chapter Seventeen

Michael had not slept well that night. Tossing and turning on the narrow sidebed, thoughts chased dreams chased memories: His home, and little Ginny, and was she all right? His first night on a boat, after Billy Hanney had dragged him out of the canal by this very same bridge, and his amazement at finding himself not only still alive, but catapulted into a new, exciting, unknown life. His life since that night, the hard work, the long days, the muck and grime of some of the loads they carried, the physical slog of loading and unloading – and the joy of long summer days at the tiller, the ever-changing scenery, the new places to see, new friends to meet along the way, old friends like Stevie and Jack to greet eagerly as they passed, to play with when they happened to be at the same stop together...

Around six o'clock, he'd given up the unequal struggle and climbed out onto the counter. It was another fine morning, the sun already up, striking over the cutting beyond the bridge and just clipping the chimney of the old wharfinger's house. The air was warm against his skin, the gentlest of breezes stroking him, making him glad, oh so glad, just to be alive. He sat on the cants, dabbling his toes in the water of the canal, enjoying its slight chill, his thoughts once more returning to the events of that night...

They'd passed this way many times over the last six months, of course. But their schedule had never included a stop anywhere near, the need to 'get 'em ahead' paramount, ruling their days and their night-time resting-places. It was just chance that that stoppage at Stoke had held them up, made this a logical place to spend a night... Or was it? Was fate rather telling him that now was the time to make contact with his family, let them know he was all right, find out how they were faring? He pondered, disturbed by his uncertainty, knowing that Gracie and Mr Baker had been throwing such hints at him the night before – if he went, would they wait for him? How long? It would be an ironic disaster if he went to find his own family, only to be left behind by the people he was now thinking of as his new family... Gracie was still very much, in his eyes, somewhere between a big sister and a surrogate mother; and he found himself ever fonder of Mr Baker, at times almost thinking of the boatman as his new father, even if the man himself kept a slightly formal distance between them.

Let fate decide! His mind made up, Michael rose to his feet and stepped down into the cabin again. He slipped on his cleanest shirt, plain white, with no collar, and rolled up the sleeves; rooting through the drawer under his bed, he dug out his old school trousers – a bit rumpled, but still smarter than the ones he wore most of the time! Socks and boots on his feet, he climbed out once more, stepped gingerly over the butty's stern and out onto the bank. As long as they'd wait for him! He could leave them a note! He shook his head at his own stupidity – that wouldn't do much good, would it? Even now, he found it difficult, at times, to remember that those around him couldn't read. He stepped back for a moment, descended into the motor cabin, found his most prized possession, a carved model aeroplane which Mr Baker had made for him, knowing his fascination with that part of the war, the heroics of Britain's fighter pilots. He placed it prominently on his bed, where it would be seen – that should tell them that he would be back!

On the bank again, he began to walk away, up to the bridge. As he turned underneath it, he glanced back at the boats, sitting deep-laden by the towpath, suddenly anxious, knowing that he mustn't let them down, hold them up for too long... What if they *didn't* wait? What if he came back to find them gone...? He almost gave up, turned back; but no, they'd wait, they wouldn't desert him! He turned and went on. At Suicide Bridge, he climbed up the bank, crossed over and found the footpath, followed it through to Stratford Road, saw no-one in that early-morning hour on the pavement all the way along the wall of the railway works until he reached the junction with Windsor Street. He crossed over the road, and stood for a moment, looking around, remembering... He walked on along the silent, deserted street of his childhood, feeling the house that had been his home for so long drawing him closer with every step...

...100, 102, 104, 106...108! He turned in through the garden gate – and stopped dead. The windows were boarded up, the plants in his mother's two big pots overcome with weeds, grass creeping out between the flagstones – what was happening? He checked the number, almost thinking he'd stopped at the wrong house – 108! He stood in the gateway, a hand on each gatepost, feeling small, lost, shattered...

Janet Eastwood was up, as always, at six that morning. Life had settled back into its everlasting routine – nothing had ever been heard of little Michael from next door, most people now assumed that he was dead. They'd searched for him everywhere, dragged the canal and the river, but his body hadn't been found, either – so it was all a mystery, really. Nettie had never quite got over it, still mourning her eldest son; and Ginny was so quiet, these days, not her old self at all even after six months... Reg had just got even angrier with everyone, especially himself, of course, until...

She shook her head, went downstairs to put the kettle on for Eric's tea; she'd let him sleep a few more minutes, there was time enough for his breakfast before he'd have to set off for work! Kettle on, toast under the grill, she went into the front room to quickly sweep the floor, tidy up ready for the new day. Movement beyond the window caught her eye a she drew the curtains back, took down the blackout screens – a youngster, walking past, something familiar about him… The boy turned at the next house, stopped in the gate; she leant forward for a better look, then hurried, unbelieving, to the front door, snatched it open, stared…

It wasn't until she spoke that Michael saw the woman in the doorway of the next house.

'Michael?' Her voice held disbelief, amazement; he looked around:

'Hello, Mrs Eastwood.'

'Michael! It's really you?' He smiled, nodded:

'It's me, Mrs Eastwood, really!' He looked up at the house: 'What's happened – where's my Mum, and Ginny, and…?' The woman gazed at him, her eyes suddenly full of compassion:

'Come in Michael. I'll… Come on in, please?' He hesitated:

'I mustn't be long, they're waiting for me.'

'Who, Michael? Who's waiting for you?'

'Oh – I'll tell you in a minute!' She looked flustered:

'Yes – come on in, Michael!' He did as he was bid; she ushered him inside, led him through to the kitchen, clucking over him:

'Just look at you! You're so brown – and you've grown! Taller than ever; and I swear you've filled out a lot, too…' She sat him in a chair by the table, then snatched the pan out from under the grille where Eric's toast was beginning to smoke, tutted at her own inattention as she replaced the ruined bread with two fresh slices. Impatient for her news, Michael prompted her:

'What about Ginny, and Mum, and Andy, where are they? And… and my Dad?' Janet turned from the cooker, her eyes full of sympathy again, and took a seat facing him over the table. She reached across, took both of his hands in her own:

'Oh, Michael! They're not here, any more…'

'I can see that, Mrs Eastwood – but where are they?' She

held his eyes for a moment longer, squeezed his hands:

'Oh, Michael! I don't know how to say this!' She paused, then plunged on: 'Your father's dead, Michael, that's why your Mum moved. He… he got into a fight, at the pub, one night after work. It was no-one's fault, he fell over, hit his head on the edge of the bar, as they were arguing. They took him to hospital, but he died the same night. I'm so sorry, Michael!' The boy looked down at his hands, raised his eyes again:

'I'm not. He only ever got angry with me, and everyone! He used to hit me, all the time; and Mum too, he used to beat her up, sometimes! He…' He hesitated, feeling tears beginning to spill from his eyes despite his words: 'What about them, are they all right?' Janet squeezed his hands again, then got up to turn over the toast:

'They're doing all right, Michael! They went to live with your Gran and Granddad in Buckingham, after the funeral. I see them now and then, and your Mum writes to me, sometimes. Ginny's in a new school, there; and Andy's doing well, too. Your mum's got a little job, at the printing works. They're fine! And they're going to be so pleased to know you're okay, you're *alive,* after all this time!'

'No! I mean… You mustn't tell them… Oh, I don't know!' She turned to him in surprise:

'Whatever do you mean, Michael – of course I've got to tell them, they've been so worried about you!' He held her gaze for a moment, then shook his head:

'No… I'm – not ready. I mean – they'll only try and make me go home…'

'And you don't want to?'

'No. I've got a new life, Mrs Eastwood, I… I'm a boater, now – and that's what I want to be! When I'm older, I'll have my own boats, and… I don't want to go home.'

Janet stood, looking down at the boy, seeing the determination in his face; he seemed different, somehow – more grown up, as well as taller, fitter:

'So what *about* you, Michael? Where have you been, all this time?' Those suddenly-adult grey-green eyes held hers for a moment:

'If I tell you – will you promise not to tell *anyone?*' She studied him, not sure if she should accept those terms; but the appeal was still in his eyes: 'Promise?' She hesitated, but then gave in:

'Okay – I promise! But can't I at least let your Mum know that you're all right?'

'No, please! Not yet – I'll get in touch with them one day, but not now. She'd only try and persuade me to go home with them, and… I'll go and see them, one day, I promise – but please don't say anything to them, not yet, *please?*'

'All right – if you're sure, Michael…?'

'I'm sure! You see, what happened was…' The tale took almost half an hour to tell, as Janet bustled about preparing Eric's breakfast; then she had a whole raft of questions for him. Aware of passing time, he eventually ducked out, saying that he had to go, that he couldn't keep the boats waiting any longer. Just as he stood up to leave, the kitchen door opened:

'Good God – *Michael?*' Eric Eastwood stood there, ready for breakfast and quite unready to find a supposedly-dead child in his kitchen.

'Hello, Mr Eastwood – I've got to go!'

'What…How…Michael…!'

'Let him go, Eric, I'll tell you all about it.' Janet ushered the boy to the door, quickly drawing him into an embrace as he turned to go: 'Take care of yourself, Michael – come and see us again, when you can, okay?'

'Thank you, Mrs Eastwood, and – not a word to my Mum, or anyone, please?' She nodded:

'You can trust me, Michael – but you will get in touch with them soon, won't you?'

'I promise!'

The boy was gone; she turned to go back to the kitchen and try to explain his resurrection to her flabbergasted husband.

Chapter Eighteen

''E'll not be mooch longer!' Gracie's voice held a hint of impatience as Albert Baker looked at his watch, dropped it back into the pocket of his waistcoat, for about the hundredth time since breakfast.

It was a rare treat for them to eat the first meal of the day sitting down, in the butty cabin – usually, they would be well on the way, and eat on the go: Routine was for Albert to begin the day steering the motor, while Michael rode the butty with Grace; when the breakfast was ready, he would take his own and the captain's, run forward along the top-planks to the fore-deck, and jump across as Albert let the motor slow until the butty caught up. Then on, they would share the steering on open pounds, leaving the butty to Grace, who, with the consummate skill of the born-and-bred boatwoman, would manage to steer, tidy up, cook the next meal, even wash some of their 'smalls', all at the same time.

'We should be gettin' on, girl.' Albert withdrew his watch again, glanced down at it. Grace just gave him a pitying look; she got to her feet:

'Oi'm goin' ter sweep out in your cabin, Ooncle Alby – Oi don't suppose the two o' yeh've doon it fer ages! Yew could busy yerself polishing the brasses or soomat, instead o' sittin' there frettin'.' She left the cabin; he shrugged his shoulders, got up to follow her. As he climbed out into the well, she stuck her head back out of the motor's cabin:

''E's left 'is Spitfoire 'ere, on the soidebed!'

'Yeah – Oi saw it ther', before.'

'Well, doon't yeh see? 'E's left it wher' we'd see it to tell oos 'e'll be back!'

'Yeh think so?'

'O' course! 'E thinks the world o' that – if 'e was goin' off, 'e'd a' teken it wi' 'im, would'n 'e?'

'Mebbe…'

'O-oh!' She turned and flounced back down into the cabin, out of patience with her uncle's lack of understanding. Albert stepped around the gunwale to the engine-hole doors, swung them open and began to lower himself inside, going to get the cloths and metal polish as she had suggested; but he looked up quickly at a hail from the bank:

'Coom on, we should be gettin' 'em ahead by now!'

'Moichael – yeh're back!' He quickly extinguished the delighted smile which had sprung unconsciously to his face.

'Of course – did yeh think I might not be?'

'Course not – not fer a moment. Git on oover 'ere, 'elp me git the motor started – Gracie! We're away, girl!' Her head appeared from the cabin; she gave Michael a big grin as she climbed out, stepped back over to her own boat and onto the bank ready to loose them away:

'Everythin' h'okay, Moikey?' He shook his head:

'They're not there, Gracie. My Dad'd dead, and my Mum's moved – our next-door-neighbour's been telling me all about it.'

'Oh, Moikey!' She put an arm around his shoulders, held him tight for a moment.

'I'll tell you all about it later, Gracie. We'd better get goin' now.'

'Yes – h'okay, Moikey. Yew go 'n 'elp wi' the motor – 'ave yeh 'ad any brekfuss?' He shook his head.

'Oi'll get yeh soomat, when we're away, roight?'

'Okay – thanks.'

Under Galleon Bridge, then Suicide Bridge, and all around the back of the railway works, Michael steered the butty while Gracie bustled below, making him some breakfast. She felt his unusual silence, sensed his preoccupation with his thoughts; when she stepped out again, took the tiller from him while he ate, she prompted him gently to tell her what he'd found. Between bites, he passed on all that Janet Eastwood had told him; when he'd finished, she regarded him with a deep sympathy in her eyes:

'Oi'm sorry, Moikey – about yer Dad. Will yeh get in tooch wi' yer Mum, 'n Ginny?' He sat silent for a moment:

'Yeah – I guess I will, one day. But – I don't feel ready to see them, now… Can you understand?'

'Yeah – Oi think so. Boot, yeh should let 'em know yeh're all roight, stop 'em frettin' about yeh, don't yeh think?' He shrugged:

'Maybe – but not yet! They'd only put pressure on me, to go back – and I don't want to, I want to stay here, with you, and Mr Baker!' One arm resting on the tiller, she drew him into the other's embrace, squeezed his shoulders:

''N we wouldn't want teh be without yeh, Moikey. Boot Oi'll be away, oone day – Oi'm goin' teh marry moy Joey, 'n then we'll 'ave our own boats. Oh, not yet awhoile!' She assured him, seeing the stricken look on his face: 'Mebbe boy then, the war'll be oover, 'n Alex'll be 'ome. 'E's gooin' ter marry Iris Ward, 'n then they'll coom on the boats wi' Mr Baker, Oi 'spect. Yeh'll loike Alex, 'e's 'a foine feller!'

'Yeah…' Michael had formed an impression of an upright, strong young man from the few letters he'd read out to Albert, the replys he'd written for the boatman: 'But – when he's back, will Mr Baker need me as well? Will he *want* me on the boats, then, if his son's here?' Grace glanced down, saw the impending sadness in the boy's eyes:

'If 'e don't, Moikey, yew coom wi' me 'n moy Joey – we'll foind work for yeh!' The sparkle came back to his face:

'You mean it? You'd have me with you?'

'Course Oi mean it, Moikey – yeh're me spare little brother, ent yeh?' He threw his arms around her not-insubstantial waist, hugged her tight:

''Ey, lit go! Yeh'll 'ave me oop the bank!' He sat back on the gunwale, smiling up at her; then he said, thoughtfully:

'I'd miss him – Mr Baker, I mean. He's been very good to me, and… and…'

'Yew loike 'im a lot, don't yeh?' The boy nodded:

'Yeah – but I'm not sure if he likes me much. I mean, he never says anything…'

''E loikes yeh more'n yeh think, Moikey. Yeh should'a seen 'im this mornin', frettin' 'cause yeh weren't back!'

'Yeah – I suppose…' Michael sat in thought for a moment: 'He's been almost like a new Dad for me – I mean, he's taught me so much, showed me so much about the life here, given me a new home – but if I say anything, he kind of brushes it off, you know? And now my *real* Dad's dead…'

'Oi oonderstand, Moikey – boot give 'im toime? 'E's not long lost 'is woife, remember – Rita was a lovely woman, 'n Oi'm certain 'e still misses 'er. 'N 'e woories about Alex, too, in case 'e gets 'urt, or worse – 'e's got a lot on 'is moind, yeh see? Doon't expect too mooch from 'im – boot 'e doos loike yeh, a lot, Oi knoo that.'

'Yeah… Thanks, Gracie!' He looked up at the girl: 'I love you, big sister!' She laughed:

'Oi love yeh too, little brother!'

The next couple of hours were spent in a gentle, companionable silence. Michael had climbed up onto the cabin roof, sat himself on its front edge, legs dangling down over the open hold above the piles of steel tube stacked below; he seemed deep in thought, and Grace had the sensitivity to leave him be.

He thought, remembered times past, his old home, his mother, Andy, especially Ginny – *should* he get in touch with them now, or leave it? His conscience said now – but he knew that they would only insist on him going home again, against his will – and could he resist their pleadings? He doubted it – so, better to leave them in ignorance of his survival, at least for now. Later, when he was more settled, more established...

He thought of the Hanneys, of Bill and Vi, of their kindness to an unknown runaway; of Billy, quiet, self-possessed master of the boating craft at the ripe age of fourteen; of Stevie and Jack, so unstoppably full of life, so proud of their *way* of life, their growing abilities in the world that was their home. And Gracie: He turned to smile at the girl, leaning capably on the heavy curved tiller of the butty, was rewarded with one of her wide, beaming smiles in return. Since they had together crewed for Albert Baker, his feelings for her had grown to something close to love – the deep bond of a younger brother for his older sister, for the girl who would treat him anywhere between a friend and a child, as she sensed his need.

He thought of Albert Baker, the man he had come to trust so implicitly that he would do anything the man bid, even if it seemed crazy, dangerous, to him. As he'd said to Gracie, the man had become like a surrogate father to him, filling the void of instruction and inspiration that his own father had never offered; he found himself wishing that the man *was* his father – why couldn't he have been born to a boater, instead of...? He felt a great sympathy for him, too – he'd known, understood, the gap left in his life by the death of his wife, of course, but before Gracie's words that morning, he hadn't really thought about how the absence of his son must affect the man, the knowledge that Alex was always in danger, at risk of injury, even death, in the cause of peace and justice for the world.

Alex knew about Michael, of course – the first letter he'd written for the boatman had included an explanation of his own arrival, of how he and Gracie were to be a crew, were to ensure that his father could continue his career. The reply which eventually came had been close to ecstatic, the young man delighted that his father was going to stay on his beloved boats after all. And there had been a note for Michael, too:

'Michael – I'm so grateful, so happy, that you and Gracie are going to work with my Dad. It would kill him, I know, if he had to leave the boats, and it means so much to me to know that the two of you will be there with him, looking after him, while I'm away. I don't know if I'll get any shore leave, any time soon – we're a long way away at the moment, and I don't know when we might get back to England – but I'm really looking forward to meeting you, one day, and thanking you properly. Until then, take care of yourself as well, and give my love to Gracie.'

There had been only a couple more letters from him; each time, there was a note for Michael, a few lines of such amusing anecdotes about the war at sea as would pass the censor's erasing pen. In the last, he'd signed himself as 'your new big brother, Alex.', a fact which had boosted Michael's spirits to level almost as high as the snarling Spitfires which so held his imagination. He'd not read these notes out to Albert, accepting them as his own private communications – not wishing to be secretive, he'd told the man of the first one, but Albert had simply said 'if it's for yew, boy, then yeh can tell me about it or not, as yeh loike.' So he'd chosen to keep them to himself, hugging them to his heart as something precious, even if they were only casual jottings from someone he'd never met.

Approaching Fenny Lock, he'd jumped off under the awkward, angled bridge and run forward, windlass in hand, to set it ready. Once through the lock, so shallow as to be almost insignificant, which began their climb up from the Ouse valley into the Chiltern Hills, Albert had had him take over the motor, while he pottered about, checking the engine and cleaning the brasses, the job he'd not got started on before their delayed departure from the Galleon.

The climb continued all day: Talbot's Lock, Hammond Three, Leighton, Grove, Church, Slapton, Horton, Corkett's Two, Nag's Head Three, Peter's Two, and at last, Maffers - the delightful, twisting flight of seven that led uphill from Marsworth to Bulbourne. They tied that night opposite the canal company works in Bulbourne, still echoing so late in the evening to the manufacture of lock gates for the Grand Union Canal. They'd eaten, as they often did, earlier, taking the meal Gracie had prepared in the short spells between locks; now, they tied the boats, breasted, the butty to the bank as usual.

Albert swung himself down into the engine-hole to still the aging Bolinder; re-emerging, he gestured at the Grand Junction Arms which loomed over the canal by the bridge:

'Coom on; quick wash 'n broosh oop, 'n we'll goo fer a drink in the Joonction.'

'Roight yew are, Ooncle Alby.' Michael, his mind still partly absorbed in his earlier musings, replied without thinking:

'Okay, Dad.'

An instant silence fell. Gracie looked at Michael, at first thunderstruck, but then with a smile spreading slowly across her homely face; Albert's jaw dropped, and he stood gaping at the boy for a moment, a variety of expressions chasing each other through his eyes:

'Oi'm not yer father, boy, 'n Oi never will be!' Michael felt stricken, wishing he'd switched his brain on before opening his mouth:

'I'm sorry! I didn't mean... Oh!' Gracie, for her part, was glaring at the boatman:

'Albert Baker!' He glanced at her, turned back to the boy, realising how much his gruffness had upset him:

'What made yeh say *that*, Moikey?' His voice was softer now, gentler.

'I... You've been almost like a Dad to me, since... you know! I'm sorry, I didn't mean to upset you...' Albert walked around the gunwale to where he stood on the counter, took the boy's shoulders in is hands:

'Yeh're *not* moy son, Moikey – boot whoy any man wouldn't be proud ter 'ave yer fer 'is son, Oi'll never know. Now go on, git yerself clean 'n toidy!'

'Yes, Mr Baker!' The boy dived down into the cabin, stripped off his sweaty shirt and grabbed the handbowl ready for a quick wash. Albert looked at Gracie:

'Oi don't mean ter be grumpy wi' the kid, boot…'

'Alex?'

'Yeah. Yew oonderstand?'

'Oi think 'e doos, 'n all!' She gestured with her head at the open cabin doors.

'Yeah. Mebbe 'e doos, at that.'

Chapter Nineteen

That trip was to suffer further hold-ups. The next day, they'd barely cleared Cowroast Lock, at the far end of the Tring Summit, when the Bolinder began to cough, and then died altogether. Muttering curses under his breath, Albert dived down into the engine-hole while Michael and Grace brought the boats in to the bank; a couple of minutes later, his head appeared in the side doors:

'It's only a bit o' moock in the oil loine, Oi reckon. Tek me 'bout 'alf an hour, if we're loocky.'

'Is there anythin' I can do to help?' The boatman shook his head:

'Not really, Moikey – ent room fer two of oos in 'ere, any road. Boot Oi'll show yeh what ter do, one day when we've got toime, h'okay? Fer now, yew two sit 'n h'enjoy the soonshoine!'

'Coom on, Moikey, we'll goo fer a walk, stretch our legs, shall we?'

The two of them strolled away, to Albert's ''Alf an hour, moind!', along the towpath towards the locks of Northchurch. Michael was still feeling somewhat bereft, following the news of his family; after a few steps, his hand sought Gracie's, and they walked on, hand in hand. At last, he broke the friendly silence:

'Am I a really bad person, Gracie?' She turned to him, surprised at such a question:

'Whatever d'yeh mean?'

'Well – I ought to feel sad, that my Dad's dead. But… I don't, not really. I'm… almost pleased – not for me, but… because he can't hurt my Mum any more, or get angry with Ginny, now that I'm not there… I must be pretty bad, don't you think?' She stopped, took his other hand as well, shook him gently:

'Yeh're *not* bad, Moikey! 'E was a tyrant, from what yeh've told oos, 'n Oi don't think 'e deserves yeh ter be sad fer 'im. So yew stop worryin' about it, yeh 'ear?'

He looked into her eyes for a moment, then gave her a thin smile:

'If you say so!'

'Oi do!' She smiled back; they walked on a little further, then:

'I do love you, Gracie – not, like a girlfriend, kind of love, you understand?'

'Oi should 'ope not! Moy Joey'd 'ave a thing or two ter say about that!' She chuckled: 'Loike Oi said before, yeh're moy extra little brother, aren't yeh?' He just nodded, happy in their mutual affection. They strolled on; after a while, Gracie said:

'We'd better be getting' back, see 'ow Ooncle Alby's gettin' on.'

They could hear his muttered curses as they approached the boats; Michael put his head around the engine-hole doors:

''Ow's it going, Mr Baker?'

'Almoost doon, Moikey. Took me a whoile ter foind the problem, boot Oi've got it now. Joost got teh put these poipes back, 'n we'll be off.'

Ten minutes, and he was proved right – the engine settled again to its reliable thumping, and they were running down the hill, into the Thames valley.

* * *

They'd unloaded the boats, were relaxing with a cup of tea while Gracie tackled their pile of dirty clothes, pounding them in the old barrel which she kept on the butty for the purpose, soapsuds blowing into the gentle breeze. The local traffic manager bustled up:

'Steerer Baker – you've orders to load at Regent's Canal Dock, a shipment of some special alloy, urgent, for Fazeley Street Wharf.'

'Oh, ar? Goin' empty ter Loime'us, then?'

'That's right – they want you there as quickly as possible.'

'Better git gooin' then. Yew doon there, Gracie?'

'Foive minutes, Ooncle Alby!' He nodded to the manager:

'We'll be away, then.'

'Very good – here's your starting money.'

Ten minutes, and they were on their way, the butty on cross-straps, pulled up tight behind the motor's stern, both stems riding high out of the water. Gracie hung the washing out as they went, on spare ropes slung along the butty's empty hold; there was a twinkle in her eye:

'Gracie seems pleased, Mr Baker?' Albert chuckled:

'Aye, I'll bet! If we're on a Birnigum run, she'll 'ave more chance o' runnin' across Joey Caplin!'

The young couple's romance had been making very slow progress – since Baker's new crew had been formed, they had been running between Nottingham and Brentford, sometimes loading at City Road Basin in Camden for the Northward trip, while Henry Caplin ran a pair of Grand Union boats, on a regular run between Birmingham and London – so, for more than half of each trip, their boats had been on different water. Their meetings had been few, and mostly fleeting as the pairs passed in the usual haste to 'get 'em ahead'.

The next day, they were loading in the riverside dock at Limehouse. In the distant sky, from time to time could be seen the twisting vapour trails of aircraft; sometimes, the aggressive snarl of an engine, Merlin or Daimler-Benz, would sound over the constant clamour and clatter of the dock, causing Michael to pause in his work and look up to the battle raging above the horizon:

'Fascinates yeh, doosn' it, boy?' Michael looked around at his captain, a grin on his face:

'If I was old enough, I'd be a fighter pilot!'

'Would yeh now?' The boy nodded, turned his attention back to the distant dogfight, cheered as one trail suddenly turned to black smoke, a stricken plane spiralling down. He looked around, the light of his excitement shining in his eyes:

'We got one!' Albert regarded him, reluctant to shatter his illusion; but then he said:

'Ow d'yeh know that's oone o' theirs, 'n not oone of ours?'

'I… Well…'

'Whether it's ours or theirs, Moikey, there's a yoong feller in that aeroplane, mebbe more'n oone. A yoong feller, 'oo's p'raps 'urt, p'raps even dead.' Michael stared at him, as the meaning of his words sank in; Albert went on: 'That's what war's really about, boy – men gooin' off, smart 'n proud in their uniforms, 'n a lot of 'em never coomin' 'ome again. Yeh see?' There was a deep sadness behind the man's eyes; Michael put down the heavy ingot of metal he'd been holding, went over to his mentor:

'Alex is goin' teh be all right, Mr Baker – 'e'll be 'ome, right as rain, you'll see!' Albert looked down at him, nodded:

''Course 'e will, Moikey. Oi'm joost bein' silly.' Impulsively, Michael put his arms around the man's waist, held him tightly for a moment before going back to his job, carefully not looking him in the eye. The boatman watched him go, turned his smile away so the boy wouldn't see it.

* * *

They'd made good progress, heading North with their special cargo. Back around the Regent's Canal, up the Paddington Arm and so onto the Grand Union; over the steady rise of the Chilterns, and running down again into the Ouse Valley. They were in the rolling farmland, heading to Horton Lock, when Michael turned his gaze to the East:

'Look, Mr Baker!' Albert, standing on the gunwale, puffing at his pipe, glanced over his shoulder:

'Oi think 'e's in trouble, Moikey.' A lone aircraft was approaching, slowly losing height over the gently sloping fields, aiming to cross the canal not far in front of them. Its engine sounded rough, hesitating, coughing, running on for moment before coughing again. They watched as it came closer; then the engine gave a last splutter and fell silent – the propeller windmilled to a halt, and the Spitfire, gliding now, drifted lower and lower. It skimmed over the canal, no more than fifty yards from them; its underside, the radiators slung below the wings, snagging in the top of the towpath hedge; further slowed, it touched down in the adjacent field, a thick cloud of pale yellow dust billowing up as the ripening wheat cushioned its impact, braked it quickly to a halt.

'Roon 'er inteh the soide, Moikey, we'll go see if we can 'elp!' He wound back the throttle, knocked out the clutch and allowed the boat to run along the towpath edge, the friction quickly bringing it to a halt; behind, Gracie was doing the same with the butty.

'Yew stay 'ere wi' the boats, Gracie!' Albert and Michael struggled through the hedge, ran across the swath of flattened crop to where the aircraft had come to rest; as they came close, Albert stopped, put out a hand to halt his companion:

'Wait 'ere, Moikey, let me go fust.' He'd seen the bullet-holes peppering the side of the fuselage, realised the likely meaning of that awful pattern; he went on, but Michael, not to be put off, followed close behind. Albert went up to the side of the plane, looked in through the Perspex of the canopy, and turned away, shaking his head; Michael ducked under his arm, and looked in also:

'Oh, my *God!*' Albert grabbed the boy, pulled him into his arms to stop him looking, held him close. The pilot had to have been hit a number of times; the cockpit was a horrifying sight, liberally sprayed with blood. Now, he hung in the restraining straps, unmoving, beyond any help they might have been able to give. Whether he had survived long enough to turn away from the fight, head back inland, or whether the plane, following some incomprehensible mechanical instinct, had sought to return its dead pilot to his home, no-one would ever know.

Albert gently led Michael away, back to the boats, passed him over to Gracie while he set off on foot to the next lock, where he could get the keeper to telephone the news of the plane's whereabouts to the correct authorities. Returning, half an hour later, he found the boy still shocked, sitting quietly in the cabin with Gracie's arm around his shoulders, holding the toy plane he'd made for him in his hands. Tear-stained eyes lifted to meet his:

'Mr Baker…'

'It's all roight, boy, yew tek yer toime.' *'E's still only a kid, fer all that! 'N a kid shouldn't see things loike that…'*

Albert Baker was no craftsman, with wood. That model aeroplane could as easily have been Spitfire or Hurricane; or even, truth to tell, a Messerschmitt 109 – that had never mattered to Michael. But from that day, it was never played with again; no more imaginary dogfights took place while they were waiting for orders, no sorties over occupied France ranged across the towpath at the end of the day. Sometimes, in moments of quiet contemplation, he would be found in the cabin, sitting silent on the sidebed, turning it over in his hands, sadness for all those young men who wouldn't be going home wetting his cheeks.

Chapter Twenty

The summer of 1940 had been long, dry, hot. Hermann Goering's attempt to steamroller the Royal Air Force out of existence had been frustrated by those brave, talented few whose dogged determination had seen off the hordes of the Luftwaffe; talking of it in a speech, Winston Churchill had coined the phrase 'Battle of Britain'. Now the Reichsmarschall's anger was being turned on Britain's industry, her cities. In North Africa, two armies struggled back and forth across the desert, like two well-matched wrestlers in an unbreakable clinch; the continuing cat and mouse game of convoy, escort and U-boat made up the war at sea, enlivened occasionally by the appearance of one of Hitler's powerful surface raiders.

September had long been swallowed by the winds; now October saw the amber tints of autumn darkening towards the colder shades of winter. Hallowe'en: A pair of boats, heavy laden, running down the thick of Hatton Locks; three locks ahead, another pair, bearing the same gold-lined red and green livery. Knowing they were followed, and having the larger crew, the leading pair were setting the locks back for their fellows; friendly rivalry meant that, while they strove to pull away, the second pair were trying just as hard to catch up. A boy in his mid-teens stood at the helm of the first motor boat, taking the breasted pair while his parents and younger brothers formed the crew on the bank; the captain of the second steered himself, while an older girl and a slim, wiry lad wound paddles and pushed gates for him.

That night, both crews met in the Cape of Good Hope. Chance had brought the Hanney family together for this trip, Grace, with Albert Baker's boats, rostered on the same job as her father's; both were carrying empty shell cases from Birmingham to Brentford, and the evening was spent in high merriment. Gracie had been in good spirits for some time – since their special cargo, back in the summer, Albert's boats had been engaged on a regular run to and from FMC's Fazeley Street depot in Birmingham, back-loading from Brentford or sometimes the City Road Basin. The fact that Henry Caplin's Grand Union pair were on a similar schedule made for frequent meetings, and her romance with Joey was blossoming, the young man often hopping on his bike and cycling for miles to see her of an evening, if their respective boats were within striking distance.

The next morning, a Northbound pair, headed to New Warwick Wharf with cocoa for onward shipment to Manchester, set away early and left the two locks in their favour. The *Acorn* was first away, Bill Hanney anticipating Albert's intention to sneak past before he was ready; as they dropped through the first lock, the two younger boys ran ahead to set the second. Michael and Grace stood ready, windlasses in hand, while Albert kept the *Sycamore's* engine idling, waiting for the lock to be reset for him.

All through the morning, they ran in convoy, across the valley floor through Warwick and Leamington Spa, and then began the climb up towards the Braunston summit: Radford and the Fosse, Welsh Road, and so to Bascote, all locks, like the flights of Knowle, Hatton and Stockton, rebuilt in the 1930s with the distinctive 'Candlestick' paddle gear. At Bascote, Bill's pair had managed to be a little way ahead, working through the two separate locks below the riser; now, they were in the lower chamber of the staircase as Albert ran his pair into the bottom lock. Pulling the paddles to fill the lock, Michael and

Grace both became aware of something amiss in front of them, shouting, figures running:

'Stay 'ere, keep an eye, Gracie!' Michael ran ahead to see what was wrong; as he reached the other boats, Vi grabbed him by the shoulders, stopped him:

'What's oop, Mrs Hanney?'

'Oh, Moikey! It's Jack – 'e's gone in the lock!'

'What happened?' She shook her head in disbelief:

''E was follerin' Stevie, loike always – they went ter cross the gates, 'n 'e slipped. Bill 'n Billy are oop there wi' the keeper, troyin' ter fish 'im out!' As she spoke, her eldest son ran to her; she turned, and he flung himself into her arms:

''e's gone, Ma, 'e's gone!' She held him as he sobbed into her shoulder:

'Got 'im out, 'ave they?' The boy just nodded.

'Look after Billy fer me, will yeh, Moikey?' She eased out of his embrace; Michael put his arm around the older boy's waist as she hurried away to where her husband and the lock-keeper were bent over a still form, laying on the ground beside the top gates. He eased the teenager around, made him sit on the boat's gunwale, holding him all the time; Gracie came running up, sat the other side of him, slipping her arm about his shoulders:

'What is it, Moikey?' He looked at her, unsure what to say; then, seeing no option, blurted it out:

'Jack – he's fallen in!' Her dark eyes held his gaze; she read the truth in his face:

''E's dead, ent 'e?' Michael could only nod as tears sprang to his eyes; he saw their brightness gather in hers, and then she bent to her brother, murmuring inaudible words of comfort. Michael left them, went up to where the adults were gathered around the child's still figure; as he approached, the lock-keeper got to his feet, shaking his head:

'It's no good, Bill – I'm afraid 'e's gone.' Vi gave a huge sob, turned to her husband and drew him into her arms; Stevie, standing to one side, a horrified, bewildered look on his face, desperate for comfort, ran to Michael and flung himself upon him. Michael put his arms around the other boy, aware of the trembling of his body, his heaving breath as he cried for his little brother, feeling worse than useless, wishing there was something he could say to ease Stevie's pain. From the corner of his eye, he saw the lock-keeper go to his cottage, to telephone the authorities.

* * *

They were tied there for two days, the boats dragged above the locks, waiting while the police and the coroner's office put in their appearances, gave their agreement for the boy's body to be taken for burial. The lock-keeper had called around, found a suitable coffin; when they left, it was carried with honour, tied to a top-plank laid from beam to beam, just above the empty hold. Two pairs had been sent, post-haste, to take over their trip, the families commiserating in the Hanneys' grief, and bringing the news that the boats they had passed at the Cape had also suffered disaster – they had been tied in the New Warwick Wharf, at Fazeley Street in Birmingham, the previous night, when a stray bomb had hit it, destroying the roof and sinking both them and another pair:

'No-one was 'urt, thank God! Vi'let 'n Dolly Beechey were in the *Robin*'s cabin, boot they got out before it sank!'

During that time, Michael found himself with an unshakeable shadow. Stevie attached himself to the boy who had once been his eager pupil, stuck with him everywhere – Michael didn't mind, after all, it was a long time since he'd had the company of another youngster, except for the occasions when they'd been tied up briefly, loading, unloading, or waiting for orders. Not that either of them felt much like playing – rather, they would wander together in the autumn countryside, or sit on the boats, in the empty holds or the cabin, talking infrequently, finding solace in each others presence, sharing their unspoken emptiness at the absence of the youngest of their clan.

Jack's funeral was a simple, moving affair – Ben Vickers had made all the arrangements before the boats returned. Michael found himself included as part of the family, caught up in their sorrow, but pleased to be able to make his own farewell to the boy he'd come to think of as his little brother. Dressed in his smartest clothes, hand in hand with Stevie, he followed the small coffin up the hill from the canal to Braunston's elegant church, stood with bowed head through the interment, and returned to the Old Plough with a crowd made up of all the boaters whose movements allowed them to be there, to celebrate the youngster's short life.

And the next day, they were on their way again, sent back to Birmingham for a fresh load:

'Loife 'as ter go on, Moikey. The job's still got ter be doon – we've said goodbye teh 'im, 'n now we owe it ter 'im as mooch as ter ourselves teh git on wi' things.'

'Can Oi go wi' Ooncle Alby, Dad? Joost fer a day or two?' Stevie asked as they prepared to turn the boats and depart. Bill looked around, surprised, caught the pleading look in his son's eye:

'What d'yeh say, Alby? We'll be goin' tergether, any road – can 'e ride wi' yew?'

'Oi don't see whoy not – Yeh'll 'ave ter sleep on yer own boat, boy, not ter oopset the arrangements, though?'

'H'okay, Ooncle Alby.'

'Coom on, then! Let's be gettin' on wi' it!' The two men exchanged glances which said that they both knew the boy really wanted the comfort of Michael's company, rather than his uncle.

The two empty pairs ran quickly, back along the Oxford Canal length to Wigrams, then on the Northern Grand Union, down

Stockton and into the Avon valley. Bascote locks were worked in a solemn, fragile silence; then on down to the bottom level, on to the long pound from Radford which would lead them to the beginning of the uphill work at the Cape.

The locks done for the time being, Michael and Stevie sat side by side, huddled in their coats against the chill of the dull grey day, on the back-end planks, their backs against the front wall of the engine-hole. Neither spoke; the Bolinder's steady beat drew them into the outskirts of Leamington Spa.

'Yeh miss 'im, don't yeh?' Michael broke the long silence.

'Soomat cruel, Oi do.'

'Me too.'

Another half-mile of silence:

'Oi love moy Ma, 'n moy Dad. 'N Billy, o' course.'

''Course yeh do.'

Two hundred yards:

'Boot – Oi doon't want ter *be* wi' them, not roight noo. D'yeh oonderstand?'

'Not really…?' Stevie looked at his companion for the first time since they'd sat there:

'It's *moy fault,* doon't yeh see?'

'How's that, Stevie?'

''E was *moy* little brother – Oi should'a bin lookin' out fer 'im!'

'You couldn' be watchin' 'im all the time, Stevie!'

'Boot Oi *should* 'ave bin! 'E was follerin' me, loike 'e always did, acrorss the lock; 'n then 'e wasn't there anymore!' The dark eyes took on a haunted look; Michael stared at him, realising at last the boy's torment:

'Oh, Stevie – even if yeh'd been watchin' 'im, what could yeh 'ave *done?'*

'Oi don't *know!* Boot Oi still should'a bin…' His voice trailed off; tears welled in his eyes, ran down his cheeks, and Michael found his own grief surfacing again. He put an arm around Stevie; the younger boy turned into his embrace, and then they were

124

crying on each other's shoulders. Minutes passed; trying to ease his friend's guilt and sadness, Michael told him:

'You gave 'im so much, *taught* 'im so much, Stevie – just like you did me. I don't know where I'd be if it wasn't fer you.' The heavy head lifted from his shoulder:

'Yeh mean it?'

''Course I do. It's not your fault, if you couldn't save 'im, in the end – even if you'd bin *followin'* 'im, instead o' the other way round, yeh couldn't 'ave *done* anythin'.'

'Mebbe not...'

'You *couldn't!*'

They sat in silence again, Michael's arm still about his companion, until Stevie spoke up again:

'Yeh're a good boater – even moy Dad says so.'

'S'all down ter you, Stevie.' A hint of a chuckle:

'Yeh're even beginnin' teh *sound* loike a boater!'

'Oi am?'

Chapter Twenty-One

They loaded with steel tubes again at Coombeswood, and had an uneventful trip to London. Stevie stayed with the other boats, at least during the days, until they had unloaded; they continued to run in convoy, and he still felt happier in the company of Michael and his older sister, but once reloaded, this time with sugar bound for Birmingham's Crescent Wharf, his father insisted that he return to his own pair in case they became separated.

The natural rivalry of the cut re-established, Albert had managed to get in front of the Hanneys after an early start from Winkwell; but a message was awaiting him at Marsworth:

'Steerer Baker? Mr Vickers says you're to stop at Braunston and see him, on your way by!' The junction-keeper's voice carried across from the maintenance yard.

'What fer, d'yeh know?' The man just shook his head.

They worked hard and fast for the rest of that day, and tied overnight in Stoke Bruerne. The *Acorn* and the *Angelus* had kept up, and the hospitality of the Boat Inn was enjoyed that night, even if Albert was still a little concerned at the import of that uninformative message. The next day, they made Braunston in the early afternoon; Bill gave them a wave as he swept past, Vi called out a cheery 'see yeh in Birnigum!' from the tiller of her butty. Albert made his way quickly to Vickers' office, while Grace and Michael tied the boats up.

'Come in, Alby! Everything okay?'

'Foine, Ben – What did yeh want me fer?' Vickers laughed:

'I've got you an extra crewman, Alby! Only for a couple of days, mind – but I think he'll come in useful.'

'Oh? 'Oo's that, then?' He turned, as the side door of the office opened:

''Ello, Dad!'

'Alex? Coom 'ere, boy!' They embraced, slapping each other's backs in their delight at the reunion:

'What're yeh doin' 'ere, boy?'

'Oi've got a few days leave, Dad. Moy ship's in fer a refit – we got a bit knocked about on the last run, 'n they're postin' me to oone o' the big 'uns!'

'Oh ar? When's that, then?'

'Oi've got teh report on board on Froiday – so Oi've got three days wi' yeh!'

'Coomin' teh Crescent Wharf wi' oos, then?'

'Yew bet! Oi'll get a train from Birnigum!'

'You'll be wanting to get on, Mr Baker?' Vickers queried.

'Oi will that, Mr Vickers! 'N thank yeh!'

'Go on, Alby – enjoy your trip, Alex!'

The two left the office, hurried back towards the boats:

'So what's this noo boat o' yours, Alex?'

'I'd best not tell yeh 'er name, Dad, yeh know what the censors are loike! Boot she's a big battle-cruiser, proide o' the Navy! 'N they're mekin' me oop teh leadin' torpedoman, 'n all!'

'Good fer yew, boy! Gracie! Moikey! Look 'oo's 'ere!'

They were sat in the butty cabin, enjoying a cup of tea in the captain's absence, when they heard his call. Both quickly climbed out:

'Alex!'

''Ello, Gracie – 'ow are yeh?'

'Foine – it's good ter see yeh! 'Ow about yew?'

'Oi'm grand – got a few days leave, so Oi'm coomin' teh Birnigum wi' yeh. 'N yew moost be Moikey?'

Michael stepped out of the well onto the bank, held out a hand to the stocky young man in the smart navy-blue, the simple legend 'H M S' in gold on his cap-band:

'Alex? I'm pleased to meet you!'

'Me too, Moikey – it's grand teh meet yeh at last!' They shook hands, but then the matelot put his arm around the boy, gave him a firm hug: 'Oi'm so pleased yeh turned oop when yeh did – moy ol' man needs someone teh keep an oiye on 'im!'

''Ave yeh seen Iris, Alex?' Gracie asked.

'Yeah! Her folks coom boy yesterday, whoile Oi was waitin' fer yew to turn oop. She's foine – with a bit o' loock we'll pass 'em again, 'cause they're on their way ter Sherbo'n Street, 'n they'll be on their way back as we're goin' oop!' He paused: 'Oi 'eard about Jack, Gracie – Oi'm so sorry.' She nodded:

'Thank yeh, Alex – 'e was an aggravatin' little beggar at toimes, but Oi do miss 'im!'

'We all will – 'e was a good kid. 'Ow are yer Mum 'n Dad?'

'Oh, they're h'okay; they're on the same roon as oos, joost gone past – yeh'll see 'em later, Oi 'spect.' Through this exchange, Albert had stood to one side, his expression one of undiluted pride in his son; now, he chivvied them up:

'Coom on, we 'aven't got all day ter be chatterin'! Moikey – can yew share wi' Gracie, fer a day or two, 'n let Alex 'ave the soidebed?'

The rest of that trip was passed in high good humour; Albert and his son were so obviously delighted to be boating together again, even if it was only for a few days, that the tragedy of Jack's death, while by no means forgotten, could be remembered with a better degree of acceptance under the sheltering umbrella of their joy. Even Stevie, when they met up again at that night's stop, seemed to come further out of his still-present mood of quiet gloom in the young man's company.

Once unloaded, and reloaded for the return Southwards, Alex

left them in Birmingham, stepping off at Old Turn Junction, bag in hand, to walk to New Street Station and his train. He had spent a lot of time with Michael, talking about the boating life which they now shared, about his parents; Michael learnt a lot about Rita Baker – Albert had hardly ever mentioned his dead wife in the boy's hearing. He, in turn, told Alex much about his own family, his life before his desperate escape from the house in Windsor Street. He felt that strange rapport with the young man, even on such a brief acquaintance, that let him open up on the subject much more than he'd wanted to with Vi, or even Gracie.

They'd all turned to, each crew helping the other, heaving the two hundredweight sacks of sugar out of the boats' holds onto the wharfside. Michael and Alex were sat side by side on the *Antrim's* gunwales, tired, grubby, and sweaty; the sailor, his uniform carefully folded away in a drawer in the cabin for the time being, clad now in the old clothes he'd always kept for loading, smiled down at the boy. Michael returned his smile, but something that Gracie had said was running through his mind; he asked, tentatively:

'Alex – when the war's over – you're going to get married?'

'Teh Iris – that's roight.'

'Then – you'll come back on the boats?'

'O' course – what else would Oi do?'

'So there'll be you and Iris, and your Dad?'

'Yes...' Sudden understanding lit his shaded grey eyes, the same colour as his father's, as he realised what was troubling the boy: ''N you too, Moikey! Yeh're part o' the family, now!'

'Am I? I'm not sure your Dad thinks so.' Alex felt his new young friend's doubts, slipped an arm around his shoulders:

''E doos, Moikey, believe me. 'E's not the koind ter say so, mebbe – 'n Oi reckon 'e's still missin' moy Ma, joost loike Oi'm doin'.' He paused, went on: 'I want yeh ter promise me soomethin' Moikey?' The boy raised enquiring eyes to his:

'What, Alex?'

'If anythin' 'appens ter me…'

'Nothing's going to happen to you, Alex!'

'No, boot – joost in case, roight? Oi want yer teh promise that yeh'll stay wi' moy Dad, look after 'im fer me, h'okay?' Michael nodded:

'Of course I would! I wouldn't leave him, ever!'

'Then Oi promise yew, yeh'll have a place with oos, as long as yeh want it.'

They parted the best of friends, promised to meet soon again, to talk of other things they hadn't said.

Heading out of Birmingham on the 'top road' to avoid a stoppage on Camp Hill Locks, they cruised towards Kings Norton on the Worcester and Birmingham Canal. After his son's departure, Albert, never exactly loquacious at the best, stood silent and thoughtful at his tiller, puffing at his well-packed pipe. Michael, stood on the gunwale at the side of the cabin, held his own silence for mile after mile, until he ventured to say:

'You must be really proud of Alex, Mr Baker.'

'Oi am, boy. More'n Oi can tell yeh.'

Chapter Twenty-Two

The cold, dark days of Winter at last gave way to a new, burgeoning Springtime. Michael had passed his first Christmas on the boats, found more joy in it than he could ever recall feeling at any previous Yuletide: They'd been tied, by chance, in Marsworth – the Red Lion had been filled to bursting with boaters on the night of Christmas Eve, and the music, the singing and dancing, had gone on until the early hours. Even in wartime, no-one was working on Christmas Day, except for the odd pair carrying especially urgent cargoes.

He woke on Christmas morning to find a few small packages waiting for him. He'd expected nothing, knowing that his new friends had little to spare for buying presents, but there was a new pullover, knitted by Vi Hanney, a traditional-style webbing belt, surreptitiously made by Gracie. And Albert Baker had two surprises for him:

'Alex said ter give yeh this – 'e left it fer yeh when 'e was 'ome.' Michael tore off the old newspaper which wrapped the gift, to find a carved wooden model of a ship, a destroyer, painted in the dark grey of the real vessel:

''E made it fer yeh, it's 'is old ship 'e was on.' He chuckled at the boy's delight: ''E's better with 'is 'ands than Oi am, that's fer sure!'

'It's terrific, Mr Baker! I'll thank him, next time we write to him!'

'Aye, you do that, boy.' He reached behind himself, under the

131

cross-bed: ''N this is fer yew, too. Sorry Oi didn't get ter wrap it oop, proper-loike.'

A brand new windlass, Grand Union size. He'd been using one of Albert's spare ones, all this time – but this was his own! Impulsively, he stood up and put his arms around the man's neck, gave him a tight hug; Albert brushed him off:

'Git away, boy! We thought, bein' off the bank, yeh'd be used ter gettin' lots o' presents…'

'They're brilliant, Mr Baker! This is the best Christmas, ever – I've never had so many presents!'

He practically leapt out of the cabin, knocked on the butty, as ever tied alongside, and threw his arms around a startled Gracie as she emerged to see what the fuss was about.

On a wider stage, that Spring of 1941, the slugging match between the Eighth Army and the Afrika Korps continued; had the results been less tragic, the tit-for-tat bombing raids across the North Sea would have had an element of childishness about them. And, in the North Atlantic, the U-boat versus convoy war looked to take on a new dimension when the battleship Bismarck sailed from its safe haven.

As the hours of daylight slowly lengthened, Michael found his spirits lifting. Boaters born to the life seemed to take Winter working in their stride, but he had found the long days taxing, when so much of what they needed to do had to be done in the dark. Boating after dark can be a pleasant experience, on a bright, clear night when the moon lays a track of silver on the still water; but on a dark, cold morning, two hours before sunrise, when the bitter rain is running down your neck into your shirt and the headlight only gives you a tunnel-vision view of the track ahead, it becomes a far less attractive proposition.

For some time they had been on a kind of circular route: Foodstuffs, including cheese and sugar and tinned goods, from Brentford to Nottingham; a variety of cargoes, from Nottingham to Birmingham; and munitions of one sort or another, back to the South.

* * *

Ben Vickers thumbed through the day's post in his office by the dock at Braunston, sorting company business from the odd letters destined for members of his crews. One of the latter – an official-looking envelope, addressed to Mr Albert Baker: Vickers' heart sank – he'd seen envelopes like this one before. Not often, thank God, but he was terribly afraid that he knew the gist of the tidings it would prove to contain; he shook his head, hoping he was wrong, and put it to one side. He'd have to get a message to Alby, make sure he called in next time he was past...

Albert got the message as they were ready to leave Wednesbury with another load of machined shell cases. Mostly, messages to call in at Braunston meant something official, company matters; they would usually stop off quickly there, anyway, in the hope of a letter from Alex. His correspondence was always erratic, depending as it did on just where his ship happened to be, whether post could be relayed back to England.

They were in Braunston two days later. As usual, Albert hurried off to the office, leaving Michael and Gracie to tie the boats; but this time, instead of rushing back with an envelope in his hand, eager for Michael to read his son's latest missive to him, he was away for half an hour or more. And when he returned, it was with a droop to his shoulders, a shattered expression on his weatherbeaten face; Gracie went to him as he approached:

'What is it, Ooncle Alby?' Michael knew the answer, even before the boatman could get the words out; like Ben Vickers before him, he felt his heart sink into his boots:

'It's Alex – 'is ship's bin soonk, 'n 'e's' missin'.' Gracie's expression showed her horror at this news:

'Oh, no!' She took him in her arms, held him close, shaking her head in disbelief; Michael went to him as well, put an arm around his waist:

'If 'e's' only missin', there's hope that they'll foind 'im, isn't there?' Albert smiled down at him:

'Of course there is, Moikey. We moostn't give oop – 'e's probably floatin' around soomewher' in oone o' them rafts. They'll foind 'im.'

'Still an awful shock, though, ent it, Ooncle Alby? Coom on, Oi'll mek oos a coop o' tea, 'n we'll think what's ter be doon, eh?' Gracie led him down into the butty cabin, where a kettle was already singing on the range. Michael sat beside him on the sidebed:

'Shall we wait 'ere for more news?' But Albert shook his head:

'Noo, boy. We've still got a job ter do! Let's 'ave that coopa, to get oover the shock – then we'd best be getting' on.'

But even the twelve-year-old knew that their words had to be no more than bravado, that the chances of Alex coming home were so remote as to be discounted. At the same time as he admired the boatman's stoical attitude, he felt his sorrow, his hopelessness, and fought to hold back his own tears, knowing that if he gave in to them, it would shatter that fragile illusion of hope that they all needed. Then a thought occurred to him; he got up, excusing himself, and hurried to the dock office as Albert had done earlier. He knocked at the door, entered nervously at Vickers' invitation:

'Mr Vickers?' The man looked up from his desk:

'Mikey! How's Mr Baker?'

'Gracie's making him some tea. He seems okay, but…' Vickers nodded, his eyes reflecting his sympathy for his old friend:

'What is it, lad?'

'Well… Alex was on a big ship, a battle-cruiser, I think he said, wasn't he?'

'Yes – that's right, I think?'

'Has there been anything, in the news lately, about a big ship like that getting sunk?' Vickers stared at him for a moment:

'Oh, my God! Yes… It was all over the papers, last week! The Hood… HMS Hood – she was hit by the Bismarck, blown apart… You think Alex was on *her?*'

'Well – it would make sense, wouldn't it?'

'He never told you the name of his ship?' Michael shook his head:

'Were there… any survivors?' Vickers stared at him in horror:

'Three or four, I think. No more.' Michael bit his lip, nodded:

'I see. Thank you, Mr Vickers. I'd better be getting back.' The man watched him go, struck by his proud, upright carriage, aware that he was nonetheless on the verge of tears.

They stopped that night at the bottom of Buckby Locks. The journey had been done under a cloud of despondency which was at odds with the bright, clear Spring evening; no-one referred to the news they'd received, but it was uppermost in all their minds. They'd eaten, as so often, on the move, the meal which Gracie had begun to prepare before they reached Braunston simmering on the range as they worked up the locks, and finally served once they emerged from the tunnel, on the half-hour pound to the top of Buckby flight.

As they cleared the bottom lock, Gracie felt a surge of excitement despite the hollow feeling in her heart – a Grand Union pair, *Bognor* and *Bodmin*, were tied near the lock, facing North. Joey was here!

They had to go a number of boat lengths down before there was room to tie. The pair secured, she turned to Albert:

'We goin' oop the *Cow* fer a drink, Ooncle Alby?' The pub by bottom lock was the rather-inappropriately named *Spotted Cow*; he shook his head:

'Not me, Gracie, Oi don't feel in the mood. Boot yew'd better go – Oi see 'Enry Caplin's boats back ther'!' She studied him, her eyes full of concern for him:

'Yew h'okay, Ooncle Alby?' He gave her a thin smile:

'Oi'm foine, girl! Git on 'n see yer man – say 'ello ter 'Enry 'n Suey fer me, if they're there, roight?'

'Oi will. Oi'll see you later – yew coomin', Moikey?' The boy shook his head:

'No – I'll stay 'ere wi' Mr Baker.'

Talk in the bar was of the war, the job, and that boater's gossip which serves as a towpath telegraph, conveying news around the system faster than the telephone can achieve. Someone had already brought the news of Alex to the assembled clans; Gracie could add nothing to what they had heard. She sat in a corner, arm in arm with Joey Caplin; after a while, they got up and strolled out into the gathering night, walked up to the lock and sat on the balance beam. Plucking up his courage, Joey slipped an arm round her waist:

'So are yeh gooin' ter marry me then, Gracie?' The darkness hid her blush, as she averted her face:

'Yew want me to, Joe?'

'Yeh know Oi do! Yeh're seventeen now; Oi'm near Nointeen – what about it? Yeh do loove me, don't yer?'

'Of course Oi do! 'N of course Oi'm goin' ter marry yeh – boot not yet, Joey.'

''Course not – Oi'll 'ave ter talk teh yer Dad about it, won't Oi? 'N yer Ma. 'Ow about nex' year, soometoime? Yeh'll be eighteen then.' She lifted her head, gazed into his eyes:

'Yes – oh yes, Joe!' He smiled down at her, bent to kiss her cheek:

'H'okay, then! S'long as yer Dad's all roight about it, Oi'll 'ave a word wi' the coomp'ny, or get *moy* Dad teh, 'n see if we can 'ave our own boats. That'll be grand, woon't it?' She hesitated:

'It will, boot... what about Ooncle Alby, Joe? Yeh've 'eard

about Alex – it'd joost leave 'im wi' Moikey…'

'The two o' them could manage, couldn't they?'

'Yeah, boot… Fellers's loike ter 'ave crews o' three on a pair, Joe.'

'Then can't they foind 'im soomeoone? Oi want yeh wi' *me,* Gracie!'

'Mebbe… Boot it's 'ardly the toime teh tell 'im now, is it? Can we keep it secret, fer a whoile, Joe?'

'Oi 'spose so, Gracie – boot not too long, h'okay? Oi want ter know 'ow Oi stand wi' yer folks.'

'Oh, yeh'll be all roight there, Joe!'

On the boats, silence reigned in the motor's cabin. Michael, sat on the stool, his elbows propped on the lowered table-cupboard, was feeling totally inadequate, wishing there was something he could do, something he could say, to soften his captain's suffering. In fact, his own heart was heavy, his thoughts on the cheerful young man who'd accompanied them for those few short days back in the Winter, whose presence had done so much to help them all over the loss of little Jack. He desperately wanted to somehow comfort Mr Baker, but the secret knowledge he'd gained from his words with Ben Vickers would make a hypocrite of him if he tried too hard to reassure the man of his son's safety.

In the end, it was Albert Baker who broke the silence. He was hunched on the sidebed, the pipe which had long ago gone out clamped, forgotten, in his teeth, until he took it out:

''E's dead, Moikey.' The boy sat gazing at his hands, clasped before him on the table; he couldn't raise his eyes, face the man's sorrow, couldn't reply.

'Ther's no use pretendin' – 'e's' gone, boy, 'e ent coomin' back.' Now, Michael looked up into the dark grey eyes, full of nothing but emptiness:

'But, you said, before…?'

'Oi know what Oi said. Boot – Oi didn't want yew 'n Gracie

gettin' more oopset than yeh 'ad ter be.'

'But… you could 'ave been roight! Per'aps 'e *is* in a lifeboat, somewhere, per'aps they *will* still find 'im!' But Albert shook his head, and Michael saw the knowledge, the certainty, in his eyes:

'Do you… do you *know* what ship he was on?' He asked, carefully; Albert nodded:

''E tole me, joost before 'e went fer 'is train, in Birnigum. Soo proud, 'e was! Best ship in the 'ole Navy, the 'Ood, 'e said it was.'

'And… you know what's happened to it?' Albert just nodded.

Words had no more value for them. Michael got up, moved to sit next to the boatman, put one hand over his where they lay in his lap, the cold pipe clasped between them. After a minute or so, Albert slipped one of them free, slid his arm around the boy's slim waist; unable to contain himself any longer, Michael turned his face into the man's shoulder, began to cry into his shirt, feeling the stiff, upright pride that kept the old boatman dry-eyed through the depth of his sorrow.

Chapter Twenty-Three

That trip was carried on in a mood of silent determination. No-one spoke more than they had to, but they set about doing the job with a dogged eagerness, knowing that, in their own small way, they were contributing to the war effort. Gracie's joy at Joey's proposal was more than tempered by her sorrow for her uncle; she had told him, quietly, of her news without telling him when they intended to marry, received his rather distracted blessing. She had told Michael as well; the boy had hugged her tightly and told her how happy he was, although, quietly, he was wondering what this portended for his own future. Albert, never a great talker, had sunk into a deep, silent mood, his eyes clouded, the humour which would normally surface at unexpected moments vanished as if it had never been.

In the evenings, he would most often stay on the boats, sitting slumped in a corner of the cabin, his hands clasped around a mug of tea which had usually gone cold before he remembered to drink it. If he did venture to the pub, wherever they happened to be tied, he would sit in similar fashion in a corner of the bar, his pint mug similarly forgotten in his hands.

Their back-load, this time, took them directly back to Birmingham – bagged sugar, for the Fazeley Street warehouse – and so via Braunston. They flew down the flight, their rhythm as slick and efficient as ever despite the fact that, after two years of war with no money spent on maintenance, some of the gates and paddle-gear were becoming worn and leaky. Out of bottom lock, along past the reservoir, under Butcher's Bridge, and so to the Stop House…

It had been their habit, as long as Michael had been with them, to call in there and check if there was any mail. This time, habit was so strong that it didn't occur to him to vary that routine; he swung the motor in towards the bank in the first clear spot, reversing the engine to slow it down, watched as Gracie let the butty glide down his inside to tie on the bank as he snatched the motor tight against it. She gave him a strange look as she stepped off, but he gave it no mind. Albert emerged from the cabin:

'Moikey?'

'Yes, Mr Baker?' The man gave him a colourless smile:

'Ther'll be noo letters now, boy.' Michael felt his face turn red; he stammered:

'I… I just thought… we should check, see if there's… any more news?' Albert shook his head, then said:

'Go on, if yeh want, boy. Don't be long.'

'I… I won't!'

Kicking himself for his stupidity, Michael set off for Vickers' office. Why hadn't he used his brain, why hadn't it sunk in with him that there'd be no more letters from Alex, no more reason to stop here unless Mr Vickers wanted to see them? Still cursing his insensitivity, he knocked at the door:

'Come in! Michael, how are you?' Ben Vickers looked up from his desk, an odd expression on his face.

'I'm foine, Mr Vickers. I just wondered, is there any more news? I mean…'

'About Alex?' He shook his head, looking perplexed: 'Not *about* him, no…' He paused, then seemed to come to a decision: 'Sit down, Michael.'

The boy did as he was bid, puzzled at the dock manager's uncharacteristic hesitancy. Vickers opened a drawer in his desk, took out an envelope, looked up at Michael:

'I… This came, the day before yesterday, and I'm not sure what to do with it…'

'What is it, Mr Vickers?' The man showed him the envelope; he saw the style of the writing, the forces postmark; his eyes lifted to meet Vickers', joy shining in them, but the man shook his head again:

'It's dated *before* the one telling us… what had happened. Must have been held up in the Navy's post. Nothing's changed, Michael.' The boy closed his eyes – the surge of hope he'd felt, the sudden certainty that Alex had survived after all, had been so good, and for it to be so quickly dashed… He looked up at Vickers again, as he went on:

'I'm not sure what I should do, Mikey. It's addressed to Albert, of course, and I shouldn't withhold it from him – but, I don't want to make things any worse for him than they are, you understand? If he gets another letter from him, now, one written before… You see what I mean?' Having himself just put his foot in it, done something to remind Albert of his lost son, Michael understood only too well. He thought for a moment, then said:

'Why don't you give it to me, Mr Vickers? I'll keep it, try to pick a good time to give it to him, maybe when he's getting over things a bit.' Vickers looked unsure; but this was a sensible young lad, thoughtful and trustworthy…

'Okay, Mikey, you take it. But…'

'You can trust me, Mr Vickers, I don't want him hurt any more, either.'

'Oo don't yer want 'urt, boy?' Neither had heard the office door open, seen Albert appear there; both looked around guiltily. Michael stuck the envelope inside his shirt – too late:

'What yer got ther', Moikey?' He considered trying to bluff it out, but decided he wouldn't be able to do it; he pulled the letter out again, showed it to Albert:

'Ah… Better coom back ter the boat, Moikey. Thank yeh, Ben – Oi'll be boy fer a chat 'fore long.'

It was a rather embarrassed silence that held them as they walked back to the boats. Michael was mentally kicking himself again – why hadn't he thought that Mr Baker might come after him if he wasn't back right away? Why hadn't he kept his eyes open? Now, he'd insist on hearing the contents of the letter, and that could only upset him even more than he was already. He risked a glance at his companion, saw the man striding along, his eyes fixed straight ahead: *I love him like he was my Dad – don't make me hurt him any more!*

Gracie gave one look at Albert's expression and ducked down into the butty cabin:

'Oi'll mek soom tea, shall Oi?'

'Good oidea, girl – coom insoide wi' me, Moikey.' Albert sat down on the sidebed, by the end of the table-cupboard; Michael stood in front of the stove, nervously holding the envelope in both hands until the boatman gestured for him to sit on the step inside the doors:

'Well – read it to me, Moikey.' Michael regarded him cautiously, then carefully tore open the envelope, extracted the sheets of notepaper from within. Albert gestured impatiently for him to start:

Dear Dad...

The first few paragraphs were the usual mix of personal items and anecdotes of Alex's shipboard world, the little glimpses of life on one of His Majesty's Warships which Michael had always found so interesting, that now only made his heart ache. He glanced up at Albert as he read, saw the man sitting with his head bowed, his eyes half closed; his voice faltered, but he made himself carry on. Then, the tone of the writing changed:

Dad: There's something we've never talked about, and I think it's time we did. When my old ship was hit by that torpedo, a lot of men died – I knew them all, some of them were my friends. I know we made it back to port okay, that time – but next time, Dad, it could be me. I don't want to think about it any more than you do – but we've got to face it, Dad, it might happen. And if it does – there's something I want you to promise me. It's about Mikey.

Surprised, the boy stopped speaking; Albert didn't look up, just gestured for him to go on. Looking back down at the letter, he cleared his throat and picked up his thread:

He's a grand kid – and I know he thinks a lot of you, even if he doesn't say it. You've given him a new life, turned him into a cracking little boater – but he's more than that, Dad. He's...

His eyes a few words ahead of his mouth, Michael froze again, his mouth open in mixed shock and trepidation – How would the boatman take *this?* He looked up, to see Albert's eyes on him:

'Go on, son.' He looked back down, went to read on; but then the man's words struck him: *Son? He's never called me that...?* Nervously, he started reading again:

He's my little brother – the brother you and Mum were never able to give me. So, if anything should happen to me, I want you to look after him, Dad, treat him like he really was my little brother. I made him promise, when we were in Birmingham together, that if I didn't come home, he'd stay with you, look after you. So you've got to do the same – please, when you write back, promise me that?

Half afraid of what the man would say, Michael raised his eyes again; Albert was smiling at him, although unshed tears were welling up in his eyes. He raised a hand to stop the boy saying anything:

''E's roight, Moichael. Oi said before, any man'd be proud ter 'ave yeh fer 'is son – so if yeh can 'andle 'aving a grumpy old cuss fer a substitute Dad...' Michael stared at him, lost for words; he dropped the letter on the sidebed, got up and went to the boatman. Albert rose to his feet, reached out to him, and he flung his arms around his neck; the man drew him down onto the seat beside him, enfolded him in his arms as his tears began to flow.

Michael himself didn't know, couldn't tell, in his confusion, if he was crying for sorrow or joy; he felt Albert's body trembling in his embrace, knew that, at last, the old man was crying too, crying for his dead son; and, just maybe, out of joy in his new son, too.

Gracie found them so, when she entered with two mugs of fresh tea. Smiling, she opened the table-cupboard and put the mugs down; Albert smiled at her, gently eased Michael away:

'Coom on, son. Drink yer tea, it'll do yeh good.' Michael turned to give Gracie a beaming smile, pick up his mug:

'Yes, Dad.' The girl looked from one to the other, saw the mixed sadness and joy on their faces; she just shook her head, and went back to the butty for her own cup.

Looking over the rim of his mug, Michael said:

'You knew, didn't you? What he was going to say?' Albert's face cracked into a grin:

'Didn't tek mooch guessin', did it?' Half-afraid of the answer, Michael asked:

'Are you… are you pleased?' Albert drew him close again:

'More'n Oi can tell yeh, Moikey. Alex's gone – but Oi've still got a son Oi can be proud of.' Michael laid his head against the man's shoulder, feeling content, settled, at last.

Chapter Twenty-Four

The run to Birmingham was completed with a new feeling of cheerful camaraderie bolstering their sense of purpose, even if their shared sorrow was little abated. In quiet moments, Michael would remember again the happy, enthusiastic young man whose company he'd enjoyed for those brief few days, who had treated him, spoken to him, as a member of his family; his pleasure at being, now, welcomed by the old boatman as such would for ever be tempered by the emptiness of knowing that Alex would never return to be his big brother.

Albert, for his part, had come back out of the shell he'd sunken into; indeed, he seemed more the robustly cheerful man he'd been before Rita's death, his humour surfacing more frequently, catching Michael especially off guard. Gracie happily accepted the new relationship between them, delighted that her uncle seemed to be coping well with his grief, and pleased for Michael that his yearning for a new family had come to be, albeit a family with only one other member. But they seemed to be so happy with each other, that she found herself with a smile on her face whenever she watched them together.

But the events of those days had made Michael think, also, of his own family. Seeing how hard Albert had been hit by the loss of his son made him realise how his mother must have suffered when he'd disappeared, how much he must have upset Ginny, and Andy of course, by his sudden absence.

They unloaded at Warwick Bar, saw their cargo safely into the Fazeley Street warehouse, then headed, empty, for Wednesbury again. Waiting there already were the *Acorn* and *Angelus;* when they'd tied up in the layby, Gracie dashed off to see her family.

Bill greeted her with a cheerful ''Ow do, Girl!', knocked on the cabinside to alert his wife to their visitor. Vi stuck her head out, clambered out with a beaming smile at the sight of her daughter:

'Gracie love – 'ow's things?'

'Oh, not bad, Ma. You've 'eard about Alex?' Vi tutted:

'Terrible business! 'Ow's Alby tekin' it?'

'Oh, not so bad as yeh moight think! 'E 'ad a letter from 'im, writ joost before… you knoo! Alex arst 'is Dad to kind of adopt Moikey, tek 'im on as 'is son, if anythin' 'appened, yeh knoo?

'And?' Gracie laughed:

'The two of 'em are loike a pair o' little kids – Oi think the letter give Alby the excuse 'e wanted to mek a big fuss o' Moikey, and o' course 'e's' bin lookin' teh Alby as 'is new Dad fer ages!'

''E moost be terrible oopset, though?'

'Oh ar – they both are. Boot, 'avin' each other 'as made it easier fer both of 'em, yeh knoo?' Vi nodded:

'That's good, love. What about yew, though?'

'Oh, Oi'm foine, Ma!' She glanced around: 'Dad, Mum: Joey's arst me teh marry 'im!' Vi threw her arms around her daughter, hugged her tight; when she finally released her, Gracie turned to her father, embraced him as he asked her:

'Yeh gooin' teh, then?'

''Course Oi am, Dad!'

'If that's what yeh want, girl…'

''E's goin' teh talk teh yew about it, when 'e can, Dad.'

'Oi should 'ope so! 'Ave yeh thought about when?'

'We thought next year, mebbe?'

'Hm… Oi'd say 'old off, per'aps anoother year – yeh're only

joost seventeen, Gracie. Besoides, it woon't do teh leave Alby wi' joost a slip of a lad fer crew; Moikey'll be a year older, 'n mebbe we can foind them a third 'and in the meantoime. 'N we doon't know 'ow this bloody war's goin' ter go, yet.' She leant back in his embrace to look into his eyes:

'Oh, Dad…!' His love for his daughter showed in his smile:

'Oi know, girl! Boot if 'e looves yeh, 'e'll wait.'

'Yes… If that's what yeh think, Dad?'

'It is, loove. Oi'll talk teh Joey, don't worry – we'll be meetin' oop wi' them 'fore long, Oi'm sure.'

The call came for Steerer Hanney to load; they parted with a last kiss.

With a fresh load of shell cases, they were mopping the boats down, preparatory to setting off Southwards once more. Michael looked over the cabintop to where Albert was giving the porthole a quick polish:

'Dad?'

'Yes, Moikey?'

'Could we… I mean, if it's possible…'

'What is it, son?'

'Would it be possible to stop in Wolverton, on the way boy? Joost fer a few minutes…' Albert regarded him over the cabin, an understanding look in his eyes:

'Oi 'spect we could do that, if yeh want, boy.' Michael's face broke into a smile:

'Thanks, Dad!'

* * *

Three days later, a pair of boats were tied up by the massive blue-brick bridge which spans the London & North Western Railway as well as the Grand Union Canal, near the centre of Wolverton:

'This is closer teh wher' we used ter live, Dad.' Albert gave his adopted son a sympathetic look:

'Yeh woon't be too long, will yeh?'

'No – 'alf an hour, maybe. Oi just want teh see our old neighbour, mek sure my Mum's okay.' At this, the old boatman felt a sudden pang of what was close to being jealousy. He had, as Gracie had surmised, welcomed Alex's insistence that he should take the boy as his adopted son, allow the affection he already felt for the youngster to come to the fore, and the reminder that there were others who could call on the kid's love and respect unsettled him oddly.

Wednesday was Janet Eastwood's day for cleaning the kitchen. When the knock came at the front door, she ducked out of the oven, which she had been scrubbing, knocking the back of her head as she did so:

'Who the blazes can that be?' she muttered to herself, rubbing the painful spot; she hurried to open the door:

'Hello, Mrs Eastwood!'

'Michael! Come in – how are you?'

'I'm fine, thank you.' He followed her into the front room: 'I'm sorry I haven't been back to see you – I know I promised to get in touch, with my Mum, but...'

'You've been too busy with your new life, have you?' He smiled, nodded:

'I guess so!' She took him by the shoulders, studied him:

'Just look at you! So tall – and you look... I don't know, so fit! This boating obviously suits you.' He just smiled again:

'Mrs Eastwood?' She raised an enquiring eyebrow:

'Did you tell my Mum, about where I am?'

'You asked me not to.'

'Well – I think I ought to let her know I'm okay, don't you?' She gave him a rather stern look:

'I do, Michael! I think you should have done, a long time ago...

Are you saying that you want me to let her in on your secret?'
He nodded:

'Yes, please – will you?'

'Of course I will! Do you want to see her?' He averted his
eyes, shook his head:

'No – not yet. But – I've written her a letter. Will you give it
to her for me?' He withdrew an envelope from inside his shirt,
held it out to her; she took it with a smile:

'Of course, Michael. I'll take a bus over there, maybe
tomorrow, and make sure she gets it. Have you told her where
you are?' He nodded:

'Yes – and about… my new Dad.'

'Your new *father?*' He grinned:

'It's all in there!' He indicated the letter: 'Mum'll tell you –
I've got to get back, he's waiting for me with the boats. There's
an address, too, where she can write to me, if she wants to.'

'I'm sure she will! I'll be sure to pass this on as quickly as
I can.'

'Thank you, Mrs Eastwood. I'm sorry to be a nuisance…'

'You're not, child! I'm so happy that you're all right – your
Mum's going to be so pleased to hear from you! She never gave
up on you, you know? Even when everyone else thought you
were dead, she wouldn't have it – and now she'll know she was
right all along!'

Chapter Twenty-Five

'Coom on lad, give oos a song!'

At the beginning of the evening, Michael had somehow let it slip that he had once sung in his school choir, that he loved Christmas Carols.

'Well, give 'im room ter breath, then!'

The canalside bar of the Boat Inn was crammed to the rafters with people, boaters all. Perched in the old pews, reused here after being removed from the local church, standing in front of the open fire, squeezed into every available corner. There weren't many other kids there – only a few in their mid-teens. It was getting late – everyone was in jovial mood, even if their throats were beginning to feel the effects of too many choruses, backed by an assortment of Melodeons and Accordions. Henry Caplin had laid his banjo aside, his fingers aching; his son and Grace Hanney were squashed into a corner by the fire, looking not at all unhappy with the situation.

Six months had seen many changes in the wider world, even if life on the cut went on much as before. The endless cycle of load, journey, unload and reload, continued under the relentless pressure of earning a living as well as that knowledge that what they did was in their own small way helping to fight the war. The long, bright days of Summer had faded through the burnished gold of Autumn; now the cold, dark Winter had them all in its grip once more, their routine a round of rising before dawn, working on through the few hours of grey daylight until long after darkness had fallen again. Thankfully, such frosts as there had been so far had not hindered them.

Christmas brought a welcome break to this unending labour. The length from Stoke Bruerne top lock to the Blisworth tunnel was crowded with boats – Fellows, Morton & Clayton, Grand Unions, a couple of pairs of Barlows coal boats, Harvey-Taylors, L.B.Faulkners… And tomorrow, Christmas Day, most would remain where they were, their crews taking a long-deserved rest.

Brief talk of the war, earlier in the evening, had had a new feel to it, a different, perhaps less fatalistic, tone. The conflict was now truly global in scope: In June, Hitler's ambition had turned to the vastnesses of the Soviet Republic, taking the pressure off of the cross-channel threat and unleashing the enormous might of the Russians against the Wehrmacht, even if, for the moment, they seemed to be falling back on all fronts. And, scant weeks ago, the infamy of Pearl Harbour had pitched the wealth and resources of the USA into the fight on the side of the allies – there was talk of American forces joining in the fight against Germany, although they had what was almost their own war to handle in the Pacific.

The atmosphere in the bar was thick with smoke; Michael got to his feet, the scratchiness in his throat also in part due to the long night's singing. He was very tired – it had to be nearly midnight! He'd take himself off, back to the boats, to the comfort of his bed, before long, even if Gracie and his Dad decided to stay on longer. He looked around, at the sea of laughing faces, felt a surge of happiness: *These are my people, my neighbours, my* friends! His eyes lit on Alby Baker, repacking his battered old pipe, a proud smile on his lips as he focussed on what he was doing, his face averted, and love swelled in his heart: *My Dad!*

Since that last visit to Janet Eastwood, the note he'd left for his mother, they had exchanged regular if fitful letters. His note had been brief, an apology, mainly, for the pain and suffering he'd caused her and his brother and sister by running away; her reply had been full of love and understanding, her wish to see him again unsaid but clear in her tone. He'd resisted that, knowing it would only upset them both, risk putting a strain on his relationship with his new Dad; their letters since, his sent to his Grandparents' address in Buckingham, hers care of FMC at Braunston, had limited themselves to exchanges of news. He had been happy to hear of how Andy was getting on, how well Ginny was doing in her new school; news that his Grandma hadn't been well in the cold weather prompted him to include a special note to her in his last letter before Christmas, together with a card he'd made himself.

Now, tired, sleepy, but oh so happy, he took in a lungful of that heavy, smoky air, and prepared to give vent to his favourite carol, which he'd saved up for last.

Albert glanced up as Michael drew breath, caught the boy's eye, smiled. *Oi loove yew, kid – yeh mayn't be moine, boot Oi loove yeh all the same!* At first, after Alex's last letter, he'd worried that he was allowing his grief to take control, using the boy's affection for him as a way of softening his anguish at his own son's death. But he'd soon come to accept that his feelings for the kid were genuine, that he did indeed return that affection, and loved the boy's company to the point that he couldn't imagine not having him around. Each time Michael received a letter from his mother, the boatman felt a flutter of fear that she would press him, that he might give in and return to his roots. He'd even asked, once or twice, if Michael thought he might one day go back, only to get that shake of the head, that *you must be joking!* expression; and he'd felt his heart lighten with pleasure and pride in the boy who now called him 'Dad'.

Now he smiled up at the youngster, so tall, so proud, so straight, saw the love in his bright eyes, felt it reflect in his own.

> *'Si-ilent night, Ho-oly night,*
> *All is calm, all is bright...'*

Chapter Twenty-Six

Dear Michael,

I know you didn't expect to hear from me, but your Mum has asked me to write this letter for her. She's not very well just at the moment – I'll tell you more about that in a minute, but first, I'm afraid I have some bad news for you.

You remember that she told you Andrew was ill? There's no easy way for me to tell you this, Michael – I'm afraid he died yesterday. He'd got a bad chest infection, and it just got worse and worse, and then the doctor said it was pneumonia; I'm so sorry. The funeral will be in three days time, on Friday – is it possible you can get here? I know it might be a while before you get this.

In any case, can you come and see me the next time you are passing this way? As I said, your Mum is not too well, either – she insisted on nursing Andrew herself, and she's caught the same infection. Please don't worry too much, the doctor says she has a much better chance of getting over it, as she is stronger in herself than he was; but they've taken her into the hospital in Buckingham, just to be on the safe side. She'd love to see you, Michael – if you can come to my house, I could take you over on the bus? I know it means holding up your journey, but it would mean so much to her.

Ginny is fine; so is your Grandad, although he has his work cut out now looking after your Granny.

> *Hoping to see you very soon – I'm sorry to have to give you such terrible news.*
> *With my love, Janet Eastwood.*

Michael had paused in his rush back to the boats, tied between the Stop House and the main road bridge; he stood stock still, disbelieving, and re-read Janet's letter. They had maintained their regular quick stop in Braunston each time they passed, although now it was in the hope of a letter from his mother; the last had come two weeks before, bringing him the latest news, such as it was, and yes, telling him that Andy had been taken rather poorly. He had written back, posting his reply in Rickmansworth as they had passed through, on their last trip South.

Since Christmas, their exchange of letters had continued thus, slow but steady; now, with Easter not long past, the sudden, awful news set him back on his heels. Now, he read the letter a third time, then looked at the date at the top – four days ago! Yes, if he thought about it, today should be Friday; it wasn't always easy to keep track of the days of the week when you worked all days the same as the rest. He'd not make the funeral, a thought which made him even more dejected – but they could stop in Wolverton tomorrow...

Back at the boats, Gracie handed him a cup of hot tea before noticing the expression on his face; she looked closer at him:

'What is it, Moikey?' He drew a deep breath and told them; Albert reached out to put a hand on the boy's shoulder:

'We'll stop ther' tomorrer, Moikey, in the mornin'. You go 'n see yer Mum, tek all the toime yeh need, h'okay?' He swallowed, holding back his feelings, and nodded:

'Thanks, Dad. I think now, I ought to go, don't you?'

''Course yeh moost, son. It'll do 'er a power o' good teh see yeh, Oi'm sure.' He just nodded again; then asked, tentatively:

'Would you... come with me? I'd love her to meet you.' Albert hesitated, surprised and unsure whether it would be wise; but then he gave in to the appeal in the boy's eyes:

'If yeh're sure yeh want me along wi' yeh?'
'Please, Dad?' It was Albert's turn to nod:
'All roight, if that's what yeh want, boy.'

The bus ride had been rough, the ancient Albion jouncing along as if its suspension had long given up the struggle. They made their way into the hospital, followed Janet to the ward where Nettie was lying, dozing, in her bed. She went ahead, gently roused her:

'Hello, dear – how are you feeling today?' Nettie pushed herself weakly upright, gave her a wan smile:

'Oh, not too bad – thank you for coming again, Jan.' Her voice was thin, husky; Janet smiled down at her:

'I've brought some other visitors for you!'

'Oh? Who's here?' Nettie looked around, caught sight of the two standing by the door; her jaw dropped in amazed delight: *'Michael! Oh, Michael...'* Tears rose in her eyes; Michael felt his own spill down his cheeks:

'Mum!' He dashed across the room, bent to take her in his arms as she reached for him. They embraced, held each other for a minute or more, both crying with the joy of being together again, until she pushed him away:

'Stand up, Michael, let me look at you! You're so tall, so strong – so *handsome!* Oh, it's so good to see you!' He wiped the tears from his face:

'You too, Mum – I'm sorry I haven't come before...' She smiled again:

'I know! Too busy with your new life to come and see your old Mum!' She broke off with a fit of coughing, waved away the concern that manifested itself on his face:

'It's okay, Michael, I've just got a bit of a bad chest. It'll blow over.' He looked over his shoulder, beckoned Albert forward:

'Mum? I want you to meet... Mr Baker.' He'd nearly introduced him as 'Dad', but thought that would sound too silly. Nettie smiled up at the boatman, held out a hand; Albert took it gently:

'Hello, Ma'am. Oi'm really pleased ter meet yer – Oi'm sorry, I don't know what teh call yeh; Moichael's never told us his oother name!' She essayed a husky laugh, looked accusingly at her son:

'It's Thompson – but I'm Nettie, please?' He echoed her smile:

'Nettie – Oi'm Albert. Alby, s'what folks call me.'

'Alby! I'm so glad to meet you. I want to thank you for what you've done for my boy – you've turned him into a fine young man!'

'That was 'is own doin', mostly. 'E's a grand kid, and a real good boater, inter the bargain!' She shook her head:

'He's told me so much about you; and he's so proud of you, you know?' Albert laughed:

'Not 'alf as proud as Oi am of 'im, oi can tell yeh!'

The door of the ward opened, to admit the sister in her stiff starched uniform. She came over to the bed, her manner almost as starched:

'What's this? It's two visitors to a bed, you know!' Nettie gave her a smile:

'I'm sorry, sister – this is my son, Michael!' The nurse turned to him, nodded rather formally:

'Hello, young man. I'll give you another minute or two – but then you'll have to go, your mother needs her rest.'

'Yes, Ma'am!' He shared a slightly guilty smile with those around him, gestured to Albert: 'This is my Dad.'

'Your father? I understood Mr Thompson was dead?'

'He is, sister.' Nettie confirmed.

'So this is your stepfather?' She asked Michael; he couldn't contain a quick chuckle:

'Sort of! It's very complicated to explain.'

'Oh! Oh, well, it's your business, I'm sure. Two minutes, now!' She turned and left them; Michael looked back to his mother:

'Where's Ginny, Mum?'

'She's at home with Grandad, Michael; though he's struggling a bit, to look after her as well as Granny while I'm in here.'

'How is Gran?'

'Not too good – she has to use a wheelchair to get around now, you know?'

'Yeah – is she going to get better?' Nettie shook her head:

'She won't walk again, I'm afraid.' She patted the bed next to her: 'Sit here with me, Michael, for a minute?' He sat; she slipped her arm around his waist as he bent to kiss her cheek. They sat together, their love needing no words; Janet and Albert exchanged understanding glances, stole quietly out to stand in the corridor. In the ward, Michael and his mother chatted quietly, he talking about his life with Albert, telling her about Gracie and the Hanneys; she spoke of his sister, and of Andy, her voice frequently petering out into a fresh bout of coughing. He was careful not to let his distress show in his face – she looked so thin, so pale, compared with the way he remembered her, and the coughing, the obvious way it exhausted her, upset and frightened him.

After a few minutes, the sister returned and shooed Michael out, the smile on her face more sympathetic than might have been expected.

They passed the bus journey back to Wolverton mostly in silence; Michael's concern for his mother was clear in his expression, although he kept his worries to himself. At one point, Albert spoke up:

'We'll stop 'ere on the way back to Birnigum. Yeh can coom 'n see yer Mum agen, Moikey.'

'If yeh're sure, Dad? I don't want ter 'old us up.'

''Course yeh moost, boy.'

'When will that be, Mr Baker?' Janet asked; he thought for a moment, calculating:

'Foive days, if we load from Brentford. Oi'll ask at the office if they've got soomethin' ther' fer oos.'

They had indeed – mixed tinned foods to go to Fazeley Street. But their stop in Wolverton was only to cause Michael more anguish...

Chapter Twenty-Seven

Five days after their trip to the hospital, Janet was on tenterhooks, looking out for Michael to knock at her door, minute by minute lifting the net curtains at the window to watch for him. At last, she saw him approaching along the street, and hurried to the door, opened it before he could knock:

'Michael – come inside!' Puzzled and worried by her anxious greeting, he followed her into the house, through to the kitchen:

'Mrs Eastwood – what is it?'

'Sit down, Michael…' He did as she bid, sitting at the scrubbed oak table; she drew up a chair opposite him, reached out to take his hands in her own, her troubled eyes holding his:

'Michael… Oh, Michael!' Her voice broke; she averted her eyes for a moment, raised them to his again: 'Michael – it's your Mum…'

'What's wrong?' His concern was turning to real fright.

'Oh Michael! She's… She died, the day after you came to see her. I'm so sorry…' He stared at her, uncomprehending, then withdrew his hands, buried his face in them. She got up, went around the table and put her arms around him from behind, held him as he sobbed.

'I'm so sorry…' she whispered again. After a minute or so, he staggered to his feet, turned to her, a question clear in his eyes.

'She went peacefully, in her sleep. She didn't suffer, Michael.' He nodded; she drew him into her embrace, held him, felt his body trembling, his tears soaking into the shoulder of her dress.

After an unconscionable time, he eased out of her arms, looked at her:

'I'm sorry...'

'No, don't be, Michael. I hate to keep bringing you such awful news...'

'It's not your fault, Mrs Eastwood.' He brushed the tears from his face: 'When's... when's her funeral?'

'They set it for tomorrow, but I told them they'd have to postpone it if you weren't here.' He nodded:

'Thank you – where is it, in Buckingham?' She nodded:

'Eric's arranged to borrow a car from work, so we can take you there – you can stop until then?'

'I'm sure Dad won't mind, even if we do lose a day on the trip.' A thought struck him: 'What about Ginny?'

'She'll be there – your Grandad will bring her.' This elicited a thin smile from the boy:

'It'll be good to see her again! But – I meant, afterwards?'

'Oh, yes. I don't know, Michael – Grandad can't really manage both her and your Granny, so I don't know...'

'Oh...' He lapsed into a thoughtful silence; then: 'I'd better go and tell Dad, and Gracie.'

'Are you all right, Michael?' He nodded:

'I'll be okay, don't worry.'

'You could stay here, tonight, if you like?' He smiled, shook his head:

'Thank you – but my home's on the boats, now. That's where I belong – and Dad would miss me, anyway.'

*　*　*

It was a beautiful Spring day, when the mourners gathered to bury Nettie Thompson. Most of them, friends and acquaintances from Buckingham and Wolverton as well as the few members of the family, were already there when Michael, Albert and Gracie arrived, squeezed into the back seat of an old Austin Ten saloon with the arms of the London, Midland and Scottish Railway emblazoned on the door. Michael, dressed in his finest, the spiderwork belt Gracie had made for him around his waist, was stretching cramped muscles when a squeal went up:

'Michael!' An eight-year-old in a pretty floral dress ran down the church path and flung herself into his arms.

'Ginny!' He held her tight, felt her arms trying to squeeze the breath from his lungs.

They were still entwined moments later, when the hearse drove up. Suddenly solemn, hand in hand, they led the procession into the church, behind the coffin, stood close to it throughout, accompanied it back out into the churchyard. After the interment, they stood side by side, hand in hand still, beside the open grave, gazing down, each lost in their own thoughts. Michael broke the silence:

'Ginny?' She raised eyes bright with tears to meet his, as he asked: 'What's going to happen to you now?' She thought for a moment:

'I don't know. Grandad can't look after me, he's too busy looking after Granny now. There was a lady, came to see us yesterday – she wants me to go and live in a home.'

'An *orphanage?'*

'I suppose so.'

'Do you want to go there?' The little girl shook her head vehemently:

'No!'

'What do you want, Ginny?' She paused:

'I don't know, Michael. Can I come and live with you?' It was his turn to pause:

'I don't know…'

With Michael caught up in his maelstrom of emotions, standing by his mother's grave, his little sister holding his hand, Albert

Baker was left to his own devices. He'd stayed with the Eastwoods throughout the service, but afterwards, in the graveyard, he went over to the tall, older man pushing the wheelchair:

'Excuse me?' The man looked around, his face an older, lined version of his Grandson's:

'Hello?'

'Yew moost be Moichael's Grandad?' The man smiled:

'I am indeed! Morris, Fred Morris – Nettie was our daughter.' He held out a hand.

'Oi'm Albert Baker – Alby teh me friends.' He took the hand, shook it.

'Mr Baker! I'm delighted to meet you – we've heard so much about you, from the letters that Michael wrote to his mother. Ethel – this is Michael's new Dad!' The white-haired lady in the chair looked up, proffered her hand too; Albert shook it:

'Deloighted, Mrs Morris. Oi'm so sorry, 'bout yer daughter.'

'Thank you, Mr Baker – but it's Ethel, please?' He smiled down at her, nodded:

''N Oi'm Alby.' He gestured towards the two children by the grave: 'What's goin' teh happen teh the little girl, now?' Morris heaved a sigh:

'I wish I knew. We can't cope with her – Ethel can't get about now, so I have to do pretty well everything, you see. We couldn't manage a kiddie in the house, as well.' A brief silence held while the three of them contemplated the boy and girl, standing hand in hand, their backs to them. Fred expressed all their thoughts:

'The two of them should be together.'

'Ar, that they should.' Albert agreed: 'Boot Moikey's not goin' ter leave the boats, now.'

'I don't imagine he would.'

A few moments of silence again, then: 'They want to put her in the local orphanage.'

'A children's 'ome?' The boatman sounded scandalised.

'Yes, I'm afraid so.'

Another pause.

'She'd 'ave ter share the butty cabin wi' Gracie.' Morris turned to him:

'You're saying…'

'What else can we do with 'er?' Albert laughed: 'Oi've ended oop adoptin' 'im, Oi moight as well 'ave the pair of 'em!' Morris frowned:

'I doubt if the local authorities will like that.'

'Do we 'ave ter tell 'em?' Morris gave a bark of laughter:

'If she's not here, when they come for her…'

'Exac'ly!' The two men shared a conspiratorial grin:

'If she stays with Janet Eastwood tonight… I could bring a suitcase with her things in the morning… Can you wait until then, Alby?'

'Oi don't see whoy not, Fred.'

The little girl did not demur at the idea of spending the night with their old neighbours; and Janet, let into their plans, was only too eager to help. Back on the boats, unaware of their scheming, Michael tackled Albert:

'Dad?'

'Yes, Moikey?'

'We goin' off straight away?'

'No – Oi'm stayin' 'ere til termorrer mornin'.'

'Oh – Whoy's that? I thought yeh'd want ter get ahead.'

'Yew joost be patient, boy – yeh'll see!'

'Dad?'

'Yes, Moikey?'

'Do you think – could we use someone else, in the crew?' Albert kept his amusement to himself:

'What, 'ave four on the boats, yeh mean?'

'Yeah – the extra 'and would be useful, don't yeh think?' Albert scratched his head:

'Well – Oi don't know… We'd 'ave ter feed 'em, ooever it was. 'N where would they sleep?'

'Suppose it was another girl – she could sleep in the butty, with Gracie, couldn't she?' Albert made show of rubbing his chin thoughtfully:

'Mebbe… yeh're suggestin' we foind oos a spare girl teh join oos, are yeh?'

'What do yeh think, Dad, could we?'

'Oh, Oi don't know, Moikey. We're a pretty good team a'ready, ent we?'

'Yes, but…' Michael was lost for further arguments for a minute; then he thought of something:

'Dad – Gracie's goin' ter get married, sometoime soon! We'll *need* someone else then, won't we? If we had someone now, she could be taught what teh do, ready for when Gracie goes, couldn't she?' Albert gave up, unable to contain himself any longer; he burst our laughing:

'What d'yer think Oi'm waitin' 'ere *for,* Moikey? Yer Grandad 'n me've got it all arranged!'

'You mean…?'

''E's bringin' 'er things – yew can go 'n pick 'er oop from yer neighbours, soon as 'e gets 'ere.' Michael stared at him, eyes wide, a happy smile slowly spreading across his face; he threw his arms around Albert's waist, looked up into his face:

'Thank you, Dad!' Albert held him close:

'Oi've alwes wanted a daughter – now it looks loike Oi've got one!'

Chapter Twenty-Eight

Michael was knocking on Janet Eastwood's door before eight the next morning. Only sleeping fitfully in his excitement, he'd had to contain his impatience until after daybreak; she let him in, ushered him into the kitchen where Eric and Ginny were at their breakfast. The railwayman greeted him with a wave of his fork; Ginny leapt up and grabbed him into an eager embrace:

'Michael! I thought you'd gone?' He shook his head, laughing:

'I'm still here, Ginny! Are you ready?'

'Ready? What for?' He looked at her, mystified; Janet chuckled over the tea she was pouring:

'We didn't tell her, Michael, we thought you'd like to do that!'

'Ginny – you're coming with me, on the boats!' She just gaped at him, her mouth open; he pulled her into his arms again: 'We're going to be together again – you're going to live with me and Dad and Gracie!'

'You mean it? I'm coming with you? I'm not going into that home where the lady wanted me to go to?'

'You'll live in the butty with Gracie – you met her yesterday, remember? I live in the other boat – but we'll always be together, now!' The little girl didn't speak, but the light in her eyes shone forth her delight at the prospect.

'Sit down, Ginny, finish your breakfast, there's a good girl. Have you had something, Michael?' He shook his head, and Janet waved him to a seat: 'Sit down – there's toast and marmalade on the table, you help yourself. Grandad will be here soon.'

He did as she bid him, found himself suddenly ravenous; Ginny finished hers, and sat gazing at him as if she couldn't believe what was happening. They were sipping at steaming cups of tea when another knock sounded at the door; Janet went to answer it, came back with their grandfather in tow. Ginny jumped to her feet again, threw her arms around him:

'Grandad! I'm going to live with Michael!' He laughed, eased out of her embrace and put her case down by the door:

'I know, darling! I've brought some of your things for you.' Michael had got to his feet as well; now, he went to shake hands with his grandfather, but the man drew him into his arms, held him tightly for a moment before releasing him, holding him at arms length and gazing into his eyes:

'Michael. It's up to you, now – you've got to look after your sister. I'm… not sure, whether this is the right thing to do – but we all feel that you two ought to be together, we don't want Ginny put in some council home where she'd be unhappy. I know she'll miss out on going to school, just as you've done since… well. You'll have to teach her what you can, won't you? I know how happy you are now, with this strange life of yours – I only hope she'll take to it as well as you've done, that she'll be happy too. Look after yourselves, and each other – and you will keep in touch, won't you?'

'Of course we will, Grandad. I'll write to you, I promise – and we'll come and see you when we can.' Fred Morris nodded, holding his doubts, his fears, to himself:

'Go on, then. Go with our love, and our blessing. I like your new Dad, he seems an honest and straightforward man, Michael – give him your love and respect, both of you?' Two heads nodded solemnly.

The toast was eaten, the tea all drunk; Michael took up his sister's suitcase, turned to the door:

'Michael?' He turned back at the sound of his grandfather's voice.

'Good luck, my boy; and…' he sounded choked; Michael smiled, dropped the case to put his arms around him:

'I know – I'll write soon, I promise!' Fred nodded, released his grandson, turned to Ginny:

'You be good – and look after your brother, okay?'

'Okay, Grandad!' She embraced him in turn.

And then they were gone, headed eagerly away, he to return to the life he loved, she to the excitement of a whole new world.

'Another cup of tea before you go, Fred?' Morris sat down heavily at the table, nodded gratefully: Janet turned to the teapot, smiling gently at the sheen of tears in the old man's eyes.

* * *

In the organised confusion of the funeral, Ginny and Albert had not actually met. Now, Michael passed her case to Gracie, down in the butty cabin, as Albert emerged from the motor. He turned to his sister, helped her over the gunwale into the stern well of the butty; she gazed up with frank curiosity at the man who was to be her substitute father. He squatted on his heels, on the counter, reached across with one hand to her; she took it, tentatively, returned his smile nervously:

'Should I call you Daddy?' His smile widened:

'Only if yeh want teh, Ginny. Moikey called me Mr Baker, at fust – mebbe that'd be easier fer yew, too?' The little girl contemplated this, her head tilted on one side; he found himself looking into bright blue eyes which held his, thoughtfully:

'Okay – That'd be best, I think. 'Til I get to know you.' He nodded, looked up at Michael:

'We'd better git goin', boy, we've lost days a'ready!' Michael gave him a grin:

'I'll go 'n start the engine, shall Oi?'

Chapter Twenty-Nine

Through that Spring and early Summer of 1942, there were times, many of them, when Albert began to regret the hastily-conceived conspiracy which had led him to be the custodian of Michael's younger sister. He got on well enough with the child herself, even if she remained for a long time quite shy of him, unsure of exactly how to treat him. And the presence of an eight-year-old girl in his crew caused him no direct qualms – Gracie was only too delighted to have the domestic charge of her, relishing her acquisition of a little sister after so many brothers.

Ginny herself, however, didn't seem to settle. Unlike her brother, who had almost gleefully grasped the unfamiliar life of a boater after escaping from the household and habits he had come to hate, she had been torn from a settled, loving home in the most painful way possible. She continued to mourn for her mother and her handicapped brother, and found the sudden, dramatic change in her lifestyle very difficult to cope with. Young boys are rather less concerned with such minor conveniences as a bathroom, or a flush toilet – little girls, however, are inclined to enjoy such luxuries, and miss them if they are abruptly withdrawn. Having to manage with a strip-wash in the cabin, with a hand-bowl of warm water and a sponge, came as something of a shock; and she treated the bucket in the engine-hole with undisguised horror.

To find herself suddenly sharing a space six feet by eight, with a girl in her late teens, also gave her pause for thought. She had had to share with her mother in their grandparents' house, but that had been a moderate-sized room, and even though Gracie made a huge fuss of her, quickly settling into her role as big sister, she found the close confines rather oppressive: 'Gracie's lovely, and she doesn't mind, but there's no *room!*'

At first, Michael eagerly adopted the role that Stevie had played for him, on his first trips, becoming a teacher to her as well as big brother. She tried very hard to learn, to do all the jobs she could manage which were a part of the working boat trade – to begin with, she tired easily, but soon began to develop the same wiry tenacity that had so endeared Michael to Bill and Vi Hanney. In the locks, she would work with him, doing what she could alone and appealing for his help when a paddle proved too stiff for her, or a gate too heavy to move; she quickly showed a dexterity with the ropes which had Albert grinning with delight, and a sure-footedness about the boats the equal of many born-and-bred boat children.

But within herself, she remained unsettled, her happiness at being reunited with one brother tempered by her ongoing pain at the absence of both her mother and her other brother. To Albert, and to Michael, she seemed withdrawn, almost unhappy; only with Gracie did she relax, only to her could she talk openly about her loneliness without her mother. And, it seemed, only the older girl could comfort her, make her smile freely.

Michael found her reticence upsetting – after their joyful meeting, her aloofness from him, except when they were working, began to play on his mind, making him think he was to blame for it. And, truth to tell, he had his own difficulties. On top of the sorrow of his mother's and Andy's deaths, he couldn't rid himself of feelings of guilt – guilt that he had delayed so long over getting in touch with them, guilt, especially, that he had made no effort to see them, that he had never seen his brother again after walking out on that fateful night, that he had only met his mother on her death-bed. *If only...*

With so much preying on his mind, it is perhaps not surprising that Albert began to find his new son also becoming withdrawn, almost sullen. He tried to jolly him out of his dark moods, using the kind of banter which had always in the past got the boy laughing, but was lucky now to elicit a weak smile. He'd even tried a new jest, only to be rebuffed with an aggression he hadn't seen in Michael before: Setting away from the top of Camp Hill locks, heading out of Birmingham towards Warwick, he'd handed the tiller over:

'Ther' yeh go, Mr Thompson, she's all yers!'

'Don't call me that! My name's *Baker,* now, don't *ever* call me that!' Michael had grabbed the tiller from him, staring straight ahead in furious silence. Albert stood on the gunwale, took out his pipe and filled it slowly, lit it. Then he looked back at the boy, saw the pain in his face, and reached out to put a hand on his shoulder, only to have Michael shrug him off. But then he glanced around, and their eyes met:

'Oi'm sorry, boy, Oi didn't mean ter hurt yeh.' Michael shook his head, gave him the first real smile he'd seen in weeks:

'I know yeh didn't Dad. Sorry I shouted, but…' Albert saw the brightness of tears in his eyes, replaced the hand on his shoulder:

'Things'll work out, son, yew see if Oi'm not roight. Give it toime, eh?' Michael nodded; and then the tears were spilling down his cheeks. Albert moved closer, slipped his arm around his shoulders and gave a quick squeeze before walking around to the engine-hole and disappearing into it to allow the boy his privacy. Once out of sight, he heaved a sigh of frustrated sympathy.

Given the turmoil in his mind, perhaps it was no surprise that Michael's patience with his sister often balanced on a knife-edge. He had appointed himself her chief instructor, only allowing Gracie to take charge of her on the butty, showing her how to handle the boat itself, the tricks and knacks of living in a confined space; in other things, she would do her best to follow his teaching, but her small physique and lack of experience would frequently let her down. And it was at these moments that he would all too often snap or snarl at her, pushing her aside to do the job himself with an expression of impatient annoyance on his face.

She took this, not allowing her feelings to show in front of him; but Gracie would find her crying quietly in the cabin, try to comfort her without knowing the cause, assuming it was her continuing anguish at the death of her mother which was the source of her pain. It was Albert who had noticed the way he would let his anger show, who had been tempted several times to intervene, but then refrained, afraid of making the schism worse.

As if to reflect the fraught, tense atmosphere on Albert's boats, the news from afar was universally depressing during that Spring. The battle of the Atlantic was being lost in spectacular fashion, the wolf-packs sinking allied shipping faster than even the shipyards of America could replace it. A new offensive in Southern Russia had the German army pushing quickly, and apparently easily, to the gates of Stalingrad, with the oilfields of the Caucasus eagerly in sight; and in North Africa, Rommel's divisions had fought back again, and looked to be well on their way to the Nile.

* * *

They were heading North, loaded with bagged sugar again, for Fazeley Street Wharf. It had been a trying day; blustery showers appearing with a suddenness which had them diving for their coats at frequent intervals, and a hold-up for a displaced paddle-board which had lost them more than an hour. Tempers, if not exactly frayed, were at least a little worn.

'We'll toy at Fishery, Moikey.'

'Roight y'are Dad.' Michael handed the motor's tiller over to Albert as they came past Boxmoor, went forward ready to snatch the fore-ends together as they tied; on the butty, Ginny did the same, preparatory to taking the line off to tie off to the bank. Albert slowed the motor almost to a standstill, as Gracie slid the butty along his inside; he coiled in the seventy-foot snubber, then took the breasting string from her, dropped it over the dolly, bringing the sterns together. Michael dropped the fore-end line off the motor over the butty's t-stud, hauled the bows together, tied them off. Ginny took the butty's line, stepped off onto the bank; but she missed her footing, fell forward as one foot slipped into the water, landing heavily and grazing her knee quite badly.

'Ginny!' Far from sympathetic, Michael's shout was one of anger. He stepped over, across the butty and down beside her, snatched the rope from her hands and pulled the boats in: 'Can't you even get off without messing things up?'

She picked herself up, biting her lip to hold back the tears, brushed her pinafore down and ran to the other end of the boat and climbed aboard, ignoring Gracie's startled question. The older girl followed her down into the cabin, repeated her words:

'Ginny – yew all roight?' This time she got an answer:

'I fell over and hurt my knee.' She lifted the hem of her dress, showed her the scrape, the blood beginning to trickle down her shin.

'Coom 'ere, loovey.' Gracie sat beside her, reached for a scrap of clean cloth from the soap-hole in the back wall of the cabin, set about cleaning the wound. When she was satisfied, she asked:

'That better, Ginny?' The little girl nodded:

'Thank you, Gracie.' Her own anger surfaced: 'I could've *broken* it, for all *he* cares!'

'Oh, Ginny! He doon't mean it – we've all 'ad a rough day.'

'Yes he *does!* He's always shouting at me...' Gracie put an arm around her, pulled her gently into an embrace, shushing her at the same time as looking up to meet Albert's eyes, where he had leant over to see if everything was all right. The glances they exchanged were significant, expressing their mutual despair at the tension between brother and sister.

Chapter Thirty

It was quite late. They had eaten on the move, as they did so often; minutes after they had tied up, Joey Caplin arrived, having cycled from Berkhamsted where he had left *Bognor* and *Bodmin,* in the hope of finding them, knowing they should be somewhere along that length:

'Yew coomin' over the Fishery, Gracie?'

'Is it okay, Ooncle Alby?' She asked. He smiled his understanding:

'Yew go on, girl! Oi'll be along in a whoile.'

The two departed hand in hand; Albert ducked down into the motor cabin, slipped on the tidier of his two jackets, picked up his old trilby and stuck it on his head.

'Can Oi coom, Dad?' Albert gave Michael a stern look:

'Yew'd be better off 'avin' a word or two wi' yer sister, boy.'

'I'll talk to her tomorrow, okay?'

'No! Yew stay 'ere, boy, sort out yer diff'rences. Oi'm sick 'n toired of 'earin' yeh snappin' at 'er.'

Their life, like their work, was usually carried on in easy companionship. Now, Albert's firm line gave Michael pause – and he knew better than to argue any further. As the boatman stepped off, made his way over the bridge to the pub, he screwed down his courage and stepped down into the butty cabin.

'Ginny?' She looked up, her cheeks still wet:

'What do *you* want?'

'Can I talk to you?'

'I s'pose – if you *want* to!' Ignoring her discouraging tone, he sat next to her:

'Ginny…' He found himself lost for words. But she wasn't – her own anger flashed to the surface again:

'You sound just like *him!*' This left Michael stumped:

'What? Who?'

'Daddy! When you get angry, and shout at me, you sound just like him!'

'What?'

'When he used to get angry, and shout at Mummy! You're just *like* him!'

'No!' Her words stung a furious, frightened response from him: 'You're wrong – I'm not like *him* at all!'

'Yes you are! You ought to hear yourself!'

'No-o…!' Now the word was a prayer rather than a denial.

'I wish Mummy was here! I wish she hadn't died, so I could go home again!'

'Oh, Ginny – I miss her too.'

'Not like me!'

'Yes I do – she was *my* Mum as well! I loved her just like you!'

'Huh!' There was a depth of scorn in her voice: 'You didn't even come and *see* us, did you? You hadn't seen her for *ages and ages!*'

'Ginny…' Her name became a supplication; her words piled on top of the guilt and remorse already weighing on his mind, and the total was more than he could bear. He turned away from her, bowed his head and, elbows on his knees, buried his face in his hands: *I can't give in – I'm not going to cry…*

Ginny stared at him for a moment, his sudden collapse taking her by surprise; then, realising if not fully understanding his pain, she hotched nearer to him, slipped an arm around his waist, felt the trembling of his body, the heaving of his shoulders, heard the sound of his sobbing through the muffling of his hands:

'Mikey...?' He lifted his face, gave her a thin smile – she'd never used what he thought of as his boater's name before. There was a compassion in her eyes which pierced his heart, made his feelings of guilt surface with even greater force. He gave one more deep, heartfelt sob:

'Don't you *see?* That's why I feel so rotten! I should have got in touch with you all much sooner – I should have come to see you! If I had – maybe things would have been different – maybe she wouldn't have got sick, maybe Andy wouldn't have either! I should never have run away and left you all!'

All the anger and resentment Ginny had felt evaporated in the face of his torment, to be replaced by love for her brother: 'Oh, *Michael!*' She hugged him even tighter; he sank his head to her slim shoulder, let his tears flow freely.

'Mikey?' He lifted his head; she looked into his wide, sad eyes: 'Mummy *knew.* She understood, why you'd run away. She always said you were still alive, even when everyone else said you were dead. And then – she didn't mind, 'cos you didn't come and see us – she said, as long as you were all right, as long as you were happy, it didn't matter, not really.'

'Are you *sure?*' He wanted, desperately, to believe her.

'I'm sure, Mikey. I asked her, lots of times, why you didn't come and see us. And that's what she always said – it was enough to know you were all right. But – she was *so* pleased, that you came to see her, before she...' Her own sorrow took over; now, it was his turn to hold her, comfort her:

'You were there for her, all the time, Ginny. It's more than I was.' She nodded:

'Yes, but – I went to see her, after you'd been – and she was so *happy!* I...'

'Shhh-shhh! Don't cry, Ginny.'

'I... can't help it...I still miss her...'

'Me too...'

Brother and sister sat side by side, arms entwined, sharing

their sadness and their love. Minutes, ages, passed; at last, Michael broke the emotional silence:

'Ginny?'

'Mm-hm?'

'Things have changed, Ginny. We can't go back, to how it was, ever.' He felt her nod, her head still resting on his shoulder:

'I know, Mikey.'

'We've got a new Dad, now. And a new life... I'm sorry – if you're not happy here...' She raised her head, smiled at him:

'I'm happy, Mikey. I thought, for a bit, you didn't love me any more...'

'I *do,* Ginny! More than ever, I promise. I'm sorry I ever shouted at you – I didn't really mean to, it was only because I felt so bad...'

'I know. But we're all right now, aren't we?'

'We're *foine!'* She giggled, to hear him slip into the boater's dialect which was becoming part of his day-to-day persona.

Albert had enjoyed a couple of beers with the small group of other boaters in the Fishery Inn. Cheerful and replete, he left Gracie and Joe to make their goodbyes, and headed back to the boats. There'd been no sign of Michael following him to the pub, which he'd half expected to happen – now, he was hoping that the boy and his sister had settled their differences.

Knocking on the cabinside of the butty, he put his head in at the hatch, and chuckled to see brother and sister cuddled up together on the sidebed. Both looked up at him, their eyes shining:

'All roight, Dad?' He nodded.

'Welcome back, Daddy!' He stopped in surprise, gazed at the little girl's happy smile; then he stepped down into the cabin, squeezed in beside her. She turned to him, threw her arms around his neck, kissed his cheek; he slipped his arm about her, held her tight. Michael reached across – their hands met, held, gripped in expression of the love which bound them.

Chapter Thirty-One

The remainder of that Summer, and the Autumn which followed, saw the four-handed crew of the *Sycamore* and the *Antrim* working and living together in a renewed harmony. With Ginny reconciled to the irrevocable change in her life, happy, now, to be with her brother, and Michael's guilt and pain in some degree assuaged, they all found a new joy in their relationships. They found themselves, for much of that time, working around to Limehouse Dock to load, carrying foodstuffs, mostly tinned, which had arrived by coaster, on to the midlands. Their backloads to Brentford or City Road were usually war materials of one sort or another; occasionally bricks or building materials needed for urgent reconstruction of buildings damaged in the blitz.

Joey was making more and more opportunities, at the expense of cycling for miles along the towpaths at the end of his days' labours, to see his Gracie, and the two of them were beginning to plan for their wedding the following Summer; their shared affection brought a paternal gleam to Albert's eye, and a rather shy pleasure to the two youngsters.

And, as if inspired by such parochial events, the news from far afield was improving: Rommel's thrust to occupy Egypt had run out of steam near a little village called El Alamein – after a couple of months of stalemate, during which the Allied forces were strengthened by convoys travelling via Malta, Montgomery's counterattack had him in headlong retreat. And from Southern Russia, news was coming back that the Soviet army had penetrated the exposed flank of the German divisions besieging Stalingrad, and was threatening to trap them in a huge pincer movement.

Christmas of 1942 found a number of pairs of boats tied up around Old Turn Junction, in the centre of Birmingham, their crews collected cheerily in the *Prince of Wales*. Among them were the Hanneys, and Albert's motley foursome, both pairs just loaded with steel tubes direct from Coombeswood Mill. Ginny, especially, loved it when they were directed to travel through Birmingham – she had that little girl's common fascination with horses, and many were still used then on the short-haul dayboats around the canals of the city. She would watch them go by, plodding stolidly, with a deep-loaded boat in tow, led by one of the crew, often a young lad; the boats themselves, with their simple squared-off lines, usually lacking any form of cabin, carrying their multifarious cargoes from colliery to foundry, from factory to railway basin.

The towpath telegraph had quickly informed the whole of the boating community on the Southern canal system that she had followed her brother away from her home and into Albert's crew, making her something of a five-minute wonder earlier in the year. The same doubters who had questioned his abilities had shaken their heads, muttered that she would never cope with the work, never take to the life of a boater, not a little girl off the bank... But she'd proved them wrong, once again. With a surfeit of fresh air and exercise, she had begun to blossom – after six months, she was taller, fitter; her physique had filled out despite their restricted diet; her gold-blond hair had bleached further in the sun, her blue eyes had a new, happy sparkle.

Shortages, food rationing, had limited their diet, as it had for the rest of the population. Left out of the government's considerations, the itinerant community of the boaters had had to be issued with emergency ration cards, and would survive on them throughout the war. Ben Vickers had stepped in to support

Albert's claim for such cards for Michael, and then for Ginny, confirming that they were his 'nephew' and 'niece' to the suspicious authorities. And, like all the boaters, they would frequently be able to supplement their supplies: Carrying foodstuffs, cases would often be broken in loading, when a free-for-all was declared, everyone on hand grabbing as much as they could – excess, gained in this way, could be exchanged for coal off of other boats, to keep the range burning. And most boatmen, tied in country areas, would set the odd trap at night, collecting the unfortunate rabbits before setting away in the morning. So, all in all, they didn't eat too badly, the stew-pot living almost permanently on the top of the stove, under Gracie's loving care.

Christmas Day had been passed in relaxed and enjoyable fashion, the gathered boaters sharing their joy in the holiday like one big family. The evening was getting late; Michael was out by the boats, talking and fooling with a few of the teenage kids from the other families, while Albert was sitting in the public bar, nursing a half-drunk pint of mild, chatting with his own contemporaries and watching Ginny playing in another corner of the big room with a couple of girls her own age.

The other two children were gathered up by their mothers, taken off to their boats and their beds; Ginny wandered over to where Albert was sitting. He looked up with a smile, saw the happy tiredness in her face. Edging along on the bench to make room for her, he patted the bare wood for her to sit with him; but, her smile echoing his own, she sat instead on his lap, twined her arms around his neck, gave him a quick kiss on the cheek before laying her head on his shoulder.

Ten minutes later, coming in from the cold, Michael found her there, sound asleep in the old boatman's arms.

Early the next morning, with dawn yet to lighten the city's skies, the boats were beginning to disperse to their various destinations.

Albert stood on the bank, the *Sycamore's* Bolinder idling beside him, as Bill Hanney walked up to him:

'Word is they han't finished the stoppage on Knowle.' A stray bomb had landed by the second lock in the flight of five, on their Southward route out of the city, close enough to damage one of the paddle culverts and knock the top gates out of their quoins.

'Will they be doon boy the toime we get ther', yeh reckon?'

'Dunno, Alby.'

'Shall oos go top road, then, go round it?'

'Hnn...' Bill's grunt sounded doubtful: 'It's getting' ter be slow goin' on the Stratford cut. Bottom's too near the top a lot o' the way – and soom o' the lockgates 'ave about 'ad it, down Lapworth. 'N the Fazeley cut's not mooch better – bottom road's too slow, any'ow. Oi reckon we'd best go fer it, 'n 'ope they're doon before we get ther'.'

'H'okay, Bill. Bloody cut's gettin' bad in lot's o' places, ent it?'

'Yeah, Alby. Be grateful we ent working the H'Oxford cut!'

'Oh?'

'Yeah. We were at Sutton's, a whoile back, 'n Oi got chattin' wi' Joe Skinner. 'E says it's ruddy awful down ther', 'n the towpath's in a state, 'n all. Reckon's their mule's been in more'n once lately, missin' 'er footin' 'cause it's getting' so bad.'

'She's h'okay?'

'Yeah. Joost cloimbs out, shakes 'erself off, 'n carries on. Joe reckons mules are better'n 'orses, fer a single boat any'ow.'

'Oi'd rather 'ave me injun, Bill!'

'Me too. Wouldn't want ter go back to an 'orse, now!'

They passed the locks at Knowle with only a slight delay. The canal company's maintenance men kept a concerned watch on the damaged gates as they and several other pairs passed through, then set back to work, strengthening them as best they could.

* * *

And so began another year. Three years on the boats, now approaching his fourteenth birthday, Michael had to concentrate now to recall his life before the night when it had all got too much for him, when he had run out of the house in distress and set off the train of events which had led him to this new world. After being the source of fascination and speculation for a while, he was now an accepted and welcomed member of the canal community, respected for his abilities and enthusiasm; Ginny, too, was regarded now as little if any different from other boat-children her age, even if her limited schooling, her ability to read, set her apart, made her sometimes sought out by other youngsters who might ask her to read a paper or comic out to them.

And the work went on. Unremitting, unrelenting, day by day, loading, clothing up, mopping down, then the journey to their appointed destination, unloading, waiting at the stop for their next orders, then into the cycle once more. Through the Winter, struggling to keep your footing in snow and ice as you lean on a heavy gate or bowhaul the butty up a flight of single locks, sheltering as best you can in the hatches of a boat from the driving, freezing rain, hanging your steaming coats around the engine at night in the hope that they will be dry by morning. But the Spring came at last; brighter mornings, longer evenings, sunshine and showers, and the relaxed pleasure of cruising a long pound with the birds singing in the hedgerows.

With brightening weather came brightening news. Hitler's armies in Russia had been defeated, wiped out, at Stalingrad; now, the Soviet steamroller had begun its slow but inexorable push Westwards. In North Africa, allied landings in Algeria had formed the second arm of a pincer which was squeezing Rommel's forces towards their ultimate collapse; and new technology, new tactics, were beginning the rout of the U-boats, taking the pressure off from the Atlantic and Arctic convoys.

And with the Spring, a growing feeling of anticipation, especially for Gracie, as her wedding drew ever closer.

Chapter Thirty-Two

Harriet Caplin sat on the roof of the butty cabin in the summer sunshine, keeping an eye, as her mother had instructed, on her younger brothers as they played happily with a few other children on the grass near the *Greyhound,* the pub at Hawkesbury Junction. The point where the Coventry and Oxford canals meet, forever known to boaters as Sutton's Stop after a Victorian incumbent of the toll-house, was where boats awaiting orders to load at the Warwickshire collieries would tie; but now, her boats were there for what she felt were more important reasons.

She had been looking forward with increasing excitement to her big brother's marriage to Grace Hanney – now, the day had arrived. She turned her head to look across the canal to where the two pairs of red and green boats were tied; FMC didn't often handle coal, and so it was unusual to see the Joshers, with their elegant fore-ends and bright colours, moored here. The adults from them, like her own parents, had gone on the bus into Coventry, to the register office for the wedding itself; only Billy Hanney stood in the hatches of the *Acorn,* puffing on a hand-rolled cigarette. Like herself, he was already dressed in his smartest clothes, ready for the party which would start as soon as the newly-weds and their escort returned. Stocky, well-built, like his father, she thought he cut an attractive figure as he leant nonchalantly on the slide.

But that thought made her turn her eyes to the other FMC

motor, the *Sycamore*. Over the cabin, she could see two lads, around her own age, standing and talking. One, with the typical build and colouring of the boaters, she knew to be Grace's younger brother; but it was the other who drew her gaze.

She could still remember the tale as it had spread around the system, of this strange boy who had run away from his home on the bank to become a boater. She had met him, of course, a number of times, even spoken to him when they had been tied at the same wharf once or twice. And now, so it was said, he'd been joined by his little sister – she glanced again at the playing children outside the pub; that was her, the slim girl with the bright blond hair. Her eyes returned to the tall, handsome boy by the boat; she heard his laughter, as Stevie Hanney cracked some kind of joke. He leant back against the cabinside, resting one elbow on the roof; looking around, he caught her eye, gave her a wave and a quick smile. She waved back, suddenly shy, feeling that the smile on her own face probably looked stupid and awkward.

The boy with the straw-coloured hair said something to his companion, pushing himself upright again. The two of them walked slowly towards the junction and its elegant iron bridge, past the traffic office; they crossed over the bridge, then strolled round, past the pub and the group of younger children, to where she sat:

''Ello, 'Arriet!'

'H-hello, Moikey.' She heard the breathless stutter in her voice, coloured at her own silliness: ''Ello, Stevie.' She greeted the younger Hanney, trying to cover her embarrassment.

'Yew h'okay?' He asked.

'Oi'm foine!'

'They'll be back soon.'

'Oi 'spect so.' A slightly awkward silence fell for a moment, before Michael asked her:

'Waitin' fer orders, are yeh?'

'Yeah – we're empty.' She gestured at the boats, cursed herself for stating the obvious. But he just smiled:

'We've got a load of tinned meat – goin' ter Fazeley Street. Boot it'll be a day late, this trip!' She smiled back, grateful for the casual way he tried to put her at her ease.

'Yeah – it's goin' teh be a good evenin', ent it?' Stevie put in.

'Should be!' Michael agreed.

'Yew goin' bottom road, then?' Harriet asked; Michael nodded:

'Yeah – we wouldn't, o' course, boot we 'ad teh be 'ere today, din't we? 'N ther'd be no sense goin' back ter Braunston.'

''Course!' She glanced around, nervously seeking for a subject of conversation:

'Did yeh see that pair over ther'?' She pointed, as the boys looked around:

'The Grand Unions, along from our'n?' Stevie asked.

'Yeah. They're roon by a crew o' them trainees!'

'Trainees? Oo're they then?' Michael put a hand on his friend's shoulder:

'Oi read about them in the paper, a whoile ago. They're women, off the bank, that're learnin' to run boats, aren't they?' Harriet nodded:

'S'roight, Moikey. Ther's three of 'em on that pair – Oone of 'em went off ter the shops a whoile ago, arst me fer the way. Talked ever so posh – boot she seemed noice, fer all that.'

'Are you talking about me, by any chance?' The three of them spun around, to see a young woman clad in dungarees, wheeling an old bicycle up behind them.

'Oh! Sorry, miss – din't mean no 'arm!' The woman laughed:

'It's quite all right, we're used to it! I'm Mary – thank you for the directions; I've got all the things we needed, now.' Harriet gave her a tentative smile:

'Tha's good. Oi'm 'Arriet Caplin – this is Moikey Baker, 'n Stevie Hanney.' They shook her hand in turn, as Harriet went on: ''Is sister's marryin' moy big brother – they're down the register h'office roight now.'

'Yeah! Big party, when they get back 'ere!' Stevie added.

'Oh – that's great! Give them our good wishes, won't you?'

'Yeh could coom along fer a drink wi' oos, if yeh loike? Oi'm sure nobody'd moind.' Michael offered; the woman smiled:

'We'd love to – but we're expecting to go and load any time.' As if to confirm her words, a shout echoed across the canal:

'Mary! Come on, we've got orders to load at Griff right away!' Mary gave the youngsters a rueful smile:

'See what I mean? I'd better go – maybe we'll meet again soon. And do wish the happy couple well for us, won't you?'

'We will – good loock!' Michael promised; Mary looked back and waved as she trundled her bike over the bridge.

''Ere they coom!' Stevie pointed, and they saw the wedding party heading up the lane from the bus stop.

It was, indeed, a good day. They were joined by all the other boaters who were tied there; the ale and stout flowed freely in the *Greyhound,* and the children enjoyed a rare day of freedom, playing in the sunshine outside. Before the pub closed for the afternoon, a number of water cans were filled with beer, so that the partying could go on until the evening opening.

It was later, with most of the adults either dancing or clapping along with the rhythm while Henry Caplin and a couple of other boaters made the music, when Harriet looked around to find Michael beside her. Without a word, he took her hand and led her to join in the step-dance, both of them watching their elders to see how it was done. They danced for a while, through three or four tunes; then Michael led her out of the melee to an empty seat. He handed her down into it; she hotched along to make room, and he squeezed in beside her:

'Thanks – Oi'm about worn out!' She echoed his smile:

'Me too, Moikey. Thank yeh fer dancin' wi' me...' His smile widened:

'Moy pleasure, 'Arriet!'

The silence which fell between them now was easy, friendly.

She looked up into his face, studied his profile as he watched the other dancers:

'Moikey?' His eyes turned to meet hers, and she thought again how lovely they were, felt her shyness come sweeping back. She averted her gaze, looking at her hands clasped in her lap.

'What is it, 'Arriet?' She looked up again:

'I joost wondered – yew use'ter live on the bank, din't yeh?'

'Long toime ago, that was!'

'Whoy did yeh want to be a boater?' He laughed:

'Oi din't! It joost koind o' happened...'

He generally didn't talk about his life before the boats; but now, seeing the real interest in her eyes, he found himself telling her about his miserable existence in Wolverton – before long, she knew the whole story. Bill Hanney, bringing them fresh drinks, commented:

'Yew two've bin thick as thieves 'ere all noight, 'aven't yeh?'

'We're joost talkin', Mr 'Anney.' Michael replied; Bill laughed, spoke to Harriet:

'Yeh'll 'ave ter marry 'im, now yeh know all 'is secrets!' She laughed, but felt the colour rising to her face, saw Michael looking down at her from the corner of her eye, and took a sip of her drink to hide her embarrassment. Michael asked her:

''Ow old are yeh, 'Arriet?'

'Th-thirteen, Moikey.' He looked up at Bill:

'We'll 'ave the wait a bit, then!' Bill laughed again:

'Aye! Tek yer toime, both o' yeh, ther's no 'urry!' He left them, to go back to join Vi. Harriet looked up again, to find Michael looking down at her:

'Doon't moind Bill, 'e's only pullin' yer leg!'

'Oi know, Moikey. It's gettin' late – Oi should be getting' 'ome. Ma'll 'ave the young 'uns in bed boy now, 'n Oi'm 'sposed ter be lookin' after 'em.'

'Okay, 'Arriet.' He stood up, took her arm to help her to her feet, and she smiled her thanks to him. He followed her as she left the pub, walked with her the few yards to their boats:

'Goodnoight, 'Arriet.'

'Goodnoight, Moikey – thank yeh fer a noice evenin'.'

'Oi'll see yeh agen, soon?'

'Oi 'spect so…'

'Goodnoight, then…' He bent to give her a quick kiss on the cheek; she stood, rigid with pleased astonishment, as he turned and disappeared back into the pub.

Chapter Thirty-Three

Their two pairs were travelling butty again that trip – *Acorn* and *Angelus,* four-handed, leading, and *Sycamore* and *Antrim,* reduced now to three crew, behind. The newly-weds had spent their first night together in the cabin of Henry Caplin's motor boat – Joe's parents and his younger siblings all squeezed into the butty; except for Harriet, the only girl, who had shared with Ginny in the *Antrim* to give them a little more room. Now, Grace and Joe were on the train headed for Bull's Bridge depot, where the Grand Union company had a pair waiting for them; Joe's younger brother, Ernie, was going with them to make up a crew of three, leaving Harriet and little Sam with their parents. Harriet had returned to her own boats after a poor night – she had found it difficult to get to sleep for the thought of the tall, handsome boy in the cabin next door.

The 'Bottom Road' into Birmingham is long, slow and tedious – the main reason why it was supplanted by the building of the Grand Junction route from Brentford, through Leamington Spa and Warwick. And now, after four years of war, with no money for maintenance, it was becoming even less favoured by the boatmen. They slogged their way along the Coventry Canal, past Marston Turn, down Atherstone, and then Glascote Two; left turn at Fazeley Junction, and then begins the uphill run onto the Birmingham plateau. Thirteen at Curdworth, then the short tunnel; three at Minworth, and the long pound to Salford Junction. And all narrow locks, so the butties had to be bow-hauled through.

They tied that night, stiff, weary and footsore, just below Aston flight. Michael, having been acting horse to their butty most of the day, collapsed onto his sidebed with a tired grin when Albert suggested a quick beer in the *Reservoir;* Ginny had already retired, equally exhausted, to her first night alone in the *Antrim.* The party which trudged over the bridge and up the road consisted of Albert, Bill and Vi, and Billy – even his mother had given up calling him 'Little Bill' now, possibly because, at seventeen, he was an inch or two taller than his father, and several inches taller than her.

A hale sounded from the bank:

'Moikey! Yew ther'?' Michael roused himself, stuck his head out of the slide-hatch:

'Stevie – yew coomin' in?' Stevie Hanney stepped over the stern of the butty, and onto the motor's counter, followed Michael as he backed down into the *Sycamore's* cabin.

'Yew wan' a beer?'

'Yeh got soom?'

'Yeah! Dad brought a few bottles o' pale ale back las' noight!'

''E woon't moind?'

'Nah!' Michael took two bottles from the table-cupboard, knocked the caps off, poured the contents into two glasses, handed one to Stevie:

'Good party, wasn' it?'

'Yeah!'

'Didn' see mooch o' yew?' Stevie took a long pull at his glass:

'Oi was outsoide wi' Jack 'Umphries 'n Ernie 'n the oothers, most o' the toime. Oi see yeh wi' 'Arriet?' Michael shrugged, trying to sound non-committal:

'Yeah.'

'Loike 'er, do yeh?' He shrugged again:

'She's okay.' Stevie sniggered:

'She fancies yew, soomat rotten!'

'Yeh think so?'

'Oi know!' Michael looked up, grinned:

'Yeah, well...'

'She's pretty, ent she?'

'Yeah... maybe.'

'Yew goin' ter marry 'er, then?' Michael grabbed his hat, lying on the bed at his side, threw it at his friend; the two of them shared a companionable laugh, before Michael said:

'Oi ent marryin' anyone, not fer a long whoile yet!'

Pleased at having successfully baited his friend, Stevie allowed the conversation to turn to thoughts of the rest of the trip, to what might follow.

In the public bar of the *Reservoir,* the latter subject was also occupying their elders:

'Bloody 'ard work, terday, Bill.' They were settled in a corner, glasses nicely filled.

'Yeah. Bottom Road gets worse 'n worse, doon' it?'

'Ah. Soom o' them gates are in a state, ent they? 'N ther's no bloody water, 'alf the toime.'

''Ard work, loike yeh say.'

'Joost the Lousy 'Leven 'n Ashted six, termorrer, 'n we can go back middle road.'

'Aye, thank God! If ther's any water in the ten-moile.' The pound above Knowle was always notorious for low water levels in the Summer.

'Top road's no bloody good, now. Lap'erth locks are in an 'Ell of a state, from what Oi 'ear.'

'Ah. Mebbe the bloody war'll be over, soon, 'n they'll get 'em fixed.'

'Yeah, mebbe. Moikey picked oop a paper th'oother day, 'n tole me the noos – 'e says we've landed troops in Sicily, 'n the Eyties are on the roon.'

'If they give oop, ther'll only be 'Itler ter beat, then?'

'Ah – 'n the Japs, o' course.'

'Yanks'll tek care o' them, woon't they?'

'Wi' a bit o' loock, aye. Ther' was another bit in this paper, that Moikey read out, 'bout the soobmarines.'

'Oh ar?'

'Yeah – they've got noo long-range aeroplanes, can stay oop fer hours 'n hours, 'n they're usin' 'em to 'unt 'em down, sink 'em. The paper said we've got them on the roon, too.'

'Cor – mebbe we'll see an end o' this bloody rationin' then, if the ships are getting' through?'

'Oi wouldn' 'old yer breath, Bill!'

'Nah, 'spose not! We'll survoive, oone way or another!' A companionable laugh, a swig of beer.

'Moikey was h'enjoyin' 'imself las' night, wasn' 'e?' Vi joined the conversation.

'Wi' 'Arriet Caplin, yeh mean?' Bill added.

'Joey's sister?' Albert asked. Vi chuckled:

'S'roight! Dancin' they was, then Oi saw 'em sittin', talkin' in the *Grey'ound*. Thick as thieves! Tellin' 'er all about 'ow 'e came ter leave 'ome, 'n be on the boats, from what Oi over'eard.'

''E *never* talks about that!'

''E was with 'er!'

'Ah! Oi shall 'ave ter watch that boy, then, shall Oi?'

'Oh, ther's no 'arm in it, Alby – they're mooch too yoong ter be getting' oop ter anythin' yet. 'N they both know the score, they're sensible kids.'

'They are that.' He hesitated: 'Oi never said 'ow mooch Oi owe yeh, fer bringing 'im ter me, 'ave Oi?' Vi gave a dismissive wave of her hand:

'Oh, we 'ad ter do soomat with 'im!'

'Oi know, boot… Oi doon' know what Oi'd a' doon without 'im, nor little Ginny, especially now Alex's gone.'

'Oh, Alby!' Vi put a hand on his arm: 'Oi'm glad it's worked out. They're good kids, the two o' them.'

'Oi'm loocky ter 'ave 'em, Oi know that. The best kids a feller could 'ave, even if they ent really moine. Moikey won' use 'is old name, did yeh know? Calls 'imself Baker, now!' The pride was clear in his tone; Vi chuckled again:

'So doos she! Oi 'eard 'er interdoocin' erself ter Lucy 'Umphries yesterday – "Oi'm Ginny Baker", she says!' Albert looked up, startled:

'She did?' Vi nodded, laughing:

'Din't yer know?' He shook his head, joined her laughter, his heart lighter than ever at the news:

'Two little di'monds, they are! Bes' fam'ly a man could 'ave!' Four glasses were raised in their honour.

Chapter Thirty-Four

'This'll do, Moikey!' Michael heaved a sigh of relief as he pushed the lockgate closed. Normally, he'd have left it, but, thinking they would almost certainly be the last boats through that night, he closed up in an attempt to save water, as Albert and Ginny took the boats along to find a tying place. Across the cut, the lights of the *Cape of Good Hope* twinkled invitingly.

Christmas Eve. They'd fought their way across the valley, after a stop at Braunston to pick up the post – Christmas cards from Granny and Grandad Morris, and a little parcel each for Michael and Ginny – with the wind whipping a cold, driving rain into their faces all the way. It was earlier than they would usually tie for the night, but too late to tackle the Hatton twenty-one – especially after such a miserable day. And anyway, Christmas at the *Cape* was an attractive prospect. They'd eaten on the level pound through Leamington Spa; Ginny was proving to have been a good student to Gracie's teaching when it came to the cooking. So now, a quick wash and a clean shirt, and they could head for the warmth of the public bar.

As he walked along to find his boats, Michael noticed the first pair moored above the locks – smartly turned out Grand Unions, which looked familiar. He looked again, then realised; they were a pair of trainee boats, the same ones he'd first seen at Sutton's, the day of Gracie's wedding. They'd crossed paths a few times since, and the women on them had always waved, with a cheerful

'How are you?'. There was a light glowing in the butty cabin; he paused, to knock on the cabinside. The sound of movement from within, and then a head appeared as the hatch slid open:

'Hello?'

''Ello, miss – it's Moikey, off the *Sycamore* and the *Antrim.*'

'Oh – yes, hello. How are you?'

'Foine, thanks. Yerselves?'

'Oh, okay, I guess. Mary and Cissie aren't here – they've gone home for a few days, for Christmas.'

'Oh – 'ow about you? No foon bein' 'ere on yer own, is it?'

'No, I… I would have…' She suddenly turned away, hiding her face from him.

'Yew sure yeh're all roight?' She shook her head, then looked up again:

'I'm fine – really.'

'Would yeh loike ter coom over the *Cape* fer a drink with oos? We'll be goin' over soon as we've cleaned oop?'

'No… I wouldn't be good company, right now, I'm afraid.' There was a catch in her voice; Michael thought she sounded as though she needed cheering up:

'Oh, coom on! It'll be good foon, music 'n dancin' 'n all, yeh'll enjoy it! Yeh doon't want ter be all alone on Christmas!' She looked at him, uncertainty in her face, but then shook her head again:

'No, I…' she drew a deep breath: 'The reason I haven't gone home… My street was hit by a doodlebug, two weeks ago. My parents, my little brother, they were all killed – I've got nowhere to go, you see.' He stared at her, shocked at her tragedy:

'No Aunties or Uncles? Or friends, where yeh could go?'

'Yes, but… like I said, I would be awful company at the moment.'

'Well, yeh can't sit in ther' on yer own, on Christmas Eve, it's not roight. Get yerself toidy – Oi'll coom for yeh in a few minutes.' It was her turn to stare, taken aback by his sudden forcefulness; but then she smiled:

'If you're sure…'

'Oi'm sure. Do yeh good, ter get out.' Still she hesitated; but then she nodded:

'All right, since you insist – I'm Sylvie.' Michael offered his hand, and she shook it:

'Oi'll see yeh in foive minutes, then.'

'Right!'

As Michael had anticipated, it was a great evening – whenever a group of boaters are together, you can assume that the beer will flow, and the music will come out, and Christmas Eve is an even better excuse than usual for such hilarity. When Michael and Sylvie entered the bar, they found Albert just inside the doors, deep in conversation with several other boaters about the state of the war. One was just talking about the news on the wireless:

'They're sayin' as 'ow the H'air Force is batterin' Germany to pieces, what wi' the Yanks goin' boy day, 'n our boys boy noight!'

'Did yew 'ear about that Dams Raid, back in the Soommer? They flattened a coople o' big dams, flooded 'alf the coontry n' drained soom o' their canals!

'Yeah – Oi 'ope that doon't gi' *them* any big oideas!'

'Roight! Ther's little enooff bloody water in our'n as it is!' Albert saw the new arrivals:

'Moikey – Coom on, let's get oos a coopl'a beers, boy!'

He introduced Sylvie, to be met with a lot of ribald comments about his new girlfriend, which she took in good part. They all squeezed in around one of the tables; as the evening progressed, she began to relax more and more, joining in the singing, banging her glass on the table to the rhythm of the tune being played.

It was after midnight by the clock over the bar, the younger children, Ginny included, all long gone back to their beds, when she got rather unsteadily to her feet, and clapped her hands to get the assembled crowd's attention:

'Lish – listen! I've had quite a lot to drink, but there's shomething – something – I want to say!' Relative quiet descended upon the gathered boaters; she went on: 'I thought thish – this was going to be the worst Christmas of my life – but you've' she gestured around the room with her half-full glass, slopping some of its contents and making herself stagger: 'You've made it one of the best ever – I jusht want to say thank you – thank you all!' This was met with a round of applause, and some whistles and catcalls. She gazed around, spotted Michael:

'Mikey – come here!' He felt himself pushed up out of his seat, propelled towards her whether he wanted to or not. She grabbed him, put an arm around his shoulders:

'And it's all 'cause of you, Mikey! I'd be shit – sitting in my cabin, feeling shorry for myself if you hadn't dragged me over here.' She pulled him close, kissed him hard, full on his lips; Michael felt the colour rising to his face, but, enjoying the sensation at the same time, put his own arms around her, to the accompaniment of more catcalls and laughter from the assembly. At last, she released him, drew back to look into his eyes; 'How old are you, Mikey?'

'F-Fourteen!' He was gasping for breath.

'Oh! You'll have to be a bit older 'fore I can marry you, then – that's a shame!' She kissed him again, just a quick peck this time. She sat down again, and he made his way back to his seat, through the sounds of hilarity that his discomfiture had aroused, feeling his back slapped by many of those he passed on the way.

The gathering broke up shortly afterwards; as they rose to go, Sylvie confronted Michael and Albert:

'I'll do Christmas dinner tomorrow – I mean today! Please join me?' They exchanged glances:

'Ginny's doin' ourn, ent she?'

'Yes, Dad – but mebbe we could koind o' join forces?'

'Yeah – yeh moostn't be alone on Christmas day, Sylvie.

Coom round ter the *Antrim,* 'n we'll 'ave it all tergether.'

'Okay! See you later, then!' She staggered off. Albert turned to Michael, a grin on his face:

'Yeh'd better go'n keep an oiye on yer noo girlfriend, Moikey, see she doon't fall in!'

'Yes, Dad!' Michael put all the irony he could muster into his voice, felt himself pushed off by the shoulders in the direction she had gone.

* * *

Christmas Day was a much quieter affair. Many of the boaters gathered again in the *Cape,* for a lunchtime drink, but some, including Albert and Michael, preferred to keep their headaches at home. As promised, Sylvie joined them, bringing her contributions to the meal and a bottle of good brandy, which was considerably lighter by the time she left. She was quite subdued, probably as a result of a headache of her own – at one point during the afternoon, she began to speak about her family, and the others, already primed on her situation by Michael, let her talk as long as she wanted, easing her mind as she did so. At last, having talked out a lot of her pain, she looked around at their faces apologetically, smiled at the understanding in their eyes.

Late in the evening, she left them to return to her own boats, saying that her companions would be back in the morning, ready to carry on with their trip. The last they saw of her was a cheery wave from her butty's hatches as they set off at first light, to tackle Hatton in the chill mist of Boxing Day morning.

Chapter Thirty-Five

The first half of 1944 saw, if that was possible, an increase in the pressure on Britain's transport facilities. Despite all attempts to keep it hush-hush, it was soon a fairly open secret that the reason was the build-up to an invasion of Western Europe – fortunately, the details did remain safely under wraps, so much so that the Wehrmacht concentrated its opposing forces in the wrong place. On the canals, the result was more orders than could easily be handled, the traffic in munitions heading to the channel ports building up as the Spring progressed into Summer.

Mary Cavanagh was furious. Furious at the obstinately-stuck boat, furious at the dry weather which had caused the low water levels, furious at the lack of maintenance and dredging, but mostly, furious at herself.

She had managed to get the *Sagitta* effectively, and, it seemed, permanently, stuck, all on her own, with no help from anyone. Now, hot, sweaty in her dungarees, she was giving vent to her feelings with language which would have shocked her old circle of friends. Her vocabulary had expanded considerably over the eighteen months she had been on the boats – and it wasn't just the technical terms like straps and strings, 'ellums and windlasses, breasting-up and lock-wheeling, either. She managed a grin through her anger at the thought of what the Belgravia set would make of the way she had been expressing herself over the last hour!

Cissie was on the fore-deck, with the long shaft, trying ineffectually to move the bow sideways into deeper water; Sylvie had run the butty against the bank, and scrambled off with another shaft, which she was using against the counter with equally little effect. Mary slammed the gearbox into reverse once more, wound up the engine – the only result, as before, was a cloud of black smoke from the exhaust, drifting off into the summer evening.

Of all the stupid things to do! Mary mentally berated herself again. It was a cardinal sin, anyway, to take the motor in too close on a turn, if only because it would drag the butty across rather than around the corner; and to do it here, where she knew full well the channel was dangerously shallow even when the water level was well up… *Slow goin', the Jackdaw!* More than one of the fulltime boaters had warned them of that – the pound from Hammond Three to Leighton Lock had a reputation; and in mid-June, with the water level many inches off…

And where were all the other boats? They'd passed a steady stream of them, all day, but now, when they could use some help, there was no-one about! Just that one pair… *The arrogant bastard!* Most of the old boating families had taken to the trainees, accepting the need for them to take over unoccupied pairs, to help with the war effort, referring to them jocularly as the 'Idle Women' – whoever had designed that stupid badge with its 'I.W.' motif?. But it was her luck to meet one of the other variety just when she needed some sympathetic assistance – the pair of Grand Union boats had swept by, just after they'd run aground, the steerer's face carefully hidden behind the cabin chimney, his old trilby hat pulled down low over his eyes. *Damn him!* His wash had left them, if anything, even more firmly stuck than ever. She wound down the engine again, knocked the gears into neutral, the boat still as immovable as before. But now, she cocked her ears – was that the sound of an engine? Sylvie called out something, but Mary waved her to silence: Yes! For certain, that sounded like a Bolinder, coming from the direction of Stoke Hammond. She called across to Sylvie, cupped her hands to her mouth to shout to Cissie, to hold on for a minute.

Swinging around the long turns approaching Old Linslade, Michael saw the heads across the field before he saw the boats. When the pair, randomly stopped across the canal, came into sight, he slowed the engine to its off-beat tickover, turned to take in the tow as the butty overhauled him. Albert, standing on the gunwale, puffing contentedly at his pipe, took it from his mouth, gestured ahead:

'Looks loike they've got problems!'

'Yeah!' Michael echoed his grin, glanced back to see Ginny running the butty against the towpath to slow it down. He let the motor run slowly on, to within haling distance, then knocked out the clutch:

'D'yer need soom 'elp?' The woman on the motor had watched them approach; now, she called back, gratitude already in her voice:

'Yes, please! We're stuck on the mud!'

'Oi'm not surproised, over ther' – it's awful shaller on the insoide o' these turns!'

'Yes, I know! My own fault, I wasn't paying attention!' Michael and Albert exchanged knowing glances:

''Ow we goin' ter get 'em off?'

'They'll need snatchin' back, Moikey. Only way is ter get a line from their starn teh our fore-end, and pull 'em back'ards.'

'Can't we breast 'em on, do it loike that?'

'Mebbe – boot we could end oop stoock next to 'em, yeh know 'ow bad it is along 'ere. Better teh keep our starn in deep water.'

'H'okay, Dad.' He turned to the woman, whom he vaguely recognised, called out: 'Oi'll put our fore-end boy yer starn – get a loine around moy stud, h'okay?'

'Okay!' the shout came back.

He looked back, to see that Ginny had the butty safely by the bank, and was on the fore-end – he threw the tow line off from the stern dolly, waved to her to coil it in, then gently nudged the motor's bow as close as he could to the other's stern. Mary threw her rope, missed; she coiled it in, tried again, and got it over the t-stud on the *Sycamore's* fore-deck, quickly secured it to her own dollies, then gave Michael a wave. He waved back, and reversed his engine; dropping in the clutch, he wound up the throttle, hearing the engine on the other boat also revving hard. At first, it seemed they were still going nowhere – but then, oh so slowly, they began to move, inching backwards. He pulled out the oil-rod, further increasing the power of the Bolinder, and their progress increased. Moments later, to gleeful shouts from the other pair's crew, the *Sagitta* was floating free once more.

'Thank you very much!' Albert just waved dismissively as Michael set back to pick up the *Antrim* in the gathering dusk.

'How far are you going? We'd like to buy you a drink for your help?' Albert looked at Michael:

'It's gettin' late – the *Globe?'*

'If yeh loike, Dad.' The tow re-attached, they steered carefully past the Grand Union boats; Albert called across to Mary:

'We're stoppin' at the *Globe* – next bridge boot oone!'

'Very good – we'll see you there!'

Half an hour later, both pairs were tied outside the pub. Ginny, tired after a long day, had retired to her bed; Albert, Michael and the three women were becoming re-acquainted over beers in the bar:

''Ow are yeh gettin' on now, Sylvie?' Michael asked. She replied with a smile:

'I'm fine, now, thanks. I've kind of moved to my Gran's house, when I'm not here on the boats.'

'Yeh still goin' teh marry moy lad, then?' Albert asked her; she laughed:

'Of course! I'll never forget how he dragged me off to the pub for Christmas Eve!' This raised a laugh all round, through which Albert said:

'Oi'd better tell 'Arriet when we see 'er, then!' Michael had the grace to blush at this:

'Dad!'

'Oi've seen yer, talkin' to 'er whenever we roon across 'Enry's boats!'

'We're *friends,* all roight?'

'Yeah, o' course!' Another friendly laugh, and the talk turned to the dramatic news:

'War could be over boy Christmas, they're sayin'.'

'Yes – the invasion's going well, isn't it?' Cissie agreed; Mary had some doubts:

'Our lot's doing well, they say – but the Yanks are having a much more difficult time of it, aren't they?'

'Oh, they'll get goin' soon, you wait 'n see. 'N the Roossian's are goin' strong, too – we'll squeeze 'Itler 'tween oos 'fore long!'

'It'd be great to see the end of it, wouldn't it?' Sylvie said.

'Oh yes!' Mary agreed: 'No more rationing!'

'Eggs!'

'Bacon!'

'Coffee!'

'Big juicy sausages!' The boatmen listened through this exchange, smiling:

''N mebbe they'll start drudgin' the cut again, 'n fixin' all them leaky gates!' Albert suggested.

'Yes – that would be a big help. It's getting bad in places, isn't it?'

'Yeah. Even down 'ere, ther's gettin' ter be dodgy gates, leakin' all over the place. The Stratford cut's in a 'Ell of a state, so top road's no bloody use; 'n bottom road's not mooch better!'

'That's the Birmingham and Fazeley?'

'Yeah – 'n the Coventry cut. Shaller as 'Ell, that is, now.'

'I know!' Mary exchanged looks with her crew: 'We go that way sometimes, from Birmingham to load from the coalfields.'

'S'not seh bad if yeh're roonin' empty – Yeh daren't put a full load on, if yeh 'ave ter go that way.'

'It's all down to the war, I suppose?'

'S'roight. They say ther's no money fer drudgin' or oother jobs.'

'It'll cost a fortune to put everything right, when it's over, won't it?'

'Ar. Mek our loife bloody 'ard, fer years n' years, Oi reckon. Yeh'll go back teh yer old jobs, will yeh?'

Mary nodded:

'I expect so – I was a teacher, in a primary school, in London.' Cissie chuckled:

'I hope you remember to watch your language, then!' Mary blushed:

'Yes – I was rather letting rip earlier, wasn't I?' They all laughed; Cissie added:

'I was a secretary, for a firm of solicitors in the city – they said they'd have me back after the war, if I wanted to go. This has been great fun – most of the time, anyway! – but I expect I'll go back there.'

'How about you, Sylvie?' Their third companion looked thoughtful:

'I don't know – My old life's, kind of gone, you know? I'd just finished college – then losing Mum and Dad and Jonathan… Maybe I'll stay, if anyone'll have me!'

'Soomeoone'd tek yeh on, Oi'm sure, Sylvie – if Gran' Union's don't want yeh, yew talk teh Mr Vickers – 'e's Fellerses manager at Braunston. Oi'll bet 'e'd 'ave a place fer yeh!'

'Thank you, Albert – I'll remember that!'

'I'm getting hungry, girls – how about you two?' Mary asked; she explained to the others:

'We'd intended to eat after we stopped – but then getting stuck like that's put us all behind. And now I'm starving!'

'Yeah, me too!' Sylvie agreed: 'I'll be cook, if you like – you two stop for another drink I'll go and get it ready. Give me half an hour, okay?'

'Okay – thanks, Sylv!' She got up, left them with a cheery wave from the door.

'Poor kid – losing her family like that!' Sympathy furrowed Mary's brow.

'Yeah – 'appened ter lot's o' folks, though.'

'Yes, I imagine so.' A sad silence prevailed while they contemplated the tragedy of war, until Michael spoke up:

'Alex was killed, in the Navy. 'E was… moy big brother.' The women's eyes turned to Albert:

'Oh – I'm so sorry!' Mary said.

'Oh, it was a long whoile back. 'E was on HMS 'Ood, when it was 'it boy the Bismarck.' Mary just reached across the table, took his hand in her own:

'Better times are coming, Albert.' He smiled:

'Oi know. 'N Oi've still got Moikey 'ere, 'n little Ginny. They're all the family a man could want.' He smiled at Michael, who reached out and took his other hand.

Chapter Thirty-Six

Harriet Caplin stood in the butty's stern well, scanning the line of boats tied above Stoke Bruerne top lock. It was bitterly cold, with a steady drizzle adding to the misery, but her heart gave a quick leap as she spotted a Fellows, Morton and Clayton pair; then it sank again – wrong boats! A few more lengths – they'd end up right by the tunnel, if they didn't find a tying-space soon – then she saw them: Was it? Maybe... Yes! The *Sycamore,* breasted on the outside of the *Antrim* as always. He was here!

Suey Caplin noted the brightness in her daughter's eyes as they found and filled a space on the towpath, smiled as she guessed what it meant. She slid the *Bodmin* against the bank, as Henry held the *Towcester* outside – the old *Bognor* had gone, taken away after the engine had died in spectacular fashion a few months before, but Henry was more than pleased with his new motor boat. She'd heard, a week or two ago, that the *Bognor* was back in service, being used by a group of the trainees, now.

They'd eaten, coming along the six-mile from Cosgrove – now, a quick wash and brush-up, and they'd head back to join the celebrations in the *Boat.*

Christmas Eve, once again – Albert's hopeful prediction hadn't come to pass, the fighting still going on in Europe and the Far East. The war in the Pacific seemed too remote to generate much interest, even if the news of American successes added to the general feeling of hopeful, even eager, optimism. But the approach of the allied armies to the borders of Germany itself was discussed at great length:

'Whoy don' they joost give oop? It moost be obvious they've 'ad it, moostn' it?'

'Seems crazy ter go on loike this, don' it?' Joey Caplin concurred, with a glance down at Gracie, sat quiet in the corner by the bar.

'Yeah. But 'Itler's a bloody nutcase, ent 'e? 'E won' *let* 'em surrender, from what Oi 'ear. 'S what the papers say, any'ow.'

'Moikey got a new oone, 'as 'e?'

'Yeah – 'e picked oone oop the oother day – arsk 'im, 'n 'e'll read it to yeh, Oi'm sure.'

'Wher' is 'e, Alby?'

'Oh, 'e'll be along in a whoile. Ginny din't feel loike coomin', she's very toired, so 'e's staying with 'er fer a bit.'

Michael looked up as a knock sounded on the cabinside. He gave his sister a puzzled glance, stood up and put his head out through the hatch.

'Ello, Moikey.' Harriet sounded her usual shy self.

''Arriet! Noice ter see yeh!'

'Yew coomin' fer a drink, fer Christmas?' Michael looked down at Ginny:

'Go on, Moikey – Oi'm goin' ter bed, Oi think.'

'Oh, coom on, Gin – joost fer oone?' He'd been trying to persuade her anyway.

'Oh – all roight, then. Joost oone, okay?' She got to her feet, slipped her bonnet back on, followed him as he climbed out onto the towpath:

'Ello, 'Arriet – 'ow yeh bin?'

'Foine, thanks, Ginny. Ow's yerself?'

'Grand! Oi'm joost a bit toired, we've 'ad a long day.'

They set off; Michael threw an arm around each girl's

shoulders, eliciting a shrug from Ginny, and a shy smile from Harriet. Singled out once more, they crossed the lock gates to the *Boat Inn,* pushed through the door into the bar.

'Coom on in, 'Arriet – Mum 'n Dad 'ere too, are they?' Joey asked.

'They're joost gettin' changed, they'll be along in a minute. 'S good ter see yer, Joey!'

'Yew two, Sis!' He grabbed her into a warm embrace; Gracie got to her feet, gave her a hug too:

'Oi've got soom noos fer yeh, 'Arriet!'

'What's that, then, Gracie?' She laughed:

'Oi'll tell yeh when yer folks get 'ere!'

'Wher's your Mum 'n Dad, 'n Billy 'n Stevie?'

'Oh, they ent 'ere, they're oop Birnigum.'

'Beer, Moikey?' Albert asked: 'N what would yeh loike, 'Arriet? Ginny?'

'Please, Dad.'

'Could Oi 'ave a shandy, Ooncle Alby?'

'Lemonade, Dad, please.' He turned to the bar, waved to the lady behind it:

'When yeh're ready, Zoe!'

'Coom 'n sit 'ere wi' me, Moikey, Ginny – 'aven't seen yeh fer ages!' Gracie suggested, hotching along the bench; then she chuckled to see the doubtful look in the boy's eyes: 'Oh-ho, loike that, is it? Yew'll join me though, won'cher, Ginny?' the girl smiled, squeezed in beside her.

Albert had procured their drinks; he handed a glass of lemonade across to Ginny, passed a pint of ale to Michael, a half-pint of bitter shandy to Harriet:

'Appy Christmas, everyone!' They raised their glasses to his toast. Michael looked over the rim of his, at his companion, was suddenly struck by a realisation: *She* is *very pretty, isn't she? Teks after 'er Mum!* Suey Caplin was a handsome woman, on the short side as were most of the boat people, but without Vi or

Gracie's roundness. Strong and robust of figure and feature, with a ready smile and big dark brown eyes; now, her daughter was growing into a younger, lissome echo of her. On impulse, he slipped his arm around her waist, was rewarded with a flash of her eyes, a repeat of that warm, shy smile.

''Arriet?'

'Yes, Moikey?'

'Could Oi... Oi mean, would it be okay, if...' He broke off, not sure how, or even if, he should continue.

'What is it, Moikey?' She put her own hand over his, on her waist, squeezed it gently. He cleared his throat, tried again:

'Can Oi... see a bit more of yeh? Oi mean, we've got the boike, Oi could coycle along, when we're toied oop soomewher' close...' Harriet dropped her eyes from his face:

'Oi'd loike that, Moikey.'

'Yeh would?' He sounded almost surprised.

'Yeh'll 'ave teh arsk moy Dad, though.'

'Arsk me what, girl?' The door had opened behind them; both turned, embarrassed:

'Dad! Mum!'

'Good evenin', Mr Caplin.'

'Ello, kids – what was it yeh wanted ter arsk me, then, Moikey?'

'Er – Mr Caplin...'

'Go on, Moikey!' Harriet's whisper was all too audible.

'Mr Caplin – would it be h'okay if Oi coom ter see 'Arriet, soometoimes?' Henry glanced at his wife, chuckled:

''Ow old are yeh, Moikey?'

'Near sixteen, now.'

'Our 'Arriet's fifteen, boy. Yeh're still too yoong teh be gettin' too mooch in tow, Oi reckon.'

'Oh, Dad! Please?'

'Let 'em see each oother when they can, 'Enry!' Suey put in her views: 'They're only yoong oonce – it moight coom ter nothin';

boot then, 'oo knows, eh? 'N they're sensible kids, they'll not get oop ter nothin' silly.' He turned to his wife, nodded, a smile creasing his weather-beaten features:

'Yew 'eard yer mother, 'Arriet – no moockin' about! Boot yes, then Moikey, we'll be pleased ter see yer, from toime teh toime.'

Michael looked down at Harriet, gave her waist a gentle squeeze; her brown eyes smiled up at him:

''Appy Christmas, Moikey.' Her voice was quiet, but happy.

''Appy Christmas, 'Arriet.' He bent, kissed her cheek, then looked up in surprise as a round of applause echoed around the little bar, grinned in embarrassment as he acknowledged it. Gracie got to her feet, went to stand with her husband:

'We've got soom noos fer yeh, 'n all! 'Aven't we, Joe?' He nodded, smiling down lovingly at her.

'Well, out with it, then!' Suey was smiling too, guessing what was coming.

'Oi'm 'avin' a babby!'

A chorus of congratulation broke out; everyone trying at once to give her a hug, to shake Joey's hand. Suey embraced her daughter-in-law:

'Oh, well doon, loovey! D'yeh know when?'

''Bout May, Sister Mary reckons.'

'That's wonderful, loove! Oi'm so pleased fer yeh!'

Henry took her in his arms too, gave her a tight hug, kissed her cheek:

'A grandsoon fer me, eh?' She laughed:

'Moight be a grand-*daughter,* Dad!'

'Oi don' care, girl, either oone'll be grand!'

Chapter Thirty-Seven

The war was over – and yet it wasn't. Hitler's thousand-year Reich had vanished amid the dust and rubble of the destroyed city of Berlin, its dictator dead by his own hand before he could be taken by the advancing Russian army. The celebrations of what they'd called VE Day had lasted rather more than a day, in the end. Both Albert and Bill had been at Catherine de Barnes that day, on the ten-mile pound between Knowle and Camp Hill, and the festivities in the pub had lasted well through the night.

But around the Pacific Ocean, the fighting was still going on. Allied forces, British, Australian, New Zealand, and others, but primarily American, were knocking on the door of the Japanese home islands; but, like Hitler before him, the Emperor Hirohito wasn't about to give in. Now, towards the end of May, there was a growing sense that it couldn't go on much longer, that the Empire of the Rising Sun would have to accept its approaching dusk sooner or later.

Michael skidded the bike to a halt, leant forward over the handlebars and hung his head between his shoulders, breathing long and deep: *This courtin' business is bloody 'ard work!* A smile crept slowly across his face, the twinkle returning to his soft green eyes: *Boot it's well worth it!*

Since Christmas, he'd managed to see quite a bit of Harriet Caplin, even if it was usually at the cost of some miles spent on the rickety old bike which was intended for lock-wheeling. He glanced around, watching the scattered clouds roll slowly across the sky as the sun sank towards the horizon beyond the turnpike – it was a beautiful late spring evening, and the prospect of seeing Harriet made it unsurpassable, in Michael's eyes. He sat upright, stretching his aching back – he'd already covered nearly six miles, from Cosgrove, along the level pound; just up past the locks, about another mile, and he'd be there… He'd stopped just below Stoke Bruerne bottom lock, to have a breather before tackling the uphill part of his journey, on the old transhipment wharf which dated back to the days before Blisworth Tunnel had been finished; now, he bent to his pedals again, leaving its dilapidated, long-abandoned isolation for the hub of activity which was the village.

Oi woonder 'ow Gracie's doin'? His thoughts took a new turn as he rose from the saddle to breast the rise up to the lockside, the bike swaying from side to side beneath him. She was about due to have her baby – last time he'd seen her, just a few weeks before, she'd been even more robustly joyful than normal. She'd grabbed him, given him a huge hug and a hearty kiss on his cheek; he'd kissed her back, despite feeling rather embarrassed at being held tightly against her bulging tummy, as she'd told him that she was hoping to be at Stoke when the baby came, so that she could have Sister Mary on hand to help: *Oi woonder if they're ther'?* His smile grew even wider at the thought.

It had been a good trip – they'd loaded with tinned goods at City Road, destined for Crescent Wharf, leaving about half a day ahead of Bill and Vi Hanney, who'd got similar orders. Albert, a knowing twinkle in his eyes, had suggested waiting, running the two pairs butty all the way, but had allowed Michael to persuade him to go on ahead, knowing that *Towcester* and *Bodmin* were also travelling North, a bare few hours in front of them – the bike had seen a lot of use, the boy setting off as soon as the boats were tied to cycle ahead as far as it took to see his girl, leaving his captain's knowing grin and his sister's despairing look behind him.

The shirt was sticking to his back as he slogged his way past Major Gardner's farmhouse, under the double-arched bridge, and up the last slope at the tail of the top lock. Just along, to the right, a crowd was gathered outside Sister Mary's surgery; several faces turned to him as he hove into view, and then one detached itself and ran towards him, waving frantically: *Soomethin's wrong!* But the face in question was grinning fit to split itself in half:

'Moikey! It's a boy – Oi'm an *Ooncle!'* Ernie Caplin rushed up to him, threw his arms around a startled Michael's neck, held on to him whilst jigging up and down on the spot.

'Yeah? That's brilliant, Ernie!' The teenager released him and stepped back, suddenly embarrassed at his own excess of emotion:

'Er – yeah – well, so're yew, Moikey!' Michael felt himself echoing the other's silly grin:

'Oi s'pose Oi am, too!'

''Course y'are! Gracie alwes calls yew 'er little brother, even if y'ent, not really... Oi mean – oh, yeh know!'

'Oi know!' Michael laughed at his companion's discomfiture – Ernie had always had a knack of putting his foot in his mouth. 'Coom on, Oi want ter see!'

He dropped the bike on the lockside, took Ernie by the elbow and hurried him back to the crowded doorway of the little red-brick house. People saw them approach, made way for them to get to the door and look inside; Joey Caplin, a look of stunned pride on his face, saw Michael standing there, and beckoned him in. Joey was stood behind the chair where his wife sat, gazing raptly down at the tiny bundle she held in her arms, his hands protectively on her shoulders; at his side stood his parents, joy and pride just as evident in their expressions. Gracie looked up, gave Michael a radiant smile:

'Look, Moikey! Coom 'n see yer nephew!' He stepped forward, into the room, and knelt on the floor beside her; she eased the lacy white cloth from the baby's face to allow him a better look. He gazed down at the tiny, wizened face, brightly pink, the eyes firmly shut – and sudden memory assailed him. He'd looked down at a new-born baby once before, in a hospital ward, so many years, a lifetime, ago… His head came up, his eyes frantically searching, until they lit on Sister Mary, quietly bustling in a corner:

'Sister Mary! He's – all right, isn't he?' She looked up, a kindly if puzzled smile on her face:

'All right, Mikey? He's a lovely bonnie boy, as strong and healthy as you'll see!'

He turned back to Gracie, feeling tears gathering behind his eyes; she eased one hand from the bundle in her lap, and reached out, stroked his cheek:

'He's *foine,* Moikey. Ther's nothin' *wrong* wi' 'im, nothin' at all!' He nodded, feeling his throat tighten until he couldn't speak; he looked down again at the baby so that she wouldn't see his tears, and saw the little eyes flutter open, to look straight into his own. Gracie's voice was soft, loving:

'Jack – this's yer Ooncle Moikey.' Her hand caressed the back of his neck as he struggled to take charge of his feelings. Another voice spoke from the doorway:

'What d'yer reckon, Moichael – ent 'e wonderful?' He looked around, his heart lifting at the sound although he was still blinking back the tears:

''Arriet! 'E's marvellous!' Staggering to his feet, he bent to kiss Gracie on the cheek, then reached out and shook Joey's hand:

''E's brilliant, Joe – yeh moost be so proud!'

'Thank yeh, Moikey – Oi am, that!'

''E's lovely, ent 'e, Moikey?'

''E is, Gracie – well doon, big sister!'

'Thank yeh, little brother!'

With a last grin at the new parents, he made his way to the door where Harriet was waiting, her usual shy smile on her face. Impulsively, he took her by the shoulders, drew her to him and kissed her soundly on the cheek, to an accompaniment of quiet, encouraging laughter and jeers from those around them.

'Moichael!' Harriet's whisper sounded flustered; he just grinned down at her. She shook her head at him, well aware that her parents were in the room; he glanced over his shoulder, to see both senior Caplins watching him – the expression on Henry's face was not discouraging, and a smile was playing around Suey's lips as she exchanged looks with her daughter.

'Kettle's on, Moichael – would yeh loike a coopa?' He turned back to his girl at her question, the grin still on his face:

'Oi'm doyin' fer oone, 'Arriet – Oi've joost boiked all the way from Cosgrove!'

'Well, coom on back ter the boats, then! Yew coomin, Ma?' Her father answered for them:

'Yew two go on, we'll be 'long in a minute!'

Ernie Caplin watched as his sister led her beau outside, smiling up at him all the time, shaking his head with all the worldly-wise experience of any fourteen-year-old: *Them two'll be getting' in tow 'fore long!* His eyes stayed on them, half proud, half amused, as they strolled along the towpath towards the waiting Grand Union pair, hand in hand.

Chapter Thirty-Eight

Unfamiliar territory, unfamiliar water. The beat of a Bolinder echoed from the blackness of the tunnel-mouth into the Summer sunshine, then fell in tone and volume as the motor-boat nosed out again into daylight, its fore-end riding high out of the water. The butty followed, tight to its stern on its cross-straps; but the sound of a second engine resonated from deeper within the darkness, echoed by yet a third.

Thursday morning, and Ben Vickers had called both Albert and Bill Hanney, by chance tied up together in Braunston, to his office:

'I need three pairs, for a special job – how do you fancy a trip down the Worcester Cut?' The two boatmen had exchanged looks, raised eyebrows; Albert spoke for them both:

'Oi thought the Severn coomp'ny ran that cut?'

'They do, usually. But they've no boats to spare, and they've got a special cargo, to come to Birmingham from Diglis basin – are you up for it? I'll find a third pair to go with you.' Bill nodded to Albert as he looked around again:

'H'okay, Mr Vickers, we'll give it a go fer yeh. We're to go empty, are we?'

'Yes – can you set off today?'

'Oi reckon so – moy injun seems ter be h'okay now. 'N yeh've got the stooff out o' store yeh needed, Bill?'

'Yeah – we can go soon as yeh loike, Mr Vickers.'

'That's great! You should make Diglis Sunday night, shouldn't you?'

'Aye, reckon so. We'll load Moonday, shall we?'

'Hopefully, yes. The company'll pay you for running empty, as it's a special job.'

'That's good, ent it, Bill?'

'Tis that! Oi'll get Vi 'n the boys tergether, we'll be off in 'alf an hour, h'okay?'

'We'll be ready, Bill. Moikey's joost oop the shop, gettin' soome bits, 'e'll not be long.'

Returned from the village shop, a bag of provisions in hand, Michael received the news with mixed feelings. He'd never seen the Worcester and Birmingham Canal, beyond its junction with the Stratford at King's Norton, and the prospect of new places, a new road, with a surprise around every corner, excited him. But, the few days it would take them for the trip there and back meant being far away from Harriet, with no clear idea of when he might see her again – and he was surprised to realise just how much that bothered him. He would hardly have called their relationship a romance, feeling that they were both far too young for things like that, and they were only able to meet infrequently, as their respective orders permitted, anyhow – but he always knew, at least approximately, *where* she was. For these days, he would lose touch with her, not know, not be able to imagine, just where she was, what she was doing, at any given moment. And that idea left him feeling unsettled, distracted. But – orders were orders, and he was a company man now, so what Mr Vickers said was what they would do. And, once they were back to their regular haunts, he'd soon pick up knowledge of where she was, when they might meet…

They'd made the *Cape* that night; the *Bluebell,* on the Stratford-on-Avon Canal, for Friday night; now, Saturday afternoon, and, once out of the darkness of the tunnel, they were approaching the top of Tardebigge locks. As he slowed the boats past the old wharf, a strange sight caught Michael's eye – a butty, to all appearances, but with the sound of a petrol engine coming from its stern, and the oddest of constructions built upon it. The hull, with the sleek lines of a Shropshire Union boat, looked to be unchanged – but a full-length cabin had been added, leaving a long open deck at the stern where the original butty cabin had been, with steel hand-rails around it: *What on earth?*

As he looked, a man emerged from the doors of the strange cabin – a tall, almost gangling fellow, casually but well dressed. He looked over at the working boats, and waved a greeting:

'Hello!' Michael raised a hand in reply:

''Ow d'yer do?'

'Fine, thank you! Yourselves?'

'Good, thank yeh. That's a rare boat yeh got ther', mister?' The man laughed:

'The *Cressy?* I suppose she is, a bit! I had her rebuilt, by Tooley's at Banbury – we live on her, now, myself and my wife.'

'Joost live? Yeh've no room fer carryin', 'ave yeh?' The man laughed again:

'Just live! I'm a writer – Tom Rolt. Pleased to meet you!' Michael nodded, echoing the man's smile:

'Moikey Baker! This moy Dad's pair – we're goin' ter Diglis.' They were drawing past; the man waved a farewell:

'Good luck to you, Mr Baker! We'll see you on your way back, perhaps.'

'Oi'll look out fer yeh!'

He carried on to the top lock, which stood open and ready for them, ran the motor in at the same time as he cast off the cross-straps; Ginny ran the butty to the side, stepped off and braked it to a halt on the strapping stump placed there for the purpose. Tardebigge top lock is abnormally deep – by the time they'd worked both boats through, and Michael had set off on foot to ready the next, Bill Hanney's pair were at the top, and their third pair rapidly approaching; Jack Warden had caught them up the previous night, at the *Bluebell.*

They'd got the *Acorn* at the bottom of the lock, and Albert was running the *Sycamore* into the second, when the lock-keeper came running down from his cottage, waving at them:

''Old on, fellers! Noo orders fer yeh!' They dropped whatever they were doing, and waited for him to catch up. He stopped beside the *Acorn,* as it emerged from the lock, bent to catch his breath:

'Message for yeh from Braunston! The job's off, yeh're to turn roond 'n goo back.'

'Off? What d'yer mean?'

'All I knows is that's the message I got fer yeh – to goo back ter Braunston.'

'Bugger me! Oi 'ope they're goin' ter pay oos fer all this empty roonin'?' The keeper shook his head:

'I don't know 'bout that, Captain. All I got is what I told yeh.' Bill shrugged his shoulders:

'We'll stop 'ere, then, fer tonoight, 'n start back in the mornin'. Roon down 'n tell Alby, will yer, Billy?'

'Roight, Dad!' The teenager set off at a run; Bill turned back to the keeper:

'Thanks, mate. We'll tie all three pairs 'ere, if that's h'okay?'

'Sure thing! I'll give you all a 'and to back up in the morning, 'n turn at the wharf.' Bill nodded:

'Thank yeh.' The lock-keeper left to return to his cottage; they worked all six boats into the long pound between the first and second locks, tied them securely there for the night. Fed, watered and changed, they walked to a pub in the village for a few beers.

Sunday morning – no-one felt like an early start, after the anticlimax of their aborted trip. Everyone was up and about, breakfasts cooking, hands and faces being washed; Albert, still not entirely happy with the way the aging and tired Bolinder was running, was down in his engine-hole, once again resetting the injector pumps. He paused in his work, wiping the sweat from his brow with the back of an oily hand, and leant out into the sunshine, to see a couple walking up from the second lock. The man was tall and well-built, dark-haired, with heavily-framed spectacles, smartly dressed in an expensive raincoat; the woman, equally well-dressed, had an air of class about her, in her appearance and the way she carried herself. They approached Albert's pair, first of the three:

'Good morning!' The man greeted Albert, in the act of lighting up his pipe; he took it from his mouth:

'Mornin'.'

'Have you seen a boat called the *Cressy,* hereabouts?' Albert scratched his head – he'd been in the cabin as they passed the wharf the previous day, but Michael, eating breakfast in the butty cabin, had overheard. Now, he poked his head out of the hatch:

'Mornin'; she's oop above the top lock, boy the old wharf.'

'Good morning! Thank you – we're here to meet the man who owns her.'

'Mr Rolt, that'd be?' The man smiled:

'That's right – Tom Rolt. He's there, is he?'

'Was last noight, fer sure.'

'That's good! Thank you.'

'Yeh're welcome, mister...?'

'Aickman – Robert Aickman. This is my wife, Ray.' The woman inclined her head in greeting.

'Moikey Baker – 'n that's moy Dad, Albert.'

'Good to meet you, gentlemen!' He gestured over his shoulder: 'These locks are in a bit of a state, aren't they?' Michael grinned:

'We 'aven't seen 'em yet – we doon' usually work down this way. Boot yeh doon' surprise me – yeh should see the Stratford

Cut; or the bottom road out o' Birnigum!' The look on Aickman's face was sympathetic:

'I know – I've been to look at some of them. That's why I'm here, to meet Mr Rolt – We're hoping we might be able to do something about it.'

'Oh? D'yeh work fer the coomp'ny, then?'

'No! But – I'm thinking we might be able to get other like-minded people together, form… oh, some kind of pressure group, maybe, do something to make the authorities see that the canals are worth saving, worth investing in for the future.'

'Yeh'd 'ave all o' the boaters be'ind yeh, fer sure, if yeh can do anythin'! Good loock to yeh.'

'You too, gentlemen! Goodbye for now.' They walked on, passing the other pairs, exchanging 'good mornings' with Bill and Vi, and Jack Warden.

'Oi woonder if they'll ever do any good, Dad?'

''Oo knows, Moikey!'

Epilogue

Now, at last, it really was all over. The Rising Sun had gone down into its self-inflicted night with the ultimate persuasion of two atomic bombs, and the world was once more at peace.

The succession of astonishing news stories had broken as they were making their way back to Braunston after the abortive trip to Worcester. The *Sycamore's* aging Bolinder had begun to play up again; Albert had told Bill and Jack to go on, to get back for whatever orders were available, while he and Michael did their best to keep the tired engine going. They had lost more than a day, but made it back eventually; Ben Vickers had to send to Saltley Dock for a spare injector, and they remained tied on the towpath near the iron bridge to await its arrival.

The end of the fighting, after so many years, brought on a strange feeling of nostalgia in Albert, as it had in so many others. With little to do, they were sat in the cabin of the *Antrim* the next morning, breakfast finished, with a mug of tea apiece; he looked up at Michael:

'Oi was toied joost here, furst toime we met – yew remember, boy?' Michael nodded:

'That's roight, Dad. Oi'll never forget – Oi was so nervous!'

'Oi was pretty grumpy wi' yeh, wasn' Oi?' Michael grinned at him:

'Not really!' Albert drew on his pipe, blew out a cloud of smoke:

'Oi was feelin' so… depressed. Oi'd joost buried moy Rita – 'n Oi was worried 'bout Alex, o' course, 'im bein' away in the Navy…' He chuckled quietly: 'N along cooms Bill 'Anney, wi' this daft oidea that Oi should tek on this know-nothin' kid off the bank ter 'elp me roon the boats! 'Ow stoopid can yeh get, that's what Oi thought.'

'Boot yeh took me on, any'ow?' Albert nodded:

'Ther' was soomthin' about yeh, Moikey. A… koind o' spirit, Oi suppose. Skinny little kid, yeh was! Boot yeh had a feelin' o'… oh, Oi dunno, copin' wi things, soom'ow. 'n Bill said yeh'd doon well wi' them, on the roon from Stoke Bruin…'

Ginny had been sitting quietly, listening to their memories; now, she asked:

'Are you glad yeh did, Dad?' Albert turned to her, shook his head:

'Nah! Wurst thing Oi ever did in moy loife!' But the grin on his face told its own tale – she reached over and punched his shoulder; he grabbed her hand, drew her close and took her in his arms:

'Yew two are the best things that ever 'appened to me – 'cept per'aps meetin' Rita. 'Ow Oi'd a' coped without yeh, 'specially when Alex was killed, Oi joost don' know.' Michael felt tears suddenly burning behind his eyes, he said quietly:

'Yew saved my loife. Oh, Bill and Billy fished me out of the canal, that night – boot it was workin' with you, 'avin' a new Dad, someone I could love and respect… Yew gave me a loife worth livin', Dad.'

''N I'd be stuck in soom dreadful orphanage soomwher', if it wasn' fer yew, Dad.'

'Yeh don' regret coomin' on the boats, then? Yeh don' miss yer schoolin', toime teh play wi' yer friends?' Two heads shook as one:

'No!'

'Never!'

'Coom 'ere, Moikey!' The boy stood up; Albert's eyes followed him:

'Look at yeh, boy! So tall 'n 'andsome – no woonder yoong 'Arriet's got an oiye fer yeh! Yer Mum would be proud o' yeh, both o' yeh.' Michael slipped into the bench beside him; Albert freed one arm from Ginny, slid it around his shoulders:

'Moy son – moy daughter! Oi'm so proud o' the two o' yeh…!' Ginny wriggled closer:

'I love you, Daddy.'

Teenage boys are not given to displays of sentiment. But:

'Oi love yeh too, Dad.'

In this sequel to *A Boy Off The Bank,* published March 2008, the familiar characters of Michael and Ginny, Alby Baker, and other boating families – the Hanneys, the Caplins – continue their lives in peacetime Britain, plying their trade despite the deteriorating state of the waterways. And new faces appear, one of whom is to have a greater impact on the crew of the *Sycamore* and the *Antrim* than they could ever guess...

The pleasures and hardships of a working life on the canals, the occasional joy or tragedy, form the backdrop of a deeply human tale in which the reader becomes enmeshed in the lives of his characters. A third book, *The New Number One,* is planned for early 2009, and will complete the story of Michael's growth from the scrawny boy from Wolverton into the respected head of a boating family.

Departing from the detective novels for which he is known, in *Starlight* Geoffrey Lewis tells a tale of schoolboy friendship set against the backdrop of the Oxford Canal in the days when the commercial trade was in decline; the canal itself threatened with closure. In a story where the mood ranges from heartwarming humour to unbearable poignancy, he conjures up the world of the 1950s; factual events and real characters flit past in the background as he leads the reader through the long heat-wave of the summer of 1955, as it was seen by an eleven-year-old boy living in a little North Oxfordshire village.

Starlight was published in 2005 – for more information, please check our website at www.sgmpublishing.co.uk or telephone 07792 497116. ISBN 978-0-9545624-5-8. Cover price £6.99.